APPORTIONMENT
OF BLAME

APPORTIONMENT OF BLAME

KEITH REDFERN

THAMES RIVER PRESS

Apportionment of Blame

THAMES RIVER PRESS
An imprint of Wimbledon Publishing Company Limited (WPC)
Another imprint of WPC is Anthem Press (www.anthempress.com)
First published in the United Kingdom in 2014 by
THAMES RIVER PRESS
75–76 Blackfriars Road
London SE1 8HA

www.thamesriverpress.com

A CIP record for this book is available from the British Library.

ISBN 978-1-78308-218-6

This title is also available as an eBook

Acknowledgements

My thanks to Thames River Press for accepting my novel for publication and for their advice and assistance.

I am indebted to Felicity Collier for information on the adoption service and the process by which children may trace their birth mothers.

My editor, Angela Abid, did a wonderful job and made some very valuable suggestions. Thanks Angela.

Another friend from France (where this novel was written), Iain Wodehouse-Easton, provided invaluable insights into the process of publishing and helped encourage me through the submission process.

And to Rosemary, my wife, who has been and remains my chief source of encouragement and support, all my love.

Chapter 1

I could still make out the shape of neighbouring rooftops in the failing light. I considered putting on the lamp, but realised I could see outside more clearly without it. Anyway, it felt more atmospheric in the gathering gloom and it would do no harm to keep the electric bill as low as possible.

Stretching out my legs, I pushed against the desk and sent myself and the swivel chair pirouetting across the office. I was now sufficiently skilled at this manoeuvre to reach the filing cabinet with one deft scoot on the carpet; well, all right, vinyl.

Where was Joyce? She should have been here ages ago.

I looked at my watch once again. How long was it since I called her? Long enough for her to have caught a train to London and taken the tube to my office. Even allowing for the vagaries of the Circle Line, two and a half hours should have been plenty.

I began to rub the ends of my fingers roughly through my hair in an attempt to massage some wakefulness into my skull. It didn't work.

It was four thirty and almost dark. The day had been as busy and unrewarding as usual; then the note arrived.

A messenger in a black crash helmet thumped up the stairs to bring it.

"You Greg Mason?"

"Yes."

"This is for you."

And then he was gone.

The message said: 'IF YOU WANT TO KNOW HOW SHE DIED, LOOK UNDER THE BENCH BELOW THE FRIENDS MAGNOLIA'. It was all in capital letters cut from newsprint. But what could it mean?

Clearly it referred to Helen, no one else had died. But how did anyone know I was looking into her death?

And what bench, and what about that friend's magnolia? It didn't make any sense.

As soon as I had told Joyce, she said she would come up and join me.

"We can work this out together," she had said. "Two heads are better than one."

Certainly this head wasn't making much progress.

I looked round the office, but saw no inspiration there, just a stack of shelves above the filing cabinet, all empty; a cane chair and a desk that had looked perfect in the shop, but now seemed to fill the room.

All the walls were bare – about like my brain at the moment – but at least the white emulsion was still reflecting some light from outside, what little there was.

I tried to persuade myself that this was what detective work was all about; that I was the famous investigator, waiting to solve another case of international mystery and intrigue. Greg Mason, the good guy, the clean living idealist, struggling to fight injustice in an unjust world.

Who was I kidding? I was twenty-five, in a cheap, cramped room above an Indian restaurant, waiting for something to happen. Or, more precisely, waiting for someone to arrive.

I looked at my watch again and felt pretty useless, just standing there, waiting.

My eyes caught the first signs of a star in the darkening sky and I spent several minutes trying to work out in which direction I was looking and which star it was, before I realised it was an aircraft coming straight towards me. Some detective.

The sound of a car, moving very fast and getting nearer, pulled me out of both my reverie and my chair and I went to the window, my gaze aimed along the street. As the car reached my building I thought I heard a door slam and more out of curiosity than anything, I craned further forward to look down in front of the ground floor.

My first thought was to be glad I had not turned on the light. My second thought froze my stare. A body lay, bent like a horseshoe, against a concrete lamp standard.

I didn't want to look, yet I couldn't avert my eyes and the stare remained fixed till I couldn't really see at all.

My mind was telling me this sort of thing doesn't happen. My mind was lying.

As the focus returned to my eyes I suddenly realised who I was looking at. I'm not sure how I knew. I suppose it could have been her clothes, but some sort of instinct in me was certain; gut-wretchingly certain, and I didn't want to be. My immediate reaction was to go down and check, but something stopped me.

Perhaps whoever got Joyce was waiting for me, too. What could she possibly have done to have caused this? We'd only just started this investigation.

I was suddenly scared. Scared of what might happen to me. Scared of what I would have to tell Joyce's parents. Why wouldn't she listen to me and let me work alone?

I had to think. I should have thought before, but who could have expected anything like this? Staying in the office wouldn't do any good, but nothing would do Joyce any good, now. Oh God! What should I do?

Whoever had dumped Joyce was probably waiting just round the corner, waiting for curiosity to draw me out. They must have known I'd heard them. They probably intended that I should. No real detective would walk out into a possible trap, but I had to know for sure who it was and I couldn't leave Joyce just lying there, so I decided.

Leaving the office door open an inch, I was soon down the two flights. My soft, black shoes made no sound, and when I reached the outer door I stopped and opened it slowly and carefully. I couldn't see anything obvious to worry about, but I knew how many windows there were in that street. There could be someone behind any one of them, or peering round one of the buildings, and if they were looking for me, I would make a sitting target under that street lamp.

There was a shallow, covered area between door and pavement and I eased myself out and stood, side on to the road, my back against one wall.

I strained my eyes to see, but detected no movement, so I repeated the procedure on the other side edging my back against the doorway. Still nothing.

So, in for a penny, I crouched low and launched myself across to the street lamp and then stopped, eyes closed, expecting something violent to happen, but nothing did; nothing at all. It seemed unnaturally quiet.

Staying close to the ground I shuffled round to look at the face. It was Joyce all right and she was breathing, but harshly and she had a tape stretched across her mouth. Well thank God – at least she was alive.

"Joyce," I half whispered and half shouted. "Joyce. Can you hear me? Are you all right?"

What a stupid question. Yes, of course she's all right. She makes a habit of lying curved around street lamps in the early hours of darkness.

There was a note, safety-pinned to her coat. I tore it off, screwed it up in my hand and pushed it into my pocket.

Crouching down next to her I felt her forehead – it seemed warm. I wanted to pick her up, but recalled all the advice I had heard about not moving people too soon in case there were broken bones. So I felt along her arms and legs. They felt relaxed and I could detect no strange shapes or twists as might have been expected if something was broken.

"Mmmm....mmmm?" Joyce tried to speak.

I was so surprised, I jumped forward from my crouch and banged my head against the lamp standard. As I rubbed the bruise, I could see Joyce beginning to unravel herself.

She felt around the tape and gingerly began to peel it off.

"What exactly were you doing?" were her first words.

"What do you mean, what was I doing? I was trying to find out if you are all right. What did you think? That I thought this was the ideal place for a furtive grope?"

"No. Of course not, stupid." She tried to smile and failed. At least the attempt took some tension out of the situation, but not much.

"Well, are you?"

"Am I what?"

"Are you all right?"

"Of course I'm all right," she said unconvincingly.

Then, as if realising exactly how she really felt, she said: "Well I will be when my head clears." I took her by the arm and helped her to her feet.

"What happened to you? Where have you been? Can you walk?"

My questions came pouring out.

"I think so. And I'm not sure what happened."

"Come on then. Let's get back inside out of sight, before someone starts asking questions."

I helped her across the pavement and into the doorway, very relieved that apparently no one had seen us.

Back in the office, Joyce lowered herself into the chair - my chair, but I just stood and looked down at her, feeling rather helpless.

"So what happened?"

"I did what the note said," Joyce said.

"What?"

"And I went to the right place."

"What place? What are you talking about?"

"Just a minute." She was rubbing her hands across her face where the tape had been and I could see that she was trembling.

"Would you like a drink?" Useless question.

"What have you got?" She looked up.

"Coffee. But it's real," saying this to justify the inadequacies of my office provisions. Philip Marlowe would have produced a bottle of Bourbon and two shot glasses from his filing cabinet.

I fiddled about with the kettle and a little steel cafetière, putting in two hefty spoonfuls of ground Colombian.

Eventually I turned, leaving the kettle to boil.

"Now, if you are up to this, what place did you go to? Where have you been? You didn't say you knew where to look."

"I didn't know until I was on the train. Just as I was dozing off, it hit me. Right across the road from Euston Station is Friends House. I used to see it when I was going back to school after weekends at home."

"What does it mean, Friends House?" I asked her. "Whose friends?"

"They are Quakers. Friends are Quakers. It's the Religious Society of Friends."

"I thought they were something from centuries ago. But I think I know where you mean. "

"I don't know anything about them. Just what Friends means, and that was all I needed to know."

I heard the water come to the boil and turned to pour it on the grounds, replacing the top of the cafetière before finally sitting on the cane chair against the wall, where I sat looking at her. She was looking more relaxed and I was grateful she appeared not to be harmed in any way. All I could see was a slight red mark across her face where the tape had been.

"What are you looking at?"

"Nothing, except to check that you are OK."

I realised I had been staring at her, those deep, blue eyes and that wonderful heart shaped face. Trying to cover my embarrassment I turned back to the coffee, pushed down the plunger and poured the dark brew into two mugs.

"Do you take milk or sugar?"

"No. Neither."

"Well, thank goodness for small mercies."

I gave Joyce her coffee and sat down again with mine.

"So what did the note mean? All that about a magnolia and a bench?"

"There's a garden at the end of the building."

"This Friends' House place?"

"Yes. I used to go and sit in the garden sometimes, if I was too early for a train, and there is this huge magnolia tree, with a bench right underneath it."

"And you went to investigate on your way here?"

"Yes. I thought it would save time."

She blew on her coffee and took a tentative sip, but decided it was too hot.

"So?"

"It was all very well organised."

"What was?"

But she paused. And I waited.

"When I got there it looked like it always does. One or two people sitting eating sandwiches, or dozing. It can be quite peaceful there, despite the traffic noise.

"I walked round to the bench and I could see a piece of paper pinned underneath it. It must have been when I bent to get the paper, someone had been waiting. No, wait. It was two people, because one grabbed me and the other put the tape over my mouth. They rushed up before I could do anything about it. Then bundled me out through the back of the garden and into a car they had waiting."

"That must have been terrifying."

"Yes. It was." She sipped again at the coffee, deciding this time she could cope with its temperature.

I remembered the note in my pocket, took it out and opened it up. 'YOUR NEXT!' I read out loud in what little light there was from outside.

"Not if I see you first!" I said angrily, screwing up the note and throwing it across the room.

I was aware that Joyce was staring at me, with a mixture of amusement and concern on her face.

"Is this how investigators behave whenever something untoward happens? I must remember to stay out of range."

"Well," I said inadequately, and moved to pick up the note, which I unscrewed and read again.

"I don't like being threatened."

Joyce sipped at her coffee and watched me.

"Can we put the light on?" she asked. "I can hardly see you in this gloom."

"OK. I'll pull the blind down first."

I crossed the little office and played with the right hand string to bring the light screen down across the window. Then I turned on the lamp. It didn't make much difference to the light level, but it did make the place feel a bit more cheerful.

I put both notes on the desk to compare.

"What did the note under the bench say?"

"I don't think it said anything. I think it was just a ruse to get someone out there, to put the frighteners on. It worked quite well."

She put the coffee cup down and began to rub her hands together in a nervous way.

"It terrified me."

"It should have been me."

"The result would have been the same."

"Perhaps so, but I'd rather it had been me than you."

"Well it wasn't, so there is no point in thinking that now."

I moved the notes round to read them again and read the first out loud.

'IF YOU WANT TO KNOW HOW SHE DIED, LOOK UNDER THE BENCH BELOW THE FRIENDS MAGNOLIA.'

"The writer isn't very well educated," I suggested. "Look, there should be an apostrophe at the end of Friends."

"Yes, I'm sure we'll solve this mystery by examining the vagaries of the writer's grammar."

"No. Look. The second note says YOUR NEXT. It's very common for people to spell it like that, and not as an abbreviation for *you are*."

"You actually think this is important?"

"Well, it's something. It's a start."

"But it hardly gets us any nearer to finding out what happened to Helen, does it?"

"It tells us her death was not an accident. Because if it was we wouldn't have all this fuss."

"Are you telling me that someone killed her?"

"Well, you must have had your doubts about her death, or you wouldn't have asked me to start sniffing round, would you?"

"No. But it was only that Helen was so careful. She had far more sense than to fall in the path of an oncoming train. It just didn't make any sense."

Joyce's half sister, Helen, had died at a level crossing on a rural railway line near the Essex - Suffolk border. It had been dark. The driver said he didn't see anything until she was suddenly right in front of his cab. He didn't have a chance.

The police had concluded it was either a tragic accident or that Helen had taken her own life, and the coroner, equally uncertain, had brought in an open verdict.

Joyce was not convinced by either of the police suggestions. That's why she had called me. Why me, you might ask.

We knew each other from school. We had done some of the same subjects at GCSE and gone on together to the Sixth Form College in Colchester to do some of the same A levels. So we were old friends. But only ever that, which some of my friends could never understand.

After school we didn't see much of each other. Occasionally during holidays, at pubs or clubs, but nothing regular. After university I had gone to work in the City, while Joyce had taken up her first teaching job in the Midlands.

"What do we do now?" Joyce asked.

"Let's start by going through what's happened. Then, perhaps, we might come up with some way forward."

I thought for a moment. There was no need to think for long.

"You called me to tell me about Helen. I went to look at the scene of the accident, talked to people who live nearby, then I went to talk to the police."

"Do you still think it was an accident?"

'No. Probably not. It's just an expression."

"All right. Then what?"

"The police were not very helpful, clearly not impressed that an amateur sleuth was getting involved. But they did say there was no evidence there had been anyone other than Helen at the scene. No footprints or anything."

"But the ground would have been frozen. It was very cold that night."

"I know."

"Then?"

"Well, everything else happened today. Someone brought a note telling me about the bench and the magnolia. I called you. You went to look and got bundled off by person or persons unknown."

"There were two. I said."

"Yes. You did. And we have to assume that the whole palaver of bundling you off and dumping you here, was to give us a warning."

"To stop asking questions."

"Yes. The point is, I've hardly asked any questions yet. And then only out near the accident. So how come a note arrived here?"

Joyce just sat and looked at me. What she saw was unlikely to fill her with confidence, as I was baffled.

"There has to be a link between the accident site and here," I considered.

"Well, I have no idea what that might be.'

'No. Neither do I."

For want of anything else to do I picked up our two coffee cups and took them to the corner sink to wash them out.

"Was there anyone else in that garden when you were there?" I asked over my shoulder.

She didn't reply, so I turned to look at her. Her face was still as she stared forward and down, a thoughtful frown on her forehead.

I realised, as I had realised many times before, how beautiful she was, and how much I wanted to help her solve the mystery which had all but broken her parents.

"Can you remember anything?" I asked her cautiously.

"I am trying to visualise the scene when I arrived," she said.

I waited, drying the cups and putting them back on a shelf.

"There was someone sitting on the seat by the steps. He would have been facing the magnolia tree."

"Can you remember what he looked like?"

"I hardly saw him, except out of the corner of my eye as I came down the steps into the garden. My mind was focussed on the magnolia tree and the bench."

"Anybody else?"

"That's what's strange. The two who bundled me off came out of nowhere."

I sat down again, not taking my eyes from her face.

"They must have been waiting for ages for someone to turn up."

"And there's something else," I said as I suddenly realised. "The note implied that by looking under the bench, we would find out how Helen died."

"Assuming it referred to Helen."

"It must do. I am not doing anything else related to someone's death. And the note came here, to my office. But all that happened when you found the note was that you were bundled off. What does that tell us?"

"I told you I never saw anyone other than the person sitting to the side of the steps. What happened to me came out of the blue. Perhaps they were saying what happened to me in the garden, happened to Helen by the railway line."

"And You're next means it could happen to me as well."

"Exactly!"

"So it was a warning. A strange warning, but certainly the message was clear. Stop investigating Helen's death, or a similar fate could await you."

"Us."

"Yes."

We were staring at each other now.

"So she was murdered," Joyce said slowly, as if not wanting to have to say it, but having no option.

"It looks like it."

"I was right, although I feel no better for that." And then in a very matter of fact way, "So what do we do now?"

For once the answer came easily and quickly.

"There are two things we have to do. Find the link between Essex and here. There must be one. And try to find someone who saw what happened to you in the garden."

"OK then," Joyce said and got up.

"But not today, and take your time," I said. "Enough has happened to you for one day. We should wait till tomorrow. It will give you time to get over the shock that could easily hit you later."

Joyce nodded.

"I tell you what," I suggested with as much enthusiasm as I could muster, "let's go across to the garden. You can show me where it happened, and then we can go and have a drink somewhere. How about that?"

"All right," she said.

I got up and reached for my coat from the stand in the corner.

"Are you feeling well enough to go out now?"

"Yes. I think so."

"Come on then."

As soon as we reached the corner of Euston Road I recognised the building I had seen and walked past so many times before. White, square cut stone, greying with pollution, a pillared frontage above steps in the centre, and a flat roof. It looked quite grand – almost Greek.

"How come these Friends have a building that size? They must be pretty well off."

"I don't know."

We waited for the red light to change, then crossed and walked past the front of the building. At the far corner there was a sign for a book shop and beyond that a stone wall. Behind the wall was the corner of the garden.

It was a simple garden, but well cared for. Two squares of grass surrounded by borders of plants, with a paved path around the outside and down the centre. The magnolia tree dominated the side of the garden furthest from the building, and I could see the bench beneath it in the light of the street lamps.

We walked up to the top of the entrance way and looked down the steps to our left. The garden was deserted.

"Where's the seat you said someone was using?"

"Down there. Look," and she leaned over the balustrade to point down at the edge of the paving by the base of the steps.

I looked across the scene, wondering how I could make out anything useful; wondering if there were clues somewhere waiting to be found.

But ultimately and ironically the darkness made it clear there was nothing to see.

"There's nothing we can do here tonight," I said.

"Let's leave it till morning and see if anything can be done then."

Joyce came up close and looked up into my eyes.

"You will try, won't you?"

"Of course I'll try. I said I would, didn't I."

I said this with as much confidence as I could muster, which wasn't a lot at that precise moment.

"Come on. Let's get you that drink."

Chapter 2

That night I had a dream. It was one of those weird experiences when I was watching from above as things happened to me.

I was walking up and down inside a huge factory. It was some sort of metalworks, perhaps a steelworks as there were enormous rollers with sheets which kept sliding past me. It was all very noisy and confusing. I was looking for something, but I had no idea what. Suddenly someone was trying to push me onto the rollers and I had to fight for my life to stop it happening.

It was unusual for me to have a dream so vivid and I woke suddenly, feeling disoriented as my brain tried to drag itself back up to reality from a place deep inside my subconscious.

Sitting up, it hit me. The note was meant for me. It was supposed to be me who looked under the bench, not Joyce. Something was going to happen to me, along the lines of what happened to Helen, but they got the wrong person. That is why Joyce was just dumped outside my office.

But how did they know it was Joyce? I couldn't figure that one out, so I gave up for the time being and got up, hoping that a shower and some caffeine might kick start my grey cells.

In the shower I thought some more of what had happened to Helen and who might have caused it. Could it be someone she knew? How could I find out?

Wrapped in a towel, and with water still dripping from my hair, I retrieved my mobile and called Joyce.

"Hi. I had a thought. Did Helen have a computer?"

"Yes, a laptop."

"Great. Could you bring it with you this morning? It might just contain some useful information."

"OK. I'll do that."

"See you soon," and I closed the phone and applied the towel some more to my hair.

Down in the kitchen I waited for the kettle to boil, wondering again why I was doing this. This detective thing. It was a far cry from the city job I had recently left, and that had seemed the obvious thing for me to do at the time.

I had my Economics degree and everything seemed set for a successful career. I can't say I ever enjoyed it, though. Hard, concentrated work and early mornings were never my scene. And fighting for a seat on the seven o'clock train every day wasn't my idea of fun. Some seem to like it; at least they are happy to tolerate their working lives, but not me. All that stress and aggro to achieve a shortened life expectancy. What's the point?

Looking round at colleagues, in what few idle moments I had, I used to wonder what was the appeal. What drew them into the rat race and caught them in the maelstrom of self-perpetuating financial jugglery?

It was the money, of course, and I was well paid, with a company car, private medical care and all the rest, but I wasn't happy and became increasingly frustrated as I could see no way out and had no desire to continue going my frenetic, capitalist way until burn-out in my middle to late thirties.

Then my grandfather died and left me most of the fortune he had quietly built up from his business. Everyone in the family had considered it a small business and the amount he left caused a few eyebrows to lift. The fact that he left me the money lifted a few more.

We had always been close, my Granddad and I. I got on well with my parents too, but with him there always seemed to be a special bond.

If I had a problem, he was always the one I turned to. He was the sort of person you could totally rely on, whatever happened.

He never apportioned blame, just talked things through and made it possible to find a solution to almost anything.

The possibility of a private income caused me to reconsider my future, and when I began to feel the City work becoming even more monotonous and tiring, I began to look around for something else to do, preferably something more exciting and worthwhile.

With this intention, against everyone's advice and to the horror of my parents, I hung up my black umbrella, took my cell phone and signed a lease on a little upstairs room near Euston Station.

Granddad would have been great at detective work. It would have been good to have him there now, helping to sort out the conundrum that was Helen's death.

I realised the irony of the situation. He was not there to help me, but without him the business would not have been possible in the first place.

I had no idea how to run a detective agency, but figured it couldn't be too difficult. Always fascinated by detective novels, movies and TV series, I had some idea how to work things out from clues. Perhaps it might be a bit dangerous at times, but how hard could it be? Just advertise and see what happens, I'd thought. But little had, until Joyce called. Now I was suddenly being called upon to prove my worth. I wondered if I could.

After a hurried breakfast I left to meet Joyce at the station.

It was one of those mornings when the sun seemed to have given up. Thick clouds obliterated the sky and the late winter sunrise meant that even though it was mid-morning, it was hardly what you would call light.

The stygian gloom of the day reflected my mood as I picked Joyce out at the edge of the car park. She was wearing the same coat as the day before, at my suggestion, and carrying a brief case which she held up to show me. Then she came up and stood on tiptoe to kiss my cheek. That was new, and I looked questioningly at her.

"That's for looking after me yesterday."

"I don't feel as if I did much. I certainly didn't achieve a great deal. In fact I blame myself for spreading around my business cards. It must be someone with one of my cards who organized your kidnap. That must he the connection between Essex and London.

"It was hardly a kidnap."

"It was exactly a kidnap."

I took her spare arm and we walked together down the ramp towards the London platform. Most regular commuters had long since left for work, but there was still quite a crowd congregating in front of the ticket office, so we bought Joyce's ticket at the machine. I had my season ticket, one of the major investments arising from my decision to work from London rather than from home. Now I had to pay for it myself. There was no longer a bank to subsidise me.

"Let's go to the end of the platform. There will be more space at the back of the train and we can talk without being overheard."

We pushed our way past the few who ignored the warning line and stood near the platform's edge; past those sheltering behind newspapers in the narrow, covered waiting area, and down towards that part of the platform commuters rarely used.

"Greg?"

"Mm?"

"Those business cards you had printed."

"Yes?"

"When you went out - you know - to where Helen died. Can you remember how many people you gave cards to?"

"Everyone I spoke to near the level crossing. But there weren't many. There aren't many houses."

I couldn't hide the disappointment in my voice. The idea of the cards being the link was a good one, but perhaps it wasn't so likely after all. The chance of one out of so few cards getting into the hands of a crazy man in London, who would think nothing of taking someone by force and making serious threats, seemed decidedly remote.

"So it's not a long list," Joyce persisted.

"No."

I stared gloomily across at the small industrial unit that stood where once there had been sidings, in the days before Beeching's axe transformed the rail system from a comprehensive public service to a sparse and expensive luxury.

It had been a busy and important station once; a junction providing links between the London main line and rural Suffolk and Cambridgeshire. There had been sidings on both sides of the road bridge in those days, and even a turntable in the shunting yard.

The train pulled in with a whoosh of air brakes, its bright paint work showing off its modernity, together with its sliding doors, its lack of guard's van and its few toilets.

I recalled taking my bike on the old trains, the spacious guard's van making cycle storage easy and convenient. Nowadays cyclists were forced to lean their machines in the doorways of compartments, so they were often in the way and easy prey for complaining travellers. Another sign of progress - less common, less convenient, more trouble for most people.

As I had hoped, the carriage was nearly empty, and we sat together with our backs against the end wall.

"Can you remember all the people?" Joyce continued as if there had been no pause.

I thought for a moment.

"There's the house by the level crossing itself; one by the lane leading down to it; a large house on the corner of the lane; two cottages on the other side of the road, and that's about all.

"Oh, and I spoke to a man driving his tractor. I gave him a card as well."

"So one of those people knows what happened to Helen."

"It looks like it. And I suppose they know where to find me."

"Know where to find us," Joyce corrected.

"Yes. Us. But they didn't know it was us. I think they were after me."

"And I turned up."

"Mmm."

I couldn't get my head round the probability of one of those people being in London to snatch Joyce.

"Do you think it's likely to be someone from there?" I asked her.

"Who else could it be?"

"I have absolutely no idea."

I watched the fields pass by, and compared the speed of cars on the parallel main road with the train, a common habit of mine.

"That's interesting," I suddenly realised. "It could have been anybody finding the note under that bench. How did they know it was you?"

"They didn't wait to find out. They just bundled me off."

"But that doesn't make any sense. It might have been a complete stranger. Were they going to kidnap everyone who spotted that note?"

"I don't think the note was that visible. It's probably only because I was looking for it that I found it."

"So they were lying in wait until someone looked for the note?"

"I think so," she said.

"But if they were looking for me, why did they go for you? We hardly look alike."

Joyce smiled up at me.

"You're right."

"I mean, if they are looking for a tallish, dark, average looking bloke, why pick on a smallish, very attractive young woman?"

"Very attractive?"

"Well, you are. There's not much doubt about that."

Joyce had a strange expression on her face and looked away from me.

"What?"

"Oh, it's just that you reminded me of what someone else once said."

Joyce had been a successful music teacher, till she had a sudden rush of blood to the head with an ex-pupil and ran off with him in Corfu. It didn't last long, but it cost her the job, mainly because she was supposed to be in charge of a group of school children at the time.

So she had come back to Essex, with her tail between her legs, you might say, not knowing what her future held in store.

Then Helen had died.

Helen, her half sister, was not much older than her, and they were very close.

Joyce was shattered, and her parents were heartbroken.

Although, to an extent, I had lost touch with Joyce after school, I knew about Helen and we had met a few times. They were a very close family. I could imagine the effect of what had happened.

"I reckon," I said, "that the person looking for me sent those two who took you."

"Why?"

"Because he would know I'm male. You are fairly obviously not."

"Whoever sent them didn't give a very good description, then."

"Perhaps they didn't give any description. Just set the trap. Think about it."

I turned towards her as thoughts began to coalesce.

"They placed the note under the bench in such a way that most people wouldn't notice it. Or if they did notice it, they wouldn't bother about it.

"Then they sent the other note to my office to set the wheels in motion, and had two people wait till I came searching for the bench."

"Why not just go to your office and get you there?"

I had wondered that, and considered reasons why they chose not to.

"Perhaps the person who wants me out of the way didn't want to risk doing anything in the office."

"Surely it would have been easier to deal with you there, than in the open air with people watching."

"There would have been at least a scuffle in the office, and the noise could have been heard downstairs. They wouldn't want to risk that."

"But they were prepared to risk being seen in the garden."

"It seems like it."

The whole thing seemed so ridiculous, and Joyce obviously thought the same.

"Why go to such elaborate lengths to make a point?" she said.

"I was just thinking the same thing."

"If someone wants to threaten you, there must be more effective ways. Ways that don't involve obscure notes and kidnapping someone in broad daylight."

"As I said yesterday, I don't think we are dealing with a gifted brain. Perhaps they tried too hard to be clever."

I turned to look at Joyce.

"But the threat was effective, wasn't it? Even if it was the wrong person. It must have terrified you."

"Yes," she said. "It did."

The train pulled into a station and we stopped talking, waiting to see if anyone would get into the compartment.

An elderly lady with a shopping trolley climbed in and went to the seat next to the doors. It took her a while to get the trolley where she wanted it, and she swayed a bit as the train began moving again. I was just about to go to her aid when she flopped into her seat, gave us a brief glance, and then turned to look out of the window.

"How do you think they knew it was me in the garden?" Joyce asked. "Or if they didn't, what did they expect to achieve?"

"I don't know. It seems that someone wants to frighten me off, or perhaps get rid of me completely."

"What, kill you as well?"

The starkness of her comment brought me up short and I looked at the woman by the door, to see if she had overheard us. I realised I had not fully taken in the implications of what was happening.

"Well, it's possible," I said slowly, not wanting to believe it.

"It is fairly well known that when a person has killed once, it's easier to kill again. And if they thought we were on their tracks, they could easily resort to desperate measures."

Joyce looked up at me.

"What have I got you involved in? I never intended to endanger your life."

"I know. But you suspected someone had caused Helen's death. And there was always the chance that uncovering the truth might be potentially dangerous."

"I suppose," she said and turned away in thought.

The train had picked up speed and the Essex countryside was streaming past the window again. It occurred to me that for a county so crowded and polluted, it is remarkable how much open space still remains.

"What do you think happened?" she asked eventually.

I dragged my thoughts back to the matter in hand.

"They knew where I was from the address on my card. It must have been one of my cards that told them that," I suddenly realised. "How else could they know where to find me?

"But they needed me out in the open where they could operate more easily. So they concocted a note designed to flush me out of the office, and got a messenger to deliver it."

"And you were supposed to work out what the note meant."

"Yes, and I suppose I would have done in time. I've seen Friends House often enough, and walked past it without knowing what it was. The penny would have dropped eventually. But as it was, I phoned you and read the note out to you."

"And I worked it out first."

"So the people who were waiting must have had instructions to wait as long as necessary for the person who came to find the note."

"It could have taken days."

"Yes. Another flaw in a stupid plan. When you turned up, they assumed you must be who they wanted."

"I can see what happened next. As soon as the person in charge found out I wasn't you, they scribbled a note, pinned it to my clothes and dumped me outside your office."

"Then it didn't matter who you were. The point is, you weren't me, so they weren't interested, but took the opportunity to scare me a bit more. It could have been anybody in that garden, looking innocently at a note they had spotted under the bench. But they were prepared to use them to get to me."

I thought that through. Did it make sense?

"If you think about it," I considered, "they were lucky it was you. Anybody else would have gone screaming to the police about what had happened. As it was, it was you."

"Mm," she said, and it went quiet again.

"What are we going to do this morning?" Joyce asked eventually.

"We are going to sniff around the garden to see if we can find anything interesting. Then I want to go back there at about the time you were there yesterday, to see if the same person is sitting on that bench."

We both fell quiet again for a few minutes.

"Do you really think someone is out to kill you?"

"I don't know. I hope not," I said. "Perhaps they haven't worked out what they're going to do. But there's little doubt that my questions have scared them into action of some sort. They are definitely trying to frighten me off."

The train stopped again and a number of people joined us in the compartment.

"I think we'd better wait till later to discuss this further. There are too many other ears in here now."

Liverpool Street station was enjoying its mid-morning lull when we finally arrived. I took her bag as it looked rather heavy, and we crossed the forecourt to W.H. Smith's to buy a newspaper, then made our way down into the Underground entrance to find the Circle Line platform.

Emerging eventually from Euston Square station, we turned left, then left again and walked down the street that brought us behind Friends House and its garden. I could see there were cars parked along the roadside, so it would have been relatively easy to bundle someone out of the garden and into a waiting vehicle.

"I don't suppose you saw where the car went?" I asked Joyce.

"No. I'm sorry. The gagging and blindfolding were very effective."

I stood and looked both ways along the street, trying to gauge which direction was most likely.

"If they had a car or something ready, it would probably be on this side of the street, nearest to the garden exit. That means they would be facing east and most likely drove off in that direction."

I looked that way and could see a busy road crossing at the far end.

"We'll go and look further down the street in a minute. Let's just look around the garden first."

The grey skies of earlier were still with us and it was threatening rain. These were not the conditions to encourage people to sit in gardens, and there was no one there at all. So we returned to the roadside and made our way along to the end of the street.

Here the traffic was busy and I could see it would have been difficult to turn right. Looking left I could see the traffic lights on the corner of Euston Road, and then the road continuing northwards alongside the station.

We walked up to the corner and then crossed Euston Road and made our way to the office across the station entrance area. On the way we called at a stall for some Cornish pasties and orange juice to have for lunch.

The street outside the office was quite busy. Local Indian restaurants were popular with those seeking a low cost, but filling meal.

We climbed the stairs, and as I pushed the office door open I could hear the sound of paper scraping on the floor. Another note.

"Here we go again," I said, bending to pick it up.

It bore a similar series of capital letters cut from newsprint. 'LEAVE IT OR ELSE', it said.

"Look," I said, giving it to Joyce.

She read it, glanced up at me and I shrugged. There had been no one suspicious outside, no visible sign of anyone following or looking for us.

"This note could have been here for hours. Possibly even since last night."

I closed the door, gave Joyce back her briefcase and put the new note next to the other two which were still lying on the desk. We stood looking down at them.

"Come on, let's eat these pasties while they're still warm."

We settled back into the chairs we had used the previous evening and ate our pasties, all the time glancing over at the notes, hoping that inspiration would arrive. If everything was going to be as difficult as this, it was looking as if I'd made the wrong career choice.

"Let's go over again exactly what happened to Helen," I suggested.

I could see Joyce's expression change as I said it.

"I know you won't want to, but we need to see if there's anything we've missed."

"She'd gone out after work. No one knew where. The police found her car in the lane leading down to the level crossing. The couple in the crossing house had called them."

"You said no one knew where she had gone?"

"That's right. Mum said she had gone to work in the morning as usual and had the afternoon off. She said Helen told her she wouldn't be too late back."

"Did she know anyone in that area?"

"Not to my knowledge."

"Where does the track lead, once you've crossed the railway?"

"I don't know. I think it makes its way back to the main road. There are a few houses at the other end I think, but if you were going to one of them, surely you wouldn't approach from where Helen was?"

"No. That means she was either meeting someone there, or perhaps she had met someone who lived in one the houses."

"It's a funny, remote place to meet someone."

"I agree. So that leaves the houses. I shall have to go out there again and talk to people. See if I can pick up any hints that might lead us in the right direction."

I savoured my pasty as my thoughts moved on.

"What about yesterday? I phoned you at about two o'clock."

"Yes. I left soon after and caught the first train that came. It wasn't a fast one, but it got me in town as soon as possible."

"Then?"

"I left the tube at Kings Cross and walked along the south side of Euston Road, till I reached the garden."

"When you got there, did anything look odd? Anything out of place? Anybody loitering suspiciously?"

Joyce thought for a minute.

"I can't recall seeing anything or anybody suspicious. But I wasn't looking at things like that. I was intent on finding the note.

"I walked up the entrance area and looked straight down towards the magnolia tree. That's why I was there. I was sure I was in the right place."

"Go on."

"I remember seeing a person on the bench next to the steps, but I didn't really look that way. I made straight for the bench."

"And the two men came from where?"

"I don't know. One minute they were not there, the next minute they were, and they had me."

"So they took you out of the garden and put you into a car?"

"Yes."

"What kind of car?"

"I couldn't see its colour. I was blindfolded."

I smiled.

"What?"

"I didn't mean the colour, I meant the make."

"Well I couldn't see that either, could I?"

"I know. But could you tell if it was a big car or a small car? Did you have to dip your head to get inside?"

"No. That's interesting. It must have been quite tall. I had to step up to get inside."

"And what did the engine sound like? Powerful?"

"Yes, now you come to mention it."

"OK. That's good. They had a tall powerful car waiting at the kerb."

I shuffled the notes round on the desk top as I thought.

"They dropped you here at just after half past four. What time did your train get in?"

"I caught the 2.35, which takes about an hour."

She looked at me, clearly wondering where these questions were going.

"Go on. I'm trying to establish when you reached the garden."

"I was in the underground for about fifteen minutes, and the walk up the road would have taken about ten. That means it must have been about four o'clock."

"And I found you here at about four thirty. So you weren't in that car for very long."

"No. I wasn't."

She began to realise where I was going with this.

"So it didn't go very far," she said.

"Exactly. If I'm right, the person who set the whole thing up was waiting in the car. As soon as you were bundled in, he or she would have realised they had the wrong person, thought quickly, scribbled out a note and had you dropped off here."

"That makes sense. But you said he or she."

"Well, we don't know, do we."

Joyce looked at me.

"It just doesn't seem the kind of thing a woman would do."

"Perhaps, but I think we now know that whoever it was may not be far away."

"No. You have to be very careful."

"I think we both do."

Chapter 3

Having cleared away the wrappings from our scant lunch, I lifted Joyce's briefcase onto the desk.

"Shall we see what this computer has waiting for us?"

Joyce opened the case and took out the laptop, laying it on the desk where we could both see it.

I opened the lid, and, turning it on, was immediately faced with the File Vault screen.

"We need a password," I said, "and we have three goes to get it right. After that, we are locked out. The File Vault encrypts all the files, so there will be no other way of reaching them."

"Three goes? Is that all?"

"Yes. It's a good security system. The trouble is we have to think hard. What would Helen be likely to choose?"

Joyce looked at me and shrugged.

"She was very well organised," she said. "She will have changed her passwords frequently, as we are all recommended to do. Whatever the password is now, I'll bet it was only changed shortly before she died."

"So, assuming she chose something currently on her mind, what might that be?"

"I don't think it would be a name," Joyce suggested. "She had more imagination than that. She would have used a mix of lower and upper case letters, and probably numbers as well. So it could be any combination of those."

"Not necessarily a meaningless combination, though. Passwords are easier to use if they can be remembered somehow, so they need to mean something to the person using them. Otherwise they have to be looked up all the time and that is just a pain. So what had happened to her in the days and weeks before she died?"

"I can't think of anything."

"Think," I encouraged.

"I am," she said, the beginnings of a despairing look appearing on her face.

"Did she have a car?"

"Yes. A Golf."

"When did she buy it?"

"Er…a few months before she died."

"Was she fond of it?"

"She was. She loved her Golf."

"OK. What is the registration number?"

"God, I don't know."

She looked totally deflated now, then suddenly took out her phone.

"I'll call Mum and ask her."

She speed dialled the number and waited for only a second or two.

"Hi Mum, it's me. Can you tell me the registration number of Helen's Golf?…We are trying to think of a password to get into her laptop…You don't know? Would you mind going to look?…Thanks."

Joyce held the phone away from her ear and looked questioningly at me.

"What?"

"Mum's gone to find out. I hope it's useful. I can't think of anything else.

"Yes, Mum. Thanks. Got it," and she reeled the number off to me.

"Right. Here goes," and I typed in the registration number.

Wrong password, the screen said.

"Damn. But it would have been extraordinary to get it right first time."

"Mmm," was all that Joyce said.

"Realistically," I said, "with only three goes, the chances of us getting in are remote. If you can't think of any other point of reference for her password, let's stick with the car. If we fail, we fail. There's no use spending pointless hours over this."

I typed in VWGOLF and the first three digits of the registration number.

Wrong password.

"OK. A bit of lateral thinking, then we're done. How many doors does the car have?"

"Five. When the gang went out together, we liked being able to pile easily into the back seat."

"How old was it?"

"You can tell from the registration number."

"Yes, of course."

I thought for a moment.

"Right. One more go, then we give up. There's nothing more we can do."

I typed in 2009GOLF5dr.

It worked.

"I don't believe it," I said and punched the air.

Joyce had a huge smile on her face.

"You're going to be good at this job, aren't you? So what now?"

"Would you mind if I looked at Helen's emails? You wouldn't think I was prying?"

"We need to look wherever we can for clues," Joyce said. "Helen wouldn't mind."

I looked at her and could see she was finding this hard.

The mail icon bounced into life and I went into the inbox. The last few mails were from someone called Stuart. I opened the most recent and it gave me a record of Helen's last email conversation.

"Who's Stuart?" I turned to Joyce.

"The only Stuart I know is Stuart in our gang. Stuart Hemsley. You know him."

"Do I?"

"You must have met him. Tallish. Fair hair. He was at school with Helen."

Joyce moved her chair so we could read through the emails together. When we had finished we looked at each other a few times in surprise.

"So they were an item. And you didn't know this?"

"I had no idea," Joyce said.

"It looks as if Helen was trying to end it, but Stuart didn't want to. In fact his last two messages are quite distressing."

"Yes. He was obviously very upset."

"What does he do?"

"He works for a travel agency in the City."

"He works in London, does he? Interesting. And where does he live?"

"In one of those new flats near the station."

"Not too far from where Helen died, then."

"You don't think..."

"I don't know what to think. But those two things about him alone make interesting coincidences, if that's what they are, and it certainly opens up a possibility. It also reminds me that when I got my business going, I passed a lot of new cards round in the pub."

"So Stuart would have one and know where to find your office."

"Probably. But let's see what else there is here, before we start jumping to conclusions."

I quit the mail programme and clicked the calendar feature on the dock. Adjusting the window so it showed a whole week at a time, I examined the days and weeks immediately prior to Helen's death.

"You were right about Helen being organised. She has her calendar divided into work and personal."

Joyce watched from my side as I clicked through the weeks, moving from work to personal and back again.

There was one date with Stuart in the private section and several meetings showed up under work.

"Look at that one," Joyce said, pointing at the screen.

We read 'meeting with FJ to discuss G'.

"Do the initials mean anything to you?" I asked.

"No. But they wouldn't necessarily. If they are people at work, I wouldn't know them."

"She worked in Colchester, didn't she?"

"Yes. She was a PA. A very good one, in one of those industrial units up in the High Woods area."

We stared at the screen together, as if expecting it to reveal the reason for the meeting.

"Look at the date," I said.

"Oh, God. It's the day after...." Joyce's voice trailed off and she turned to face me.

"The meeting never happened." I said it for her.

"But it was planned and must have meant something."

We stared at each other.

"What do you know about her work?" I asked her, pulling my gaze away from her eyes with some difficulty. "If she was a PA she might have been party to information that someone wanted kept quiet."

"It's possible, but it wasn't that kind of company. It wasn't hi-tech, or likely to be involved in industrial espionage."

"What do they do?"

"They make boxes. All sorts of packaging."

"I see what you mean. It sounds innocuous enough. But I shall need to go up there and ask a few questions tomorrow. You never know. If she had a meeting with this FJ about someone called G, it suggests that G was causing a problem of some sort. What's the firm called?"

"Colbox."

"I'll look them up and go and see who FJ and G are."

I turned back to the laptop, but all I could see was personal finance stuff, files with details about holiday destinations, spreadsheets which seemed to relate to her job and nothing of any significance that we could see.

I put the computer to sleep rather than turning it off and closed the lid. Leaving it on meant I could get in again without the password for as long as the battery lasted. We turned to face each other.

"So," I said, "we may have a motive involving someone who lives near where Helen died and works in London."

"And probably knows your office address."

"That too."

I turned and stared out of the window, searching for inspiration. It seemed to be in short supply.

"What do you know about Stuart?"

"Not much. No more or less than anyone else in our gang at the pub. He seems pleasant enough. And if he had been out with Helen a few times, knowing how fussy she was." Her voice trailed away.

I put my arm round her shoulder and gave her a little squeeze.

"I'm sorry. This is hard, isn't it?"

"But it has to be done if we're to get anywhere."

"Yes. Right. I shall go and see him. See what he has to say for himself."

"You will be careful, won't you?"

"I shall try to be."

We left the office again at just after four o'clock. It was cold and grey and the pavements were damp, but there were a lot of people about, and we had to dodge between them and their luggage. I couldn't understand why so many people chose to lift heavy cases up the steps to the station concourse, when there was a perfectly good ramp. A suitcase with wheels has no benefit when it comes to climbing stairs.

Euston Road was as busy as ever and we had to wait to cross at the lights. I was hoping against hope that the person Joyce had glimpsed was on the same bench again. It seemed unlikely on that damp evening, but it was all we had to go on, and I had no idea what I was going to suggest if we came up blank.

I was very aware how much trust Joyce had placed in me, and not at all certain it was justified.

People were pouring down the stairs at the front of Friends House, and there was a lot of animated conversation as we made our way through them.

I almost didn't dare look into the garden, for fear of being disappointed, but there was someone there.

"It's him," Joyce said excitedly. "At least, I think it is," she added with more caution.

We descended into the garden and sure enough, a man was sitting on the bench to the left. He was a scruffy individual and there was a definite aroma emanating from either him or his clothing. In other circumstances I would have kept my distance, but in this case I had no choice.

"Excuse me," I began, looking down at the man, with Joyce hanging back rather nervously.

The man appeared to be half asleep, but lifted his head slowly and looked a question at me with a frown.

"I'm sorry to bother you," I persisted, "but were you here at about this time yesterday?"

"Who wants to know?"

"There was an incident here yesterday, and I'm trying to confirm what happened."

"Police, are you?"

How many times would I be asked that, I thought.

"No, I'm not the police. I'm a private investigator."

"Oh."

He didn't sound impressed and his frown deepened, but when he moved his attention from me to Joyce he suddenly came to life.

"It's you!"

Joyce edged further behind me as if frightened by his recognition.

I sat down next to him.

"So you were here yesterday."

"Yes. Why?"

"And you saw what happened?"

"I didn't see much."

"What can you remember?"

"I was eating my sandwich," he said. "It was getting cold and I was thinking about going somewhere warmer. Then she came down the steps and made a beeline for that bench over there." He pointed with an arthritic looking finger towards the magnolia tree.

"And then?" I prompted.

"It was so quick. She bent down to do something and two others appeared from nowhere, grabbed her and bundled her out to the road."

"Did you see where they came from?"

"No. It had been quiet here for a long time. It usually is. I was eating and not taking any notice of anybody else."

"Where exactly did they take her?"

"Through that gap into the road," he said and pointed again.

I turned to look through the gloom.

"Did you see the car?"

I figured that as Joyce had described a tall car, it would have been visible above the stone wall.

The man was staring past me towards the road.

"Anything you remember would be useful."

I waited and began to think I was wasting my time.

"Black," he said suddenly.

"The car?"

"It was black, and it wasn't a car."

I looked at Joyce.

"What was it then?"

Then he looked back at me, pleased with himself.

"It was one of those truck things with a big cab."

"How do you mean, big cab?"

"It had two doors each side and two rows of seats, and there was a ladder on the back, resting on the cab."

"A ladder?"

"Yes. Like builders have."

I looked at Joyce and her expression told me she had no recollection of what we had just heard. But I thought I knew what the man was describing.

"Is there anything else you can remember? You've been very helpful so far and we're grateful."

"Are you all right?" he said to Joyce.

"Yes, thanks. They didn't really hurt me. Just frightened me."

"I hope you find them. Bloody hooligans," he said.

"Yes. So do I," I replied, waiting to see if he had more to tell us. But that was it.

"Thanks again."

I got up from the bench and put my hands on Joyce's shoulders.

"Are you sure you're all right?"

"Yes. So where to now?" she said.

"To celebrate," I suggested. "We've had our first breaks in this investigation. We deserve something."

She smiled, and in one sense, that in itself was worthy of celebration as she had looked so down recently, and with good reason.

We made our way along Euston Road to a pizza place I knew and I ordered a bottle of wine - one the advantages of using public transport.

While we waited, we chatted about nothing in particular and enjoyed the Australian Merlot.

"One thing is strange," I said to Joyce. "If Stuart was involved in the garden incident, what was all that about a truck with a ladder?"

"Perhaps he has friends up here."

"Perhaps," I said. "I'll find out when I see him, I hope. Now, tell me more about your family."

An enormous pizza had materialised in front of each of us and we began to eat.

"You know most of it, I think," Joyce said.

She took another mouthful.

"Mum is from Suffolk. Dad is from Hampshire."

"Where did they meet?"

"On a train."

"Didn't you once tell me your mother was married before?"

"Yes. Helen and I were only half-sisters. Her dad died in an accident when she was tiny. I don't think she remembered him at all."

We continued to eat while I thought.

"Do you know many of Helen's friends?"

"Most of those who live near us, I suppose. You know a fair few yourself, from The Goose."

"Mmm," I agreed, with my mouth full. "But the reason I asked is that if she was killed, someone had a reason. People don't get pushed in front of trains for no reason at all. One of those friends might know something about her life which is relevant."

The thought of chasing down all her friends for question and answer sessions did not excite me. But every angle had to be covered; every possibility followed up.

I recalled how many policemen and detectives I had read about described their work as more drudgery than excitement. It was the mundane work which often brought results. Movies and TV programmes might make police work appear intriguing, stimulating and exciting as a problem solving exercise, but what they don't show is the hard slog and boring repetition of long interviews and report writing.

The restaurant was beginning to fill and the noise began to make conversation difficult.

"I think I should chat with your mother as well."

"OK."

"It might be a good thing anyway, to be out of town for a while. If someone is looking for me here, I am going to be better off somewhere else.

"I'll work from home for a day or two. I can always pick up my office messages, so I'll know if anything important comes up."

"Are you very busy doing other things?"

"Not really. A few people have contacted me for straightforward enquiries, but there's nothing so urgent it can't wait a while. As far as I'm concerned, what happened to Helen is far more important."

"I just don't want you to lose business because of me."

"Let me worry about that," I assured her, knowing I probably would worry if nothing more turned up soon.

We finished our meal and I paid the bill, then we made our way to the station and home.

I made arrangements to meet Joyce's mother the following morning, and to lunch with Joyce after that. It seemed a good idea to stay out of London for at least a few days, to see if that produced any reaction from anyone.

It was dark and even gloomier when I arrived outside the flats. I sat in the car and looked about me, considering, as I did so, how I was going to approach the interview. If Stuart was involved in Helen's death and Joyce's snatch, he would be very evasive, and also potentially dangerous.

Joyce's last words had been "Be careful". I had every intention of following them to the letter.

I could see an L shaped block which appeared to have two entrances. Which one I needed I had no idea, so I made for the nearest.

The doorway was recessed and on the side of the porch there were several bell pushes in a vertical row, each one with a name label alongside it. I counted ten labels and soon realised it was too dark to read them.

As I was stepping back out towards the car park someone rushed out of the door and brushed past me.

"Excuse me," I called hopefully.

"What? I'm in a hurry." The man turned, but continued to inch away backwards in a clumsy sort of way.

"I'm looking for Stuart Hemsley."

"Never heard of him."

His head turned back to face front, then he suddenly stopped and turned.

"No. I do know him. Over there – 7B."

He pointed briefly at the other entrance and then continued his run away from me.

"Thank you so much for your time and trouble," I muttered quietly to myself.

The other entrance was equally dark, but he had said 7B so I began counting down from the top, and when I reached the seventh label I strained my eyes to the limit to read what it said. I could see a clear H. That seemed good enough. I pressed the bell push.

"Yes?" The disembodied voice came from a metal grill speaker I hadn't noticed in the gloom.

"Stuart?"

"Yes. Who's this?"

"It's Greg Mason. I'm a friend of the Hetheringtons."

"Yes. I remember you from the pub."

"Can you spare me a few minutes?"

"I was about to go out. Will it take long?"

"Shouldn't think so. Depends."

"That sounds interesting. OK, come up. Second floor, on the left."

"Thanks."

I heard the door click open and had no trouble finding the stairs by the ceiling lights, most of which were on.

He was standing in the doorway when I reached it, straightening his shirt as if he had just dressed hurriedly. The state of his hair told me he was hot foot from the shower.

He looked fit, was certainly taller than me and had a pleasantly featured face, with piercing eyes.

I went in, and he followed me into a very masculine space, with brown leather swivel chairs, an enormous flat screen television, what looked like a top of the range sound system and a small, square glass topped dining table with a folding bistro chair at each side. Strange choice of dining chairs, I thought.

"Would you rather stand or sit?"

"I'll stand. That way I can keep up with you while you move about and get ready for wherever you are going. The Goose, is it?"

"How did you know that?"

"Well I know Joyce Hetherington. And I know you are, sorry, were a friend of her sister's and part of the gang that meets at The Goose quite often."

He was standing, staring at me, now.

"Why are you here?"

"I am looking into the circumstances of Helen's death."

"Oh, yes, that's right. You've become some sort of private detective, haven't you? So you've come here to practice on me, have you?"

"I'm speaking to everyone who had some connection with Helen. It's the only way to try to discover what happened and why."

"And are you going to question everyone who goes to The Goose?"

"That depends."

"On what?"

"On how much you can tell me."

"Does that mean I'm the first to experience your questioning technique?"

I suppose I should have expected a measure of sarcasm.

"Yes, as it happens."

He had begun to pace about the room in a rather nervous way. I just stood still and followed him with my eyes.

"So, tell me. How well did you know Helen?"

"She was part of the gang. You've been at The Goose with us sometimes. I've seen you. You know how we all get on."

"And some get on rather better than others."

"What's that supposed to mean?" He had stopped walking again and was staring at me. And if I was asked how he was staring, I would have to say defiantly.

"You tell me. Take any average group of school friends who stay in touch and meet regularly. Some male, some female. Now and again it would be natural for two of them to become particularly friendly, perhaps for a while, perhaps for good. Did you have a particular friend in that group?"

"We were all friends."

"Yes. We have established that. I am talking about special friends. Going out friends. Spending a lot of time together friends. Emailing each other a lot friends."

His head snapped towards me when I said that.

"Who told you?" he asked quietly.

"Helen's computer told me."

"You have no right to go nosing about in someone else's private messages."

"I have every right, if that person has died in mysterious circumstances and I have been asked to look into what happened."

The stare was back, but less defiant now, and Stuart flopped down into one of the swivel chairs.

"You were obviously very fond of her."

"I was crazy about her. I would have done anything for her. But she wasn't interested. Oh, she was happy to go out a few times; but as soon as she sensed something serious, she ended it."

"How soon before she died did she end it?" I knew the date from the computer, but I wanted to test his veracity. He was honest about that.

"So what did you do?"

"Do? Do?" His voice rose. "My God. You think I had something to do with her death."

"Did you?"

He leapt out of the chair and came at me, but I was too quick for him and dodged behind the dining table. We stood staring at each other. I could see his anger in the white of his knuckles as he held the back of a chair, and by the pulse at the side of his forehead.

"People can do strange, unexpected things when they are angry," I said. "When they are let down; when they lose the one thing in the world they really want."

"I wasn't angry with her, but I am angry with you for suggesting that I could hurt her. I would never have harmed her. I worshipped the ground she walked on."

He stepped back from the chair.

"OK, I was disappointed, bitterly disappointed. But I could never hurt her."

He hung his head, and I found myself believing him.

Chapter 4

Next morning I looked up Colbox online and then found them on Google Maps. It was only a short drive and I was there in ten minutes.

I hadn't made an appointment, and wondered if by suddenly turning up I might catch someone unawares.

The company was based in a metal version of its own product - a cream painted, rectangular box of corrugated steel. There were few windows except in a ground level extension which I took to be offices. A double glass door faced east and reflected the outline of trees picked out by the late rising sun.

Inside and facing me there was a hatch with a sliding door, above which it said Enquiries. There was no bell, so I tapped on the glass.

The bright and cheerful face of a young woman appeared. She looked about my age and was dressed in a tee shirt and pedal pushers. Clearly it was a lot warmer inside than out.

"Can I help?"

"My name's Greg Mason. I wonder if it would be possible to speak to your manager."

"Are you a client of ours?"

"No. I would like to speak to him about Helen Hetherington."

"Oh! So sad that was. We were all gutted. Are you with the police?"

"No. I am working privately for Helen's family."

No point in concealing the fact, I thought. My questions will make it clear why I am here.

"Mr. Jordan is in a meeting just at the moment, but he shouldn't be long. Would you like to wait?"

"Yes. Thank you."

"There are some chairs round that corner."

She pointed behind me and I turned.

"Can I get you a coffee?"

"That's very kind. Black, no sugar. Thank you, Miss...?"

"Overton. Sarah Overton."

Not G then, I thought.

As I walked back towards the waiting area I wondered how many others worked there, and how forthcoming Mr. Jordan might be.

The coffee arrived, and very good it was too, and I immersed myself in some motor magazines that would soon be as much in the vintage class as the cars they featured.

I was just glancing at my watch when Sarah came across and invited me to accompany her to Mr. Jordan's office.

"Mr. Jordan," I greeted him across his office. "Thank you for seeing me without an appointment."

"Frank, please. No need to be so formal."

That settled the FJ question.

He came out from behind a large desk; a tall, bluff man in crisp white shirtsleeves, with his arm outstretched to greet me. I took his firm handshake and held out a business card with my left hand.

"Greg Mason," I said. "I'm a friend of Helen's family. They are shattered by what's happened and have asked me to help by making some enquiries."

"Do you have any idea what happened?"

"Not as yet. I was hoping you might fill in some background for me."

"Of course. Helen was wonderful. Probably the best PA I ever had. I am finding it hard to replace her actually, and I realise now how much I came to depend on her."

"Would you say she was happy here?"

"Yes. I would. She worked hard and she was very popular with everyone. Her loss has left quite a gap here."

He was looking straight at me as he spoke and his voice carried a measure of sincerity. Either that or he was a consummate actor and I am useless as a detective.

I could see no reason why I should not come straight to the point.

"Do you have someone working here with a name beginning with G?"

"What an extraordinary question. Why G?"

"Something on Helen's laptop. Can you remember the day she died?"

"I remember how I felt when I heard. It was terrible."

"But can you recall anything particular that may have been happening here at that time, to do with Helen?"

"What do you mean?"

"Mr. Jordan. Frank," I corrected myself. "Neither Helen's sister nor I believe that Helen's death was an accident. That means someone caused it, for some reason or other. Therefore I am talking to her friends, her family, her work colleagues, anyone with any connection with her at all. I am convinced that someone knows what happened, and why."

"I see. Do the police share your suspicions?"

"Not at present, no. But I think they will when every avenue has been explored and all my questions have been answered."

He smiled.

"You sound very confident. How long have you been a detective?"

He must have seen my expression on hearing that question.

"Not very long, I'm guessing," he continued, and smiled even more.

This was another of those occasions when either I had to go with my initial judgement, or not. Did I trust this person? I couldn't trust everyone. Some people tell lies as easily as they take breath. I knew there were villains out there who could charm the birds from the trees, who could sell fridges to Eskimos and central heating units to Borneo tribesmen.

Or perhaps I didn't have to make an immediate decision.

"Do you have your diary there?" I asked him.

"Always," he said, putting the flat of his hand on the laptop which lay closed in front of him.

"Could you look at the day Helen died, and perhaps the day after?"

He looked at me curiously, then opened the computer and made a few clicks. I watched his expression.

"Yes," he said, without any apparent attempt to hide the fact. "We were due to meet that day."

"The day after she died."

"Yes."

"Why would Helen feel the need to make a special appointment to see you? She must have seen a lot of you every day, through a normal course of events."

"That's true."

He furrowed his brow and leaned forwards with his crossed arms resting on the desk.

"She said there was something particular she wanted to tell me about. No, not wanted," he corrected himself. "Needed. I remember now. I asked why she couldn't just ask me straight out. And she said it was difficult."

"And you have no idea what it was about."

"None at all," and he sat back in his chair as I continued to monitor his expression. He seemed to be telling the truth. So there I was again, not being sure about the person I was talking to.

"That brings me to the person whose name begins with G. It was that person Helen wanted to talk to you about."

"How do you know that?"

"It was in her diary. I quote," pulling out a notebook: "*meeting FJ to discuss G.* So who is G?"

"G," he said, thinking aloud. "There's a Gemma in the office and there's a Grant in dispatch. That's all, I think. We are not a large company."

"Could I speak to them both?"

"Of course, if it would help. In fact it might help me to know of something that was going on here I didn't know about."

He got up and came round his desk.

"No time like the present. Why don't you see them in here? There are other places I can be for a while."

That struck me as the offer of someone prepared to be totally open with me. Perhaps I was right about him after all.

"Thank you. That would be very helpful."

"I'll get Sarah to fetch Gemma, and then you can see Grant after that."

He was quickly at the door, leaving me to wonder how to proceed. Where should I sit? Would it be appropriate to take the boss's chair behind the big desk? I decided not, and stayed where I was.

Sarah came in after a couple of minutes, leading a young woman who looked very nervous. She was wearing a tight skirt and a white pleated blouse which extenuated her figure. Her hair was short and pulled back above her ears, with some sort of gel holding it in place. I rose to greet her.

"Gemma?"

"Yes. Mr. Jordan said you wanted to see me."

"Sit down, won't you?" I indicated the other chair provided for visitors.

I smiled to put Gemma at her ease, but she still looked wary and uncomfortable.

"My name's Greg Mason, and I'm helping Helen Hetherington's family to try to find out what happened to her."

"I thought it was an accident."

"We hope to find out one way or another. Tell me how you got on with Helen, here at Colbox."

"I didn't have much to do with her. She worked in Mr. Jordan's office and I spend my time in the main office."

The worry lines I had noticed above her nose and across her forehead were still in place. I thought her answer a little too simple and straight forward.

"How long have you worked here?"

"Just short of five years."

"Always in the same position."

"I had a promotion just over a year ago."

"A big promotion?"

"Well – more money and more responsibility, but in the same department."

"Which is?"

"Process Management."

"Which means what exactly?"

"We monitor the performance of the company and try to find ways of keeping us ahead of the competition."

"Is there a lot of competition?

"Yes. Always."

I had kept my notebook in my hand and began to write a few words.

"Do you know how long Helen has worked here?"

"Er…I should think just over two years or so."

"And was she appointed as Mr. Jordan's PA straight away?"

"No. She started in our department and was promoted later."

"How did you feel about that?"

"It had nothing to do with me."

"But were you jealous? Did you think you would have made a better PA than Helen?"

"Helen was good. I had no complaints."

"I see." I wrote a few more words.

"Now you said earlier that you didn't have much to do with Helen. Yet you worked in the same department. For how long?"

"I don't know. Several months."

"Did you get to know her very well in that time?"

"She was very quiet. A bit studious. She liked to get on with things. Most of us are a bit chatty, but Helen wasn't like that."

"So she was different. And did that create any sort of problem between you?"

"No. She got on with her work and we got on with ours."

"So there was no sense of bitterness about her being promoted, when you had been there longer?"

"No. I told you."

A slight edge had come into her voice and I wondered why. Why should she be annoyed? What was she not telling me?

"Can you remember the day she died?"

"Not really. I know it was just a few weeks ago."

"Do you know the place where she died?"

"No. Why should I? What are you suggesting?"

"I'm not suggesting anything. I'm just trying to get to know as much as I can about the people Helen knew."

"I told you. I didn't know her very well."

"Yes. Yes, you did."

I wrote a few more words in my notebook, then closed it, looked across at Gemma and stood up.

"Well, thank you for your time. You have helped me fill in the picture of what it was like for Helen at work."

She looked relieved as she got up and accepted my handshake.

I gave her one of my cards.

"If you think of anything else which might be important, or just interesting, you can reach me here."

She looked down at the card, back up at my face and then left without another word.

When she had left I read and reread what I had written, and a few minutes later Grant was ushered into the room. He looked very puzzled and not sure what to do.

I greeted him with a handshake as he looked about him at the office.

"I've only been in here once before," he said. "It's a bit more comfortable than where I work."

He didn't sound resentful, just matter of fact.

"What's this about?"

"Helen Hetherington."

"Oh, yes. She died. Very sad."

"Did you know her?"

"Not really at all. I saw her about, but not very often. I don't think we ever spoke to each other."

"Do you recall ever hearing anyone talk about her?"

"No. I don't think so. Why?"

"I'm just trying to get a better picture of her life here."

"You don't think it was an accident. Fascinating."

"Why do you say that?"

"I love a good mystery. You think someone caused her death, and you're wondering if they work here."

Then his expression completely changed.

"So why do you want to speak to me? I can't think of anyone here who would know less about her than me."

"What did you think of her?"

"I didn't think of her at all," he said and smiled. "Are you asking everyone who works here? Next you'll be asking where I was when she died."

"And where were you?"

"I have no idea when she died – or where."

"You can't remember."

"Not exactly. It was about a month ago, I would guess. Where, I haven't a clue."

"Didn't you read about it?"

"No. Why would I? I wasn't that interested."

"Most people would show a little interest in a work colleague who died in mysterious circumstances."

"Would they? Well, not me. As I said, I didn't know her. We may have both worked here, but I wouldn't call us colleagues. It was sad. What more was there to know?"

I could discern no sense of deceit in either his face or his voice. He seemed genuine. A little callous, perhaps, not to be concerned about Helen's death. But if he didn't know her, as he said, perhaps it was understandable.

"All right, Grant. Thank you for your time."

I held out another card. They were beginning to spread like confetti.

"Let me know if you think of anything, would you?"

He took the card and looked down at it.

"I'll let you get back to work."

He shrugged, rose and left. His boss passed him just outside the door and I saw them exchange glances, almost half smiles, but that was all.

Grant was gone, and Frank came back in, walking straight to his black, leather swivel chair behind the desk. His comfort zone.

Then I thought, why would he need a comfort zone?

Because he likes being the boss? Because he's more comfortable being the boss? Or could it be because he wants to maintain the dominant position over others in his office. And me.

Perhaps I was wrong to trust him. Maybe he was pulling the wool over my eyes by being co-operative. Or maybe his preference for his own chair has no relevance to the case at all. Perhaps it's just the type of man he is.

Anyway, I thought, there was no evidence to suggest that Helen did not get on well with him. I was here to investigate G, whoever G was.

"Did you learn anything?" Frank said, and I was immediately aware that I had been miles away, staring at the notebook in my lap. I looked up, embarrassed.

"Sorry. I was thinking."

He smiled.

"Were Gemma or Grant able to help you?"

"I'm not sure. If Helen wanted, or needed, to see you about G, is there anything else beginning with G you can think of? Anything to do with the firm perhaps, or customers, clients, products?"

"Nothing that occurs to me," he said.

"Then I suppose we must assume that Helen felt a need to talk to you about either Gemma or Grant."

"But why?"

"Grant says he hardly knew her. Her death appears not to have fazed him at all."

He waited before replying, while I paused and read my notes again.

"And what about Gemma?" he asked.

"She says she didn't have much to do with Helen, although, as I understand it, they worked in the same department for a while."

"Yes, they did."

"How many are there in that department?"

"Only two now."

"So there were three, perhaps, before Helen became your PA."

"Yes. That's right."

"Don't you think it would be difficult not to get to know someone if you were working with them in such a small department?"

"I can certainly see what you mean. But are you implying that Gemma had something to do with what happened to Helen."

"Not yet. It would be interesting, though, if we knew for certain that Gemma is the G that worried Helen so much. Jealousy could be a motive."

Frank shuffled in his chair.

"I'm not comfortable with the thought that someone who caused Helen's death is still working here," he said.

"Well I'm sorry to have sown the seeds of discomfort, but I'm only just at the start of this investigation. I know virtually nothing yet. Anything which might be relevant has to be taken seriously until I know for sure that there is no connection with Helen's death. I'm sure you understand that."

"Yes, of course."

His expression changed, but the signs of his concern still remained.

"When was the last time you saw Helen?"

"The morning of the day she died. She was here, at work, as usual. Then she had the afternoon off. She would sometimes work extra hours in the evening and have half days off to make up for it. It was one of those days."

"Can you remember how she was that day?"

"Not really. She always got on with her work very efficiently. She never hung around, if you know what I mean. Always busy, was Helen. It's still funny, being reminded she's not here."

He looked genuinely moved and I felt there was nothing left to ask.

I stood up and put the notebook back in my pocket.

"I'm very grateful for your time and your hospitality. I'll have another word with Sarah, if I may, before I leave. You have my card. If anything occurs to you, particularly in relation to G, please give me a call."

He picked up the card from his desk and read it.

"Yes," he said. "I will."

We shook hands again and I left him in his office and returned to the enquiries window.

Sarah responded to my tap very quickly.

"Hello. It's me again."

I saw some faces turn towards us as I spoke and thought it would be a good idea to speak to her privately.

"Could you come out to speak to me for a second? Walls have ears. You know what I mean."

She turned round, understood immediately and came out to meet me in the lobby. I held the door open for her and we went outside. Then she turned and gave me a funny look and it was my turn to recognise immediately what she was thinking.

"No," I said. "I'm not trying to get off with you." I smiled and she smiled back as if she believed me and was relieved.

"I'm just looking for some help," I continued. "You were fond of Helen, weren't you?"

"Yes. I was. What happened was terrible."

"And you would like to help, if you can, to find out what happened?"

"I would like to, but I don't see how I can."

I gave her a card and decided to be straight with her.

"In Helen's diary I found a reference to a G – something or someone that concerned Helen so much, she had made a special appointment to talk to Mr Jordan about it."

"That's why you spoke to Gemma and Grant."

"That's right. But it might not be a person. It might be a thing, or a place, or anything beginning with G. Would you have a think and see if there is anything that has happened recently which might help me. It might be about Gemma or Grant, or not. Whatever it is. If you think of anything, would you give me a ring?"

"Yes. Of course."

"Thanks. I'm grateful for your help."

I turned and walked back to my car, wondering if my visit had served any purpose. Maybe Helen's concern at work had no connection with her death. But with the planned meeting due the following day, there was always the chance.

The thought reminded me of a favourite quote of mine from 'Sherlock Holmes': 'Are there not subtle forces at work of which we know little?'

How many subtle forces are at work in this case? How much of Helen's life remained unknown to the rest of the family? No one knew she was seeing Stuart. Joyce thought she was happy at work, yet there was something worrying her so much, she felt a need to speak to her boss about it.

Gemma had called her quiet. It seemed she was also private, and I realised this might make it difficult to get at the information I would need to crack this case.

I slid a Supertramp CD into the slot and heard Roger Hodgson sing "It's raining." And so it was.

By the time I reached home it had stopped again. Wintry shower, the weatherman would have called it. It was certainly wintry and I was glad to be back indoors.

I made some coffee and read again my notes from Colbox, but I couldn't see anything obvious. Grant seemed to know nothing. The boss appeared to be honest and open, as did Sarah. I was not so sure about Gemma, but I had absolutely nothing to go on.

It occurred to me that I hadn't asked Gemma where she was on the evening Helen died. Perhaps I would need to ask her later. Or perhaps not. The case was beginning to fill with possibilities.

Chapter 5

Later, I drove out to Dedham to meet Joyce's mother. We had met a few times before over the years, but it was a while since I had seen her.

The house stood back from a long, straight road and was sheltered from traffic noise by several large trees. With its extensive garden and double garage it gave an impression of considerable financial comfort.

It made me think of the financial stability I had given up, and I wondered where I would be living when I was Joyce's mother's age. Perhaps dossing down in my London office, still waiting for clients.

When she opened the door I was shocked by her appearance. I remembered a young-looking, lively person. The woman I found was visibly ageing, with a lot of vertical lines on her face, as if the weight of concern was pulling everything down.

"Hello Greg," she said with little enthusiasm. "Come in."

I stepped into a spacious hall which was well lit from a full length window behind the stairwell. The floor was carpeted and everything looked neat and tidy as I had always remembered it.

"Joyce has gone off to the gym," she said.

She led me into a living room which my mother would have called 'lived in'. There were magazines on low tables, cushions scattered along settees, a few sports trophies on a thick mantle above a wood burning stove, all giving an atmosphere of comfort rather than opulence.

A cat which was lying in front of the wood burning stove lifted its head to look at me, but obviously decided I was neither threat nor interest and went back to sleep.

"I hope this isn't going to be difficult for you," I said, "but I think it would help if I understood a little more about your family."

"Yes, of course. Sit down. Would you like a coffee?"

"Yes, that would be good. Thanks."

"Milk and sugar?"

"Neither, thanks."

She went towards the kitchen and before I sat down, I sauntered round the room trying to build a picture.

A friend had once described a game which involved going into the living room of a complete stranger, and trying, by dint of observation and deduction, to discover the person's interests, hobbies and family details. I looked at the books, a mixture of modern novels, biography, movie history, art and travel. There were photographs of an elderly couple, someone's parents I assumed, two young girls, easily distinguishable as Helen and Joyce, and Joyce's parents leaning on a five bar gate somewhere, looking weather-beaten and happy.

There was a collection of music on vinyl and CDs, well known classical works, some ballet music and a great deal of rock music from the 60s and 70s. A Radio Times lay open at the page of an article about current film releases.

I tried to work out an obvious link between it all, but couldn't think of one, and then the coffee arrived, so I took the mug and sat down.

"If I ask you anything which you would rather not talk about, just tell me."

"All right. What do you want to know?"

"Joyce said you have no idea where Helen was going, that last night."

"No. She didn't say. She seemed quite excited about something when she left for work, though."

"Could she have been meeting someone?"

"It's possible, but if so, I have no idea who."

I sipped my coffee and thought.

"She was happy at work?"

"Yes."

"No problems there?"

"Not that I'm aware of."

"I've been to Colbox this morning. Mr Jordan was very helpful, but I didn't learn anything."

There was no point in adding to her grief by telling her of a concern which was still unknown and might be totally irrelevant. It was interesting, though, that Helen's mother thought she was happy at work. I wondered what else Helen had not told her.

"Did she have a regular boyfriend?"

"No. She had lots of friends. She was always going out with someone. But there was no one special."

Interesting again. Helen apparently hadn't mentioned Stuart to her mother, but surely that was hardly relevant to anything. Again I decided it would be inconsiderate to mention something she didn't need to know, and may never need to know. I kept quiet about Stuart.

"Joyce told me that she and Helen were half-sisters."

"Yes. I was married before. He died."

Her expression suggested little remorse at that fact, and I let it go.

"How much younger than Helen is Joyce?"

"About two years."

"So you must have met her father soon after Helen's father died."

"Yes," she said, looking hard at me.

I sipped my coffee and considered the impertinence of my last question.

"Actually, you might as well know. We knew each other before Helen's father died."

This was interesting, but again hardly relevant, and I had no reason to pry into her private life.

"You were old friends, then?"

"Not old friends exactly, but I did meet him before my husband was killed."

"Joyce said something about an accident."

"Yes. He had a motorbike."

She said no more, obviously thinking the rest was obvious. It was.

"I'm sorry," I offered.

She shrugged.

"It was a long time ago."

"And Helen never knew him."

"No. Oliver has always been," she paused to correct herself with some effort, "was always her father."

I finished my coffee. I couldn't see how anything was helping me.

"Look, would you mind if I take a look in Helen's room? You never know. There might be something that springs out at me."

"No, go ahead. I'll show you where it is."

She led me upstairs. Her movements were of someone pushing her legs through treacle. Everything a visible effort, her body weighed down by thoughts and despair. I wondered, as many others have, how any parent ever copes with losing a child. And to lose a child in such a tragic way, and not to know why.

This led me to realise again the importance of finding the truth and the responsibility on my shoulders. I hoped I could live up to it.

We came to a spacious bedroom with its bed made up as if its regular user was due back at any moment. There was a dressing table and wardrobe in matching coloured pine, and in the corner a work area with the laptop, now returned, box files and shelves of ring binders.

I just stood in the room and looked about me, wondering where to start.

"I'll leave you to it, shall I? If you need me, I'll be downstairs."

"Thanks," I said rather inadequately.

Crossing to the wardrobe I discovered Helen's clothes, still there waiting for something or someone. The drawers in the dressing table were full and well ordered – underwear mainly, some tights, lots of feminine odds and ends, sweaters – nothing out of the ordinary.

I glanced at the desk area in the corner. If there was going to be anything interesting and relevant, I would find it there.

The box files were all labelled neatly – Work, Holidays, Family, Finance. Which one first? Joyce had thought everything was straight forward at work and her mother thought the same. But I needed to know who or what was G, so I opened the work file first.

It was virtually empty. There were copies of application forms, brochures from companies, perhaps dating back to before Helen went to Colbox, but there was nothing useful that I could see. No letters, or notes, or names. I closed the file and returned it to its place.

I couldn't think of any reason why a holiday or its plans could kill Helen. So I turned to Finance.

There were bank statements going back a year or two and an assortment of letters. I shuffled carefully through them and found they were grouped together with paper clips – one lot from Helen's tax office, more from the bank, some from a loan company. I looked more carefully at them and they referred to a loan taken out six months earlier for quite a sizeable sum.

Reference to the bank statements showed me a regular salary going in, and monthly loan repayments after the date the loan was agreed, and I determined to ask her mother about that later. The bank statements also showed a regular balance each month end, with no overdraft. That was relatively unusual and quite refreshing. It spoke well of Helen. The balance was not enormous, but at least it showed she was living within her means, so that gave no clue towards a suicide theory.

The family file contained a lot of photographs and I took them over to the bed and spread them out. It was easy to recognise Helen and Joyce at various ages. Their parents were pictured in the garden, near the sea, at places which looked rather exotic – I couldn't tell where. There were a few pictures of Helen's mother with a man I didn't know, probably Helen's biological father, I wondered. The clothes suggested the pictures were taken in the sixties. He wore a sports jacket and tie, and she had hair built up into a beehive and was wearing a very short skirt in a floral-print fabric.

None of the pictures gave much of a clue. They were virtually all posed, with smiles giving an appearance of relaxation and happiness, but how much of that was artificial I had no way of knowing.

Collecting the photos together again I took them back to the box file and found an envelope I hadn't noticed before. I paused. It was one thing to look through a person's photos, quite another to read their mail. But Joyce didn't mind me reading Helen's emails, and leaving the letter in the envelope would serve absolutely no purpose.

I took out a single piece of paper. It was headed with the name of a law firm, Grace, Swindle and Little, and dated a few weeks before. It related to the will of Helen's grandmother and the person who had been the sole beneficiary. There was no name mentioned. The letter simply confirmed that the solicitor was unable to give Helen any more details than those given at the reading of the will.

What was all that about? And who was the grandmother? Her mother's or her father's mother? Something else to ask about downstairs.

I made a note of the solicitor's details and put the letter back in its envelope. Then I closed the box file, putting them all back in their original order.

The ring binders were labelled as carefully as the box files and most contained notes from various courses Helen had attended. There was nothing that looked helpful, so I left them side by side and turned again to look around the room.

Once more I found myself trying to get into another detective's shoes. What would Rockford or Colombo look for? Or Sam Spade or Poirot, or any other? Was there something about the room that I was missing? Some obvious clue? If there was, I couldn't see it, so I left the room as I had found it and went back downstairs.

Joyce's mother was ironing in the kitchen, an expression of bored resolve showed in her reflection from a small mirror. The radio was playing light music and she didn't hear me come in.

As she turned to pick up something she saw me in the doorway, and jumped.

"Sorry," I said. "I didn't mean to startle you."

"It's my fault," she said. "I seem to be always on edge just lately."

I moved into the room and leaned against the kitchen table, wondering how to ask about personal details. It was more difficult, having known the family to a certain extent for a long time, than it would have been for a perfect stranger. I hoped this wouldn't cause a problem.

"Can I ask you about two things?" I began, "And tell me if you think I'm prying into corners which you think should be left private."

She stood the iron up on its back and turned to face me.

"There's been so much happening recently. We've taken so many knocks. Losing Helen was like the last straw."

I waited for her to continue. She turned her attention to the sink, picking up a cloth and idly wiping the surround - working out how much to say, I suspected.

"When my mother-in-law died," she said, "we lost a true friend. Oliver had recently been made redundant, and the two things coming close together were difficult to cope with."

"I didn't know your husband lost his job."

"Yes. His bank was taken over, and they were rationalised - that was the word they used. Meaning slimmed down. They had too many investment managers"

"That must have come as a shock."

"It did. It came totally out of the blue. One month we were comfortably off, and the next he was unemployed."

"But not for long, I should think. If he was an investment manager, he must have a lot of talent and experience. I should think he would be picked up quite quickly."

"That's what we hoped would happen. Oliver used to talk about head-hunters in the City, but he's stopped referring to that now. He says he's too old. You worked in the City, didn't you? What do you think?"

There was hopefulness in her voice, and I knew I couldn't help, but didn't want to say anything either trite or disheartening.

"I don't know," I said uselessly. "I hope he finds something soon."

Then something else occurred to me.

"And, of course, Joyce lost her job not so long ago."

I regretted saying it as soon it came out.

"Yes. She came home, so there were now four mouths to feed, and only Helen working."

None of this had any connection with Helen, and I could see I was only making Joyce's mother feel worse. Keep to the subject, I told myself. You're trying to help her, not make her miserable. Say something positive, for God's sake.

"I found some of Helen's bank details upstairs. It looks as if she was very careful with her money."

"Yes. She was. Oliver taught her to be like that. She was a very sensible girl. We'll miss her a lot."

Her head began to drop as she spoke, and I noticed her shoulders beginning to shake. I moved up behind her and held her upper arms and she turned, her head falling on my shoulder as her body wracked with sobs.

After a few moments she sniffed very hard and lifted her head again.

"I'm sorry," she said.

"There's no need to be. I'm sorry that my questions are making you feel worse."

She pulled away from me and fished in her pocket for a handkerchief, then blew her nose.

"Do you want me to leave everything else for now?" I suggested.

"No. I'll be all right if I sit down for a bit. Let's go back in the living room."

"Don't forget the iron," I said.

"Oh, yes. Thanks. I'll be forgetting my own head soon."

She sat on a chair, her knees pulled tightly together, her handkerchief in her hand, trying very hard to hold herself together.

I took the long, leather sofa.

"What was it you wanted to ask me?"

"You've answered one of my questions already. I found a letter referring to the will of Helen's grandmother, and you told me it was your mother-in-law."

"Ex mother-in-law."

"Oh. I see. You kept in touch, then?"

"Yes. Oh, that's a whole other story," she said, her head flopping back to the cushion. We became very close during my first marriage. She was always so supportive. She came down to live near here. After her sons and husband had died, she had no one else, so she sold up and came to live near us."

"The letter referred to the sole beneficiary of her will. Was there some mystery about the person who inherited?"

"There was more than mystery. There was complete surprise. It came as rather a shock."

"Do you know the person who inherited?"

"We know her name. It was read out with the will. But we don't know who she is and why Annie left everything to her. We'd expected Helen to inherit."

"As her direct descendant?"

"Of course."

This was intriguing and again I wondered if it was relevant.

"Would you like to tell me what happened?"

Joyce's mother continued to lean back and I could see her thoughts drifting away to an entirely different time and place. When she spoke she was looking, not at me, but up to the ceiling, as if seeing a rerun of past experiences on an invisible screen.

"When Alan died, Annie's husband, he wasn't very old, and Annie was bereft. You can imagine how she felt. Although Scotland was home for her, it was now so filled with bad memories, she wanted to get away. Anyway, as she said, she had no one left up there, and we were here, so she decided to move south.

"My parents helped me find a house for her in Ipswich and she seemed to settle in quite quickly. In fact in the last few months of her life she seemed to get younger, if you can understand what I mean."

She looked across at me at that point. My expression must have shown my puzzlement.

"It was as if she had found a new lease of life. She was always fit and healthy and she made friends easily. We put it down to the effect of new interests, new friends perhaps. She used to visit us here and sometimes she would visit my parents.

"We spoke on the phone most days. She seemed very happy and settled. But then she had a fall and broke her hip. That was the start really. She never got over it and went downhill quite quickly.

"By the time she died all the flesh had fallen from her bones. She told me she was ready to go, and she died, late one night."

I could see how much Annie was missed. She was spoken about with considerable love and affection.

"Had she spoken to you about her will?"

"When she first came down, Oliver gave her lots of advice. You have to understand, she had a lot of money after selling her estates, even after buying her new house. Oliver advised her on how to invest it, how to make it work is the expression he used.

"We knew she had made a will, but she never discussed it with me. I suppose we always assumed that Helen, as her only descendant...oh dear."

Her voice trailed away and tears began to appear.

"I'm sorry." She dabbed at her eyes.

"Take your time," I said. "And if it's too hard to talk about it, we can discuss it again another time."

"No. We might as well do it now."

I waited while she collected her thoughts again.

"The reading of the will was going to be a formality. Annie had used her family's solicitors, and we went up to London to see them. When he said there was a sole beneficiary, I remember squeezing Oliver's hand.

"He had been so upset at losing his job, and Helen had planned to start a new business with him, with the money she was left. Then the solicitor said the name – Ilse Chambers. We just stared at him, and I remember, we all said 'Who?' together. And he said he was not at liberty to say any more.

"We asked him to check there was no mistake – to see if Helen had not been left at least something. But he said 'No'. We were devastated."

What a strange thing to happen, I thought. Now if Helen had inherited instead of someone else, I could envisage a possible motive for murder. But not the other way round. It didn't make any sense. Perhaps, once again, it wasn't relevant. Just strange.

It was at that moment that Joyce's father returned. He looked unhappy and a little harassed.

"Any joy, my darling?" his wife asked him.

"No. The same old story. Too old."

He came across to kiss his wife and noticed me.

"Oh, hello Greg. We haven't seen you for a long time. Pam told me you might be coming."

"We were just talking about the will."

"Oh that! What a shocker. Who the hell is that person, for God's sake?"

"You still don't know?"

"No idea," he said. "Look – does anyone fancy a drink? I'm dying for a cup of tea."

He looked around.

"Not for me, thanks. I must be going in a minute."

"I will, please," his wife said.

Joyce's father bustled off into the kitchen and her mother turned back to me.

"I was just going to ask you about a loan Helen took out a few months ago," I said.

"That was for her car. She was thrilled with her Golf. And now it's just sitting in the garage."

"Ah, that's that, then. I'll leave you in peace now."

I rose and tried to smile.

"Oh, one more thing. Do you have a recent picture of Helen I could have? You never know, it might come in useful."

"Yes. I'll get you one."

She went upstairs and returned after a minute or two, tears running down her cheeks.

"I'm sorry to have caused you to remember things," I said, taking the photograph she offered.

"It's not your fault, Greg. The memory of her is so raw, I can't stop thinking about her."

I was lost for words. Nothing would have been adequate. Best to keep quiet.

"You've been very helpful," I said. "I'm sorry you're having such a bad time of it at present." The words sounded totally inadequate, but were the best I could do.

She didn't reply, but moved along the hall to see me off.

"Say goodbye to your husband for me," I said, as she opened the front door. "And I will do all I can to find out what happened."

"I know you will," she said with about as little confidence as I had at that moment.

Chapter 6

I found Joyce already at the pub. She was sitting on a stool at the bar and I took the one next to her.

Her time at the gym had left her looking flushed, but there were still worry lines where I had seen them before.

"How did you find Mum?"

"Not as I remembered her," I said.

I ordered a pint for me and another fizzy mixer for Joyce.

"She's had a rough time," Joyce said. "We all have."

"Let's go and find a table," I suggested. "Then we can talk."

We found a relatively quiet corner, but the pub was busy and there was a lot of competing conversation.

"I went to see Stuart last night," I told her.

"Yes, there was some mention of it at The Goose. I thought you might have come to join us."

"I decided against it, having just spoken to him. It would have looked rather odd if I'd followed him there."

Joyce nodded and sipped at her drink.

"Do you think he's involved?"

"He's very convincing when he says he would never have hurt Helen."

"Do you believe him?"

"Well, I am inclined to give him the benefit of the doubt for the present. But I don't know if that's just because I don't want to think of any of your friends being involved."

"I hope it's not Stuart."

"That's what I mean. It would be even more distressing if it was him."

As I drank my pint, I pondered the difficulty of being entirely objective in this job. How to set aside friendships when guilt becomes obvious.

All I could do was leave Stuart as a possible, while following up other lines of enquiry.

"I also went up to Colbox to talk to people there."

"How did you get on?"

"The boss seems amenable and willing to help, and I felt the same about someone called Sarah who deals with enquiries as you go in."

"I see."

"What does that mean?"

"Oh, nothing," she said, and smiled.

I looked at her, mystified. Must be a girl thing, I thought.

"Anyway," I went on, "there are only two people working there whose names begin with G."

"Really?"

"Yes. There's a Gemma and a Grant. Grant says he knew Helen hardly at all, and what he said rang true. He works in a different part of the building. He's not the sort of person I would expect Helen to have associated with, and he seemed genuine when he spoke to me."

"That's what you said about Stuart."

"I know. Are you beginning to doubt my judgement?"

"Of course not. It's difficult knowing who you can believe. What about Gemma?"

"Now she's interesting. She worked in the same department as Helen for a while, and then Helen was promoted to PA virtually over Gemma's head."

"So she might have been jealous."

"She might have been, although she said not."

'She would, wouldn't she?"

"And there was something else about her whole demeanour while I was talking to her."

"What do you mean?"

"She was far from relaxed – much more wary, I would say, as if she was being careful what she said."

"So you think she was hiding something?"

"It's possible that she was, yes."

Joyce took another sip of her drink and I began to think again, particularly about the question of judging people from what they say and how they look when they say it.

"Let's leave Stuart and Colbox on the back burner for a moment," I said. "The other thing I'm trying to do is put together a picture of your family and its background. I have no idea if any of it means anything, but some interesting points came up with your mum this morning."

She looked up at me over the menu she had been studying. "Like what?"

"Well, your grandmother's will, for a start. What's that all about?"

"Oh, that."

She put down the menu.

"Granny owned a lot of land, and when her husband died she decided she couldn't cope with it any more. She had farm managers and people running everything, but she felt very cut off and lonely."

"She had lost her son as well."

"She lost both sons at once," she corrected me.

"What?"

"They were both on the motorbike when it crashed."

"God, that must have devastated her."

"I think it nearly killed them both. Grandad had worked hard keeping the estates going. Apparently he used to talk a lot about how long they had been in the family, and the importance of continuing the line."

"And they lost the next generation."

"Exactly."

We fell silent for a while and returned to studying the menus. There was something niggling at the back of my mind, but I couldn't quite reach it, so I went up to the bar to order our food.

When I returned to the table, Joyce looked up at me with rather a blank expression.

"We're not getting anywhere with this, are we?"

She sounded despondent. I tried to sort my thoughts into some kind of order.

"Your granny must have been worth a fair amount after she sold her land. Was it an estate, did you say?"

"Two estates, yes. One came from her family, and one from his. She felt quite guilty about letting them go, I think. She used to say the land was no use to her. That she had done nothing to earn it – that it was something of a burden really."

I recalled what Joyce's mother had told me.

"And if both her sons died, you would have expected Helen to inherit?"

"Of course. She was the only direct descendent, her granddaughter."

"But everything went to somebody else."

"Yes, and nobody knows who she is and why she inherited."

Our food arrived and we began to eat rather thoughtfully.

"Obviously your granny had given no indication of what was in the will."

"No. But we all assumed it would be straightforward. It was going to be something of a relief actually."

"How do you mean?"

"Well Dad lost his job. He had some ideas of things he could do, but they all required capital, and all Mum and Dad had was locked up in the house. And that was already mortgaged."

"So the inheritance would have been useful, for setting something up."

"Yes. I think there was some plan about Helen going to work with Dad. Investing in the new business. I don't know any details."

"And someone else got the money."

"Mum and Dad were furious. There was a bit of a scene when granny's will was read out."

"Were you there?"

"Yes. We all were."

"When you say 'all'?"

"I mean, all four of us."

"No one else?"

"Certainly not the person who inherited, if that's what you mean."

"So what happened?"

"We went to the solicitor's office in London. He opened the will and read it out and Dad hit the roof. He said there must be some mistake and asked who the person was who was stealing all our money."

"And the solicitor wouldn't say?"

"He said it was granny's strict instruction that no details should be given."

"Your mum mentioned her name."

"Ilse Chambers."

"Yes."

"And no one's ever heard of her."

We continued to eat.

"How long ago did this happen?"

"You mean the will?"

"Yes."

"A few weeks ago. Just before Helen died."

"I found a letter in Helen's room, from a solicitor, saying he was unable to divulge the name of the beneficiary. That suggests that Helen was trying to discover who it is."

"Do you think this has any connection with her death?"

"I can't see how or why. But it's all a bit mysterious. And if Helen was asking questions – with a lot of money involved – it's possible."

We ate on in silent thought for a while.

After the meal, I went home to think things through. Who was the mysterious beneficiary? Why had she inherited? Had Helen discovered who she was? Is that why she was killed? Why should anyone kill her anyway? Was the inheritance a red herring? Was it Stuart after all? Or Gemma? Or someone else entirely?

The more I thought about it, the more I could see no other motive for Helen's death. It was either the rage of a frustrated lover, or jealousy, or money. Three of the classic motives. But which one?

If it was Stuart, how could I break his convincing denials? If it was Gemma, how could I break her down? If it was the inheritance, why the secrecy from Helen's grandmother? What was in her past that she wanted hidden? And who was it who attacked Joyce in London, and why? That must be connected somehow. But how?

I decided to work some more on the inheritance, and tried what I often did when faced with a mysterious name. I turned to the phone book and looked up Chambers. There were several columns of them, and quite a few listed as I. Chambers. The only way to discover if one of them was Ilse, would be to call them all.

But that was assuming she lived locally. Surely that was unlikely. She could be anywhere.

If Helen's granny had moved from her home area to be near her family, the secret, whatever it was, would be where she came from. Wouldn't it?

I decided to call all the I. Chambers in the book, and it took the best part of half an hour. None of them was Ilse. At least none of them was saying they were Ilse.

Could I trust what they said? It was so easy in this business to develop conspiracy theories. Not to trust anyone. Which detective was it who said "Believe no one"? Following that philosophy to the letter would make investigation very difficult.

As I was closing my notebook, I noticed the list of names I had made when I spoke to people near the site of Helen's accident. On the spur of the moment I decided to change tack, and turned my attention back to them.

There wasn't a Chambers in the list, then, of course, there wouldn't be, if not in the phone book. None of the names meant anything to me.

I thought again of the threats in London. The source had to be one of those people, always assuming it wasn't Stuart or another of Helen's friends from the pub. But which one? Or Gemma? And if there was a link between the will and Helen's death, and I had spoken to a person involved without realising it, that might have caused them to panic. Hence the threats.

Was it possible Ilse was using an assumed name? More probable than possible, I thought, if she wanted to keep herself secret, so I went back to the phone book and looked up all the surnames from the list in my notebook in turn, running my finger down the addresses of each in search of Monks Colne, where Helen had died.

There it was. I. Lamont, Orchard Cottages, Monks Colne. Could it be a coincidence? Is there really such a thing, I asked myself.

It could be Ian perhaps, or Ingrid? I had to find out.

I called Joyce and asked her her grandmother's name.

"Glenn," she said. "Annie Glenn. Why?"

"Oh, I just had an idea, but it doesn't seem to mean anything."

"What was the idea?"

"I was trying to tie together several things; those threats at the office, the will, and the place where Helen died. But I can't seem to find any common element. I'm sorry to bother you again. I'll be in touch again soon."

I rang off. So much for that idea. Now where was I?

If the will led to a dead end, at least I could try to follow up the threats. I decided to return to Monks Colne and talk once again to people who lived near the lane.

The big house on the corner looked like a smallholding. There was an enormous front garden and a drive skirted the house to the left towards a collection of low buildings. I rang the bell and a very flustered looking woman opened the door, shouting to a dog which appeared intent on disobedience, for as the door opened, it flung itself upon me with great enthusiasm.

"Monty, come," the woman shouted, to no avail.

"I'm so sorry," she said, as I tried to retain my balance despite the legs which had been determinedly placed on my shoulders, pushing me away from the doorway.

She followed, pulling on the dog's collar, trying to threaten or cajole the creature into obedience. Neither worked.

Suddenly a male voice from the corner of the house yelled the dog's name, and all interest in me was lost as Monty sped away in search of his master.

"I'm so sorry," the woman said again as I tried to readjust my clothes.

She was middle aged and had on one of those head squares which cover the top of the head and are then tied behind on the neck. Below her neck was a long, floppy T-shirt and a rather unflattering pair of slacks.

"He's still only a puppy at heart." She had turned and was watching him disappear round the corner.

My intention of making a professional impression was totally lost as I straightened my tie and shrugged my jacket back onto my shoulders.

She turned back to face me.

"Oh, it's you."

"Yes. I'm sorry to trouble you again, but I wondered if you had thought of anything else which happened on the night of the accident."

"No," she said. "As I told you last week, we were only aware of a problem when the police came to the door and told us."

"You didn't see anyone or anything unusual."

"No. We wouldn't, you see. For one thing it was dark, and for another we live at the back of the house."

"But the back of your house faces towards the spot where the accident happened."

She paused to consider.

"Yes, I suppose it does," she said, "but there are too many trees for us to see anything. And it was dark," she reminded me.

"Yes, of course. I just wondered. Thank you."

I turned and walked back to the road feeling foolish and inadequate. The darkness, in this part of rural Essex, was complete at night. No one would have seen a thing, except the murderer, if there was a murderer.

Crossing the road, I nearly walked into a small child who was playing on a scooter.

"Hello," I said, but received no reply.

This child had been well taught not to speak to strangers.

"Where do you live?" I tried.

After a certain amount of thought the child turned and pointed at a cottage.

"Is your mummy at home?" I tried again.

At that moment I saw a flash and heard a loud rumble of thunder. The child winced and looked up.

"Sam," a woman's voice called with considerable urgency. "Sam. Where are you? It's going to rain."

The child looked towards his mother and began to run, almost too fast for his scooter which was pulled off its wheels. I followed at a walking pace, not wishing him to think I was chasing.

"Come inside. I've told you before about playing in the road."

How many children had heard that over the years?

"Excuse me," I said, reaching the gate as Sam sped up towards the house.

The woman looked harassed and not in the mood for a quiet chat.

"I wonder if.."

"No. I told you before, and I haven't the time. I've got to get in."

And with that she followed her son up to the house. I would have to get used to this sort of reaction, I thought.

Her house was one of a pair of brick built cottages; probably tied cottages originally. Perhaps they still were.

I looked up and there was the name, high on the wall in the centre of the building: Orchard Cottages.

Rain had begun to fall, but the person I wanted was either the overwrought mother or someone next door, and I had to find out which it was. So I decided to try the other house.

The gate was old and in need of wood filler and paint. It opened onto a brick footpath through a garden of dense flowers, or what had been flowers before the autumn had taken its toll.

They were dripping wet and hanging over the path, so I picked my way towards the house with care, trying to dodge spots of rain at the same time.

My knock at the front door seemed to echo through the whole building and it was quite a while before anyone responded. By this time the rain was pouring down, and as I had no hat, my hair was plastered to my head and rain was dripping from my coat to the bricks underfoot. I began to feel like the dog no one would send out in those conditions.

When the door opened a woman peered round it very cautiously. The French would have described her as 'of a certain age'. She was quite tall, very slim, and, not having the politesse of the French, I judged her to be about fifty, or possibly even older. She stood half hidden by the door, as she had only opened it a fraction, and she seemed to be using it for protection against either the rain or me.

Focussing through damp eyelashes, I realised that I remembered her, and it was mainly because of her rather bizarre clothing. Bright colours which didn't seem to match. But what did I know? Perhaps it was the height of fashion.

"Yes?" she said.

"I'm sorry to bother you again."

"Oh, it's you," she replied immediately. I supposed I would eventually get used to hearing that.

"Mrs Lamont, isn't it?"

"Miss Lamont," she said sternly.

"Sorry." Another good impression lost, as if the way I looked wasn't bad enough.

"I was wondering if there was anything you remembered about the accident at the railway."

"No. I told you," she said determinedly.

I just stood there, feeling the rain running down my face, under my collar and into my shoes.

"I wonder," I asked cautiously, "if I might come inside. It's not very comfortable standing out here."

She had to think about it, but eventually opened the door and stood back to let me in.

"Thank you. I won't go any further and drip everywhere."

She closed the door, probably against the rain, and stood in the hall with her arms crossed. I just felt a fool.

"Well?" she challenged me.

If she was I. Lamont, I needed to know if she was Ilse. Not much chance, I thought, but it would be useful to know if she was. I decided to play for time.

"Do you think I could trouble you for a towel?" I asked.

Her eyes were boring into mine, but I saw them lift to take in the state of my hair, and she appeared to relent.

"Oh, all right," she said. "Wait there."

I wasn't going anywhere. Small pools were forming around each of my shoes and I moved to pull the hair off my forehead where it had become plastered.

Looking round the hall, everything seemed bare. No pictures on the walls and no furniture save a half-moon console table, pushed against the side of the staircase.

She returned, from what I took to be the kitchen, and gave me a rather elderly, thin towel. Better than nothing.

I began to rub at my head and immediately I could feel the moisture coming straight through the towel to my hands.

"Come into the kitchen," she said unexpectedly. "It's warmer there."

I thanked her again and followed her along the hall and into the kitchen. It wasn't much warmer, and it appeared to be stuck in a 50s time warp. There was a Belfast sink with two taps high above it, just below the window sill. An aged gas cooker stood alongside it, and then there was one of those wooden kitchen cabinets with patterned glass fronted doors and a pull down hatch to form a work surface. It would have been the height of modernity soon after the war.

A plastic cloth covered the table under which two chairs faced each other.

"Sit down, if you want to."

There was something about the way she said "down" which struck me as unusual, but I couldn't place it for the moment.

"Thanks, but I'd rather stand. It will be more comfortable."

I didn't want to stay long with my clothes so wet.

Looking round, I realised there was little to see. The walls had been papered, but not very well. A picture hung on a wall, but there was nothing else which could be called decoration. And there was certainly no clue as to who she was.

She stood facing me across the room, her arms folded. Classic pose, I thought.

"Do you live here alone?" I asked her. You have to start somewhere.

"Yes."

"Have you been here long?"

"No."

This was fun. Banal questions with monosyllabic answers. Useful though. She said she had not been there long, yet she was there long enough to feature in the phone book. So not long was at least a year.

She was watching me very carefully. Perhaps she was shy and felt a little inadequate with company. But there was a certain uneasiness about her.

"Do you like country life?"

"No."

"Oh?"

"I won't be here long."

"Oh?"

Now I was being monosyllabic, and getting nowhere fast.

"It's too quiet here," she said.

"Where did you live before?"

"London."

"Ah. There's more life there."

She almost smiled. I continued to feel the water soaking from my trousers into my legs and on down.

"I wanted to see if I would like the country."

The whole sentence took me by surprise.

"And you don't?"

"No. It's peaceful and all that, but it's so dark at night."

She hadn't moved, and I could see no point in catching my death of cold waiting for this intractable woman to say something useful.

"Look. I won't stay."

I held out the towel, but she still didn't move. So I draped it over a chair.

"Thank you for this. I'd better go and get out of these wet clothes."

She moved then, past me, through the doorway and down the hall. I squelched after her, and on the little table I caught the briefest glance of an envelope. I looked up quickly, saw her back was still towards me, and looked down again.

Then she had the door open and I stepped back out into the deluge. As I turned to thank her yet again, the door closed in my face.

I ran to the car, and as I was wondering if I could ever be any wetter, dropped the car keys in my haste and had to bend to retrieve them. As I was crouching another car passed through a puddle and finished the job of soaking me.

But I didn't care. I had my next clue. The envelope had been addressed to Miss I. Chambers and was headed Grace, Swindle and Little. The firm who handled the will. So I. Lamont was Ilse Chambers, or so it seemed.

Chapter 7

As I stood in a hot shower, twenty minutes later, I began to consider my next step. I had to figure out how to work my way back into that house.

It occurred to me that if I let on that I had found Ilse Chambers, a lot of anger would come her way from both of Joyce's parents, and perhaps from Joyce herself. This might easily queer my pitch, as the only way to the truth about the will and perhaps Helen's death would come through stealth.

Furthermore Miss Chambers must not know my suspicions, so I must not let on to Joyce's family that I had found her.

I dried myself and regained the comfort of warm, dry clothes. Then I phoned Joyce.

"Hi, it's me."

"Oh, hello." She sounded decidedly low.

"I thought I'd follow up that solicitor's letter. No doubt they'll talk about client privilege, but your grandmother's will is one line of enquiry that seems promising. There's no harm in trying to find out more."

"No, I suppose not."

"Do you remember the name of the solicitor who read out the will?"

"No. Just a minute. I'll find out."

I waited as she went to look.

"Dad says it was Jocelyn Swindle, and could he meet you for a drink tonight?"

"Yes, of course. Put him on and we can arrange where to meet."

Later, I was glad the rain had stopped when I left the house for The Bull's Head. Joyce's father was nursing a pint in front of the fire when I entered the Lounge Bar. He didn't look happy as I walked across to him.

"Hello," I said. "Can I get you another?"

"Thanks. It's the special bitter."

I went to the bar and bought two pints and a bag of dry roasted nuts.

We sat in silence and drank for a minute or two. If he wanted to talk to me, I would have to wait till he was ready. I resorted to small talk, not something I'm particularly good at.

"I got soaked this afternoon in all that rain. It's good to be sitting by a fire. Much more comfortable."

"Mmm," he replied. Then out it came.

"Look, Greg, I know you're spending a lot of time trying to help us, and I know you have only recently set up your business."

He paused and took another sip of beer.

"It's just that we can't afford to pay you very much. Things really are a bit difficult at present."

"I am not doing this for the money. I'm doing it as a favour for Joyce."

"Yes. That's all well and good, but I'm not entirely happy with not paying you anything. A fair day's work for a fair day's pay, I've always thought. You've just got going. You should be working to generate new business and getting things off the ground. We're only holding you back."

"Listen, Mr Hetherington."

"Oh, call me Oliver, for God's sake."

"I've been fortunate to get the money to set up my business. We both worked in the City. We had high powered jobs, well paid, all the extras; more than I needed really, if I'm honest. You were made redundant and I left of my own accord. Now, while I'm able to afford it, I'd like to help."

"Pam's in a hell of a state," he said. "I feel responsible for that. I lost my job and I don't seem able to get another."

"What's happened to you all in the past year or so is not your fault."

But I could see the weight of family responsibilities on Oliver's shoulders. His eyes drifted away from me and seemed to stay fixed on nothing in particular. It was clear that he was recalling a painful event and thinking about his family; all the hopes and expectations that had been lost.

Joyce described to me later what had happened.

Her mother had arrived home very excited that day, having been to a travel agent and brought back several brochures for cruises.

Oliver had finally promised to take a two week break in the summer and they were determined to do something they'd often talked about, but never got round to.

She dumped the brochures on the coffee table and went to the kitchen to make some tea. Then she called up the stairs.

"Joyce. Are you home?"

Joyce had returned to live with them following the termination of her teaching contract. Having left the school under a cloud, she had not been able to find an alternative post.

For her parents it was a mixed blessing having both their children back with them. They loved each other's company and money was not a problem. Furthermore, Helen had a good job, and was therefore able to pay her own way.

What they missed was the time together which they had so valued in their early years together. Not that the girls were intrusive, but all parents look forward to the time they become empty nesters and their lives become their own again. Joyce's parents had expected this, but it never happened, or at least it hadn't happened yet.

Joyce came into the kitchen to join her mother.

"Tea?"

"Yes, please."

"I've been to the travel agent's. You know that cruise your dad and I have always promised ourselves, well it's going to be this summer. And nothing can get in the way this time."

"Great!"

"I wanted your thoughts on the Greek islands. You saw a few on that school cruise, didn't you?"

"You haven't called me down to talk about that, have you? You know I don't like to think about it."

"I only thought you could tell me where you thought it was worth visiting, or if I should think of somewhere else altogether."

"I don't know. I had too much on my mind, what with the children, and everything else."

Her mother's expression changed.

"I'm sorry. In my excitement I forgot all that. Don't think about it. I'll talk about it with your father when he gets home."

She looked across and sympathised with her daughter's downcast demeanour, knowing there was nothing she could do about it.

"What are you doing tonight? Anything?"

"I don't know. The gang will probably gather at The Goose. Perhaps I'll go and join them."

They continued to chat over their tea and the afternoon passed as most others, quietly and pleasantly.

When Oliver left the train, four hours later, even a total stranger would have known something was wrong. He walked to the car park as if in a dream, and then sat in his car, not sure if he wanted to go home.

Briefly he considered the pub, but knew that was only delaying the inevitable. What he had to say when he got home was better said sober and clear headed.

He started the car, pulled the lever to drive and made his way down the long ramped approach to the roundabout. Then he turned right and accelerated up the hill towards home.

As his car curved round the gravel area in front of the house, the security lights came on. He turned off the ignition and just sat for a few minutes, composing himself. Should he pretend nothing had happened? Would it be possible to brave it out and maintain a smile? He thought not.

Best get it over.

He pushed his briefcase off the back seat, locked the car and went into the house.

"Oliver? Is that you?"

His wife came from the kitchen to meet him.

"You didn't call like you usually do." Then she stopped. "What's the matter?"

"Come into the living room."

"Oliver. What's happened?"

He took her hand and walked her over to the sofa, then sat down next to her.

"What?" She stared at his expression.

"They've let me go."

"Let you go where? What do you mean?"

"I've been given the sack."

"What? Why?"

"The takeover. They don't need me anymore. I'm probably too expensive for the new owners."

"But!" she didn't know what to say. "How many years have you been there?"

"All my life, it seems. Apparently it means nothing. Quite simply they don't need two Managers for the Asian Portfolio, so I'm surplus to requirements."

"But that's terrible. What will you do?"

"I don't know."

"Have they been generous?"

"I have a month, and severance pay. Not bad, I suppose. But all those years, down the drain."

"But you'll find something else."

"That's the point. I'm not so sure. You know how old I am. The City is full of takeovers and talk of takeovers. It's a place for the young, up and coming executives. You don't see many older than me around Canary Wharf."

His eyes focussed on the pile of brochures on the coffee table.

"What's that?"

"Oh, Oliver. We were to have that cruise, weren't we? I went to see the agents. It seems it's never meant to be for us."

"We could use some of the severance money and go anyway."

"If you were advising someone else, would you say that?"

"No. I don't suppose I would."

"Come here."

She opened her arms and he fell into them, resting his head on her shoulder.

At that moment Joyce appeared.

"What's going on?"

"Your dad has lost his job."

"Oh God! And just today you were talking about going on a cruise."

"I know. Oh well. I've said before. It's never going to happen for us."

Later, when Helen returned home, they all sat together and talked over drinks until Pamela went to the kitchen to prepare dinner. The same question formed the recurring theme. What will you do?

Oliver had no idea. He had expected to continue for many more years with the same bank and he was now at an age when it would be difficult to start again.

They ate their meals largely in silence, the severity of the shock overwhelming any desire for light conversation. Oliver felt numb. He had a measure of pride in his ability to provide a comfortable life for his wife and daughters. Suddenly it was gone and he had a month to find an alternative.

Oliver's head turned and his eyes refocussed on me.

"No one wants me," he said. "I'm in my early fifties and too old. What do we have to look forward to? Years on the dole. Not able to pay the mortgage. Selling the house. Moving to some squalid place too small to swing a cat. Pam doesn't deserve this."

"I know. And neither do you. Neither does anyone who is pushed out before their time and made to suffer for the benefit of big business. It wasn't your fault you lost your job. Your firm was taken over. It's happening all the time these days.

"Banks are expanding and taking over other financial institutions. None of them cares about the people they make redundant. They don't care about people at all. Their bottom line is the foot of a balance sheet. They take over other companies to remove competition, to increase their share of the market and boost their profits. And if they can reduce their overheads at the same time, they will. So they let people go without giving it a second thought.

"These people are not concerned about you or I, or any other person. Oh, they play with our money, but they do it for their own benefit, not for ours. As far as they are concerned you were an expense they would rather save. So all your years of experience, all your expertise, they were prepared to forfeit."

I realised with some embarrassment that I'd been riding my own hobby horse, getting rid of the frustration I'd felt at the bank I'd worked for, but Oliver's eyes barely rose from the table top.

"I don't know what to do."

"Give me a little time to see what I can dig up. Don't worry about paying me, really," I stressed. "If I can at least find out what happened to Helen, that might make you feel a bit better."

Oliver looked as if it would take a great deal more to make him feel any better.

"What can you tell me about the inheritance?" I changed the subject, well slightly. "Are we talking a lot of money?"

"Oh yes."

He perked up a little.

"Let me get you another drink," he said, "and I'll tell you all I know."

"No. These are on me," I told him and stood up.

As I returned to the bar, I found myself hoping that with luck, there might be more to find out than what happened to Helen, and that some of it might benefit the Hetheringtons in more ways than they expected. How, though, I had no idea.

New pint in hand, Oliver began to recount the background to the inheritance.

"Annie, that's Pam's mother-in-law as was, married her childhood sweetheart during the war. As I understand it they were both the only children of parents who lived on neighbouring estates in Scotland. Their parents were old friends.

"Anyway Annie had two sons, Fergus and Archie. They were like chalk and cheese, but both adored by their parents.

Pam married Fergus, as you might know, and he was Helen's father. But both brothers were killed in a stupid accident, and their father never got over it. He became old before his time, partly worrying about who was going to run the two estates after him.

"He died, poor bloke, and soon afterwards Annie decided to sell up and move down here. She used to say there were too many unhappy memories in Scotland. I can understand that, what with her sons and Alan both being gone. So the estates were sold. She bought a little place quite near to us, and invested the rest."

He took a long mouthful of beer and looked at me.

"Why are you asking about the inheritance anyway?"

"Because I need all the background information I can get if I am going to find a reason for Helen's death."

"Are you sure there was a reason? You don't think it was all an unfortunate accident? So many other things have happened to us recently. There are so many things we've lost. It would be just our luck to have lost Helen for no reason at all."

"Joyce has never thought that, and I'm beginning to agree with her. And think about it. What are the classic motives for killing? Vengeance, jealousy, love and money. What money is linked to Helen? The inheritance she expected to get, but didn't."

"But if you follow that argument, you have a motive for Helen to kill someone else, and it's Helen who died."

"I know. There is that back-to-front aspect to the whole thing. But until I get something else to go on, I shall follow the inheritance and see where it leads."

What I didn't add, but thought, was that it was virtually all I had to go on.

"You mentioned four classic motives," Oliver said. "So what about vengeance, jealousy and love?"

"If any of those are involved, I'll found out. For the present I am concentrating on the money aspect."

The following morning was bright and fresh, reflecting my mood after the previous day's discovery.

Having identified Ilse Chambers, albeit with her name change, I had a link between the inheritance and Helen's death. Somehow Helen must have tracked down Ilse. What other reason could there be for her to be in that vicinity on the night she died?

I realised this did not automatically link Ilse with what happened, but to have died accidentally in that particular spot was too much of a coincidence for me. There was that word again – coincidence. Perhaps there were beginning to be too many of them.

Somehow I had to discover why Ilse had inherited and why it was so very important that no one should know the details. Why else would Helen have been killed, but to hide a secret, and keep it hidden?

With so much money involved, what could possibly have persuaded Joyce's grandmother to leave everything to someone unknown to the rest of the family? Who was Ilse? Surely Joyce's grandmother must have known her well. But how?

I sensed an intriguing mystery. A secret which must remain hidden. A secret worth killing to protect.

But, and there were plenty of buts buzzing around my mind at that moment, if Ilse had killed Helen, or at least inadvertently caused her death, it would probably be very hard to prove.

It had been made clear to me how dark it was that night. The spot was off the beaten track. Anyone could have done anything without being seen. Clearly the police had found no clues to suggest anyone other then Helen was there. I would have my work cut out to prove that Helen was killed intentionally.

Two ways were open to me. I could try to persuade the solicitor who dealt with the will to confirm Ilse's identity. Or I could try to get to know Ilse, to see if I could discover any clues as to the link between her and Joyce's grandmother. And I must do this without revealing my suspicions.

I did have a reason to visit Ilse again, so that would be my starting point. But first I picked up the phone and dialled the number of the solicitors in London.

"Hello. Would it be possible to speak to Jocelyn Swindle, or his PA?

"No, he doesn't know me. It's in connection with the will of Annie Glenn. I am working on behalf of the Hetherington family and I wondered if it would be possible to meet with Mr Swindle sometime soon."

I was put through to the PA, which was the best I could have hoped for. It was my experience that solicitor's PAs are as efficient, if not more so in some cases, than their bosses.

"Hello. My name is Greg Mason. I'm working for the Hetheringtons in Suffolk. You may remember the case of Annie Glenn's will...Yes. I wondered if I could have a word with Jocelyn Swindle on that subject...Yes, I am aware of the difficulty of client confidence, but if I could just have a few minutes of his time I should be grateful...Tomorrow morning? That's great. Thanks very much."

That was easier than I had expected. I could spend at least some of tomorrow at the office catching up on other cases. That would give me the chance to discover if the mysterious black vehicle and its contents were still in evidence.

Pleased with that promising start to the day, I wrapped myself up against the temperature outside, left the house and walked quickly to the car.

Tucked under the windscreen wiper blade was a piece of paper. Automatically I looked around me. There was no one I could see.

I took hold of the paper at its corner, lifted the wiper blade, turned the paper over and read I TOLD YOU TO LEAVE IT ALONE.

I looked around again, still no one there. But there wouldn't be. The note could have been put there at any time since I returned from meeting Oliver.

Whoever had taken Joyce was now here. I was being watched, not just in London, but at home.

So much for a promising start. I felt exposed and went round to get in the car, almost as if it could afford me some sort of protection.

The engine started and I put on the heater with the fan blowing hard while I waited for the temperature gauge to rise.

What should I do? What could I do? Nothing.

I didn't know who it was, or where they were. All I could do was continue with my day as I'd previously planned it, and see if anything useful came to light.

When I could feel warm air coming out of the demister and see the windscreen beginning to clear, I turned down the fan so I could hear some music and gingerly eased the car out of the drive and turned right.

The radio had come on in the middle of a rap, so I turned it off again. That wasn't music.

My destination was a nearby parade of shops, and the journey was so short it didn't give the car time to warm up properly. Parking in the last space available, I shivered involuntarily as I closed the car door, and made my way to a florist's shop I knew.

There were displays of bouquets and wreaths in the window, and a collection of galvanized buckets sitting on the pavement outside, each containing large stems of different species in a variety of colours. I wondered idly where they had been grown at this time of the year, and plumped for white roses. The assistant took them from me and I waited while she wrapped them carefully to their best effect. Now encased in a strong plastic sheath, I carried them back to the car and set off, once again, for Monks Colne.

This time I plumped for a CD and chose Rumours, beating time on the steering wheel along with Mick Fleetwood's drums.

The only evidence of the previous evening's storm were the puddles at the side of the road, and I had to park carefully to avoid stepping out into one.

I dodged the still dripping flowers along the side of the path and knocked at the door. She opened it as cautiously as before, and her surprise at seeing me again was clear in her face. I proffered the flowers.

Her eyes moved from my face to the flowers and back again.

"You were so kind to me last night in that storm," I said. "The least I could do was offer some sort of appreciation."

She said nothing, but after a long moment's pause, held the door open for me to enter. As I passed, I handed her the flowers.

It seemed she had no idea what to do with them. She just stood holding them awkwardly.

I closed the door for her.

"Would it be an idea to put them in water?" I said, more than anything to break the silence.

"Yes," was her quiet reply, and she made her way along towards the kitchen. I followed, highly aware of the care I had to take over what I said. The slightest suspicion on her part that I knew her identity in relation to Helen, would lose me what little advantage I thought I had gained.

In the kitchen she stood still, looking round, as if working out what to do with the flowers. Apparently searching her mind to see if she had anything which could act as a vase. That meant there were no vases, which seemed to confirm the simplicity of the furnishings. Did that infer that she was here temporarily for a reason.

She had admitted to not living in the house for long. Was that because she didn't like the country, or was there a more sinister reason?

Bending down to a cupboard below the sink she found a large brown pottery jug. Placing it on the draining board she began to unwrap the plastic surround from the roses.

"I don't suppose you have many callers, out here in the sticks."

"No," she said over her shoulder.

She placed the roses in the jug and began to arrange them. I had the impression she was either playing for time, not knowing what to say and not wanting me there, or she was genuinely at a loss.

I stood and waited, and eventually she turned towards me, her face suggesting it had experienced a difficult life. There were lines around her eyes and either side of her nose and mouth; all vertical lines, as if she had never ever smiled. Perhaps there had been little reason to smile in her life, and I wondered why.

It wasn't easy trying to estimate her age, but I suspected she wouldn't see fifty again. She looked the epitome of a desperately unhappy, late middle aged spinster.

"No one ever gave me flowers before," she said, as if to confirm my thoughts.

"You were very considerate to let me into your house in that storm last night. You didn't know me from Adam, although I had been before, when I was asking those questions. I could have been anyone. It was very kind."

I felt it important to distance myself from the person enquiring about Helen's death. If I was to get to know her in any way, she must have no inkling that I suspected her of anything.

She was lost for words, and the fact that she appeared unable to express her appreciation easily, hinted again at a lonely life, sad and very likely unfulfilled.

"Would you like a cup of tea?" she said it as if she could think of nothing else to say.

"Yes. Thank you."

I sat down on one of the dining chairs as she turned, a little confusedly I thought, to fill the kettle.

"You said you don't expect to be staying here very long."

She didn't reply, but busied herself with a teapot and a tin from which she extracted a couple of tea bags. Then she turned.

"Are you here to ask more questions about that girl's death?"

"No," I said, I hoped not too quickly. "I'm here to thank you for sheltering me during the storm. That's all."

"Because I don't know anything about that."

"Yes, you told me when I first came."

"But people don't always believe what they're told."

That seemed a strange thing to say and I wondered if it had any significance. But I wanted to steer the conversation away from Helen; to put Ilse at her ease, if that was possible. She looked very tense and wary.

The kettle clicked itself off and Ilse turned back to pour the water.

She was wearing blue jeans which hung loosely from her rather frail frame. Her blouse was a cotton check in a particularly unattractive colour, somewhere between yellow and brown. Old fashioned grips held her straight hair back over her ears. She really did look like someone lost in a time warp.

As she approached the table with the teapot and two mugs on a small tray, I thought how sad and downtrodden she looked. It struck me as a strange appearance for someone who had recently inherited a small fortune and made me wonder if I had made a mistake.

I decided to dig very gently for information. Here was someone very fragile, and very suspicious. The slightest error on my part would put her on her guard, or worse, and end my chances completely.

"I quite like the country myself," I said cautiously. "Life is so much slower here. It's possible to live at my own pace. Large towns are a bit of a nightmare."

"I'm used to London," she said.

"Have you always lived there, then?"

"No."

Again the appearance of suspicion. I had to go carefully.

I'd been listening for a trace of the accent I'd noticed before, but I hadn't picked it up yet. It was often just certain vowel sounds that gave away a person's origin, like the flat pronunciation of there in Beatles' songs, typical of Liverpool.

"I work in London some of the time. I think I left you one of my cards, so you'll know that."

"I didn't really look at it," she said.

Why would she say that? I was almost certain she must have done.

"But I prefer working from home. It saves all the travelling."

Her face showed no emotion at all.

"I'm sorry there aren't any biscuits."

I smiled.

"That's all right. I eat too many of them anyway."

But still she didn't smile. I began to wonder if she could.

We continued to drink our mugs of tea in a silence that remained far from comfortable. I seemed to be getting nowhere, and didn't want to make her feel too uncomfortable or suspicious, so I finished my drink and pushed back my chair.

"Thank you for the tea."

I rose and offered my hand, which she just looked at as if not being sure what it was.

"Well, I'll be going. Thanks again. Perhaps I could call again if I'm in the vicinity?"

"I don't get many visitors," she said. A strange reply. I suspected she didn't have any. Perhaps there was a tacit affirmative in her answer. I'd have to see what happened when I called again, because it was certainly necessary that I'd need to.

I led the way along the hall to the front door and opened it. It seemed necessary to take the initiative as Ilse seemed totally at a loss to know what to do with me.

"Goodbye," I said and I began to make my cautious way through the dripping flowers again. Before I had gone more than a few steps I heard the door close behind me.

I was left with a quandary. Did the rather abrupt closure of the door signify that she didn't want to see me again? Because I would have to see her again if I was to get anywhere with my investigations.

Chapter 8

The following morning I set off to catch my usual morning train. I parked across the road from the station and was just crossing when a motorbike came over the bridge, as if from nowhere.

The sight and sound of it rooted me to the spot, and I had the sudden thought that if I stood still the rider would see me and be able to steer round me. But that was the last thing on his mind. The big bike brushed past my left hand side, giving my arm a nasty blow with its wing mirror and throwing me sideways.

I twisted round to look after it, but all I saw was a registration plate caked in mud and a black crash helmet with a skull and crossbones on the back. Both receded quickly and the bike was soon gone.

No one else had seen what happened and I continued across the road to the station, brushing myself down, straightening my clothes and wondering if it was another attempt to intimidate me, or just a stupid motor cyclist. Whichever it was, I found myself rubbing my left arm involuntarily all morning. The bruise was tender and I could feel the beginnings of a swelling.

Great, I thought. Is this another occupational hazard like the occasional kidnap? Or am I getting paranoid?

On the train I sat trying to read a novel in a carriage full of rather oppressed looking travellers.

I recalled a story told me by a friend of someone who commuted from Surrey, and spent each morning's journey locked between and behind broadsheet newspapers in a First

Class carriage. He knew that his train passed a friend of his, as he waited on the platform in Surbiton, and he conceived a plan to jolt his fellow travellers out of their morning stupor.

One day, on the approach to Surbiton, he screwed up his Times, threw it on the floor of the carriage with imprecations related to the tedium of reading the same paper day after day; opened the carriage window and grabbed a copy of a tabloid which was being held out for him by his friend as the train rushed through Surbiton station. Turning to see the effect on his fellow passengers, he realised that no one had turned a hair and the other newspapers had never even budged.

The thought of this story had amused me during many a journey. I guessed it was apocryphal, but I dearly hoped it was true. Returning to my book I found myself half reading and half speculating on the case in hand as the train sped on.

There had been threats in London and now there were threats nearer home. Would anything happen now I was back in the capital? Where was the guy on the motorbike going? Off to London to bother me again, or just on his own sweet way, oblivious to the case I was working on?

Where was the truck? Lying in wait somewhere? Would I find another note at the office?

When the train arrived I soon found myself battling across the forecourt at Liverpool Street Station, but eventually I made my way down to the tube. As I crossed the bridge to the west bound Circle Line platform I realised it was even more busy than usual, and as I descended the stairs I became part of a solid, moving mass of people.

Despite all my best attempts to break free, the crowd propelled me off the staircase and onto the platform.

There was no train, but I could hear one approaching, so I tried to push my way through the crowd towards the platform edge, in the hope of finding a seat when the doors opened. Then I was suddenly aware that by pushing I was moving too quickly towards the edge. My efforts had added impetus to the current already carrying me along, and as the train was pulling into the station from my right I realised I wasn't going to be able to stop.

I tried, but my forward momentum was too strong, and just when I thought I must fall in front of the train I was grabbed by both arms and pulled back. The train rushed past my face, almost a literal close shave, and I found myself held firm, my mind a blur of thoughts and what ifs.

"You all right, mate?" said a voice to my left.

"I think so."

I looked towards the voice and saw a craggy featured, middle-aged man wearing a boiler suit covered with paint stains.

"You ought to be more careful," the craggy face said.

"Was it you who caught me?"

"Me and 'im," he said, and he gestured beyond me to my right.

I turned and came face to face with Stuart Hemsley.

"Greg?" he said.

"Surprised?" I found myself saying. Perhaps the threats were suddenly explained.

"Well yes, of course. You nearly had a nasty accident."

"I'm glad about the nearly part. What are you doing here?"

"I work near here. I'm on my way to see a client."

"And you just happened to be on a crowded platform at the same time as I was being pushed in front of a train."

"Meaning what exactly?"

I tried a sarcastic shrug, but there wasn't room enough to move.

"Come on," I said. "We need to talk. Let's try and get off this platform and find somewhere a bit more quiet."

I began to push my way back through the crowd to the stairs and climbed back up towards the upper exit. When I turned, I was rather surprised to see that Stuart had followed me. I couldn't read his expression. I was looking for disappointment, or perhaps anger, but he looked blank.

"Joyce told me you work for a Travel Agency," I said. "What sort of a travel agent makes house calls?"

"Do you think I'm following you?"

"It certainly looks as if you might be."

"Why should I want to?" The hidden aggression I had experienced in his flat was showing itself. Interesting, I thought.

But in fact he had asked a good question. If he had been involved in Joyce's snatch, his question was a bluff. If not, he could have no idea what had happened four days before. Which was it? How was I supposed to know?

"It is rather a coincidence, you being on that platform at the same time as me, after I went to see you only a few days ago about someone who fell in front of a train."

"You think there's a connection? You still think Helen died because of me?"

He said it as if challenging me to provide proof. He was either a very good actor, or totally innocent. I needed to find out one way or the other.

"Look," I said. "Can you spare five minutes to talk something through?"

"What something?" He stared at me and I still couldn't read his face at all.

"Just five minutes."

He glanced down at his watch.

"Will this help find out what happened to Helen?"

"It could help narrow things down."

"All right. Let's go out here."

We left the station by the upper exit and crossed the road to a coffee house. I bought two espressos and joined him on a black leather sofa.

"Are you able to tell me where you were four days ago during the afternoon?"

"That would be Monday?"

"Yes."

"I will have been in the office all afternoon booking winter breaks for clients."

"And can anyone vouch for that?"

"Several people can. Why? What happened on Monday?"

"Someone kidnapped Joyce, bundled her into a car, then dumped her outside my office with a threatening note pinned to her coat."

"Bloody hell! And you think that was me?"

"Whoever it was, I'm sure they had something to do with Helen's death. The threats make that clear."

"I told you before. I would never hurt her."

"I know you told me, but if I believed everything everyone told me, I wouldn't make a very good detective, would I?"

That stare of his was boring its way into my eyes. What it saw was my anger at a near fatal accident.

"No. Fair point."

"If you can confirm absolutely that you were in your office all Monday afternoon, then I shall have to try to believe that today's meeting was just a coincidence - although a very remarkable one."

"Well you can believe it, because I was, and it is," he snapped.

"Where is your agency?"

He searched for a card in his inside pocket and passed one across to me.

"Why would anyone want to grab Joyce?" he asked.

"Someone involved in Helen's death is trying to scare me off. When they took Joyce, they used her as a threat. Basically saying that what happened to Helen is likely to happen to me if I don't stop asking questions."

"And as Helen fell under a train, and you nearly did just that, with me standing next to you, I can understand what you thought."

"It would all fit, if it was you. If not, as I said, I shall have to start believing in coincidences."

I picked up my cup and drained it in one.

Was it my imagination, or was his expression softening a little?

"Of course," I said, "even if you have witnesses who can confirm you were in your office, you could have set things up. Maybe the thugs who took Joyce were just following orders, while you had a convenient alibi all prepared."

"If you think that, there's little I can say to persuade you otherwise. But I repeat, I did not and never would have hurt a hair on Helen's head."

"Just so that I know, where were you at the time Helen died?"

"I was here, in town, working late. Someone phoned me after I got home to tell me what had happened."

"And your agency staff can verify that, of course."

"Yes."

"OK, for the time being. Tell me," I said, changing tack, "who are those clients you are going to see?"

"It's a firm with offices near the Barbican. We arrange company trips for them. I was on the way to discuss some sort of junketing they want to arrange in France. They are good customers. It's worth my while to visit their place. Good for business."

I looked him full in the face and came back to the same old dilemma. How do I tell the truth from lies? What is the secret, if there is one?

"I'd better let you get on, then," I said. " Thanks for your part in saving me."

"I'm glad you think that's what it was."

"If it wasn't, you'll be hearing from me again fairly soon."

"You never give up, do you?"

"Not until I know the facts."

"You sound likely a bloody TV detective."

He got up suddenly and left, slamming the door behind him. I followed him out, but instead of returning to the station, made my way to his Travel Agency.

Five minutes later his colleagues easily confirmed his story, so I knew that unless he had phoned them before I got there, and they were all involved in some sort of extraordinary conspiracy, or he had got someone else to do his dirty work for him, I could forget about him as a suspect. My worry was that it left him with too many ifs hanging in the air.

That sent my thoughts back to the garden and the reference to a truck. My mind was conjuring up all sorts of bizarre possibilities when my Circle Line train arrived, and this time I was able to avoid its approach with ease.

As I emerged from Euston Square station the clouds were building again, and I made my way quickly to the office to avoid another potential drenching. In fact there was no rain, and neither was there any evidence of either a black truck or a motorbike, which was something of a relief.

I had not been in the office long when my phone disturbed me.

"Hello."

"Is that Greg?"

"Yes. Who's this?"

"It's Sarah, from Colbox."

"Oh, hi." Interesting, I thought.

"You said I should call you if I thought of anything."

"Yes?"

There was a slight pause, as if Sarah was collecting her thoughts, or deciding if she wanted to tell me after all.

"Are you still there?"

"Yes. Sorry. It's about Gemma."

I waited.

"It's just that I thought you should know. She's a lezzie. She likes other girls."

"Ah. And Helen?" I let it hang.

"Gemma was crazy about her. Couldn't take her eyes off her."

"I see. Were you all aware of this?"

"I think the girls in the main office were."

"And Helen?"

"She knew, but she wasn't interested. She liked boys like the rest of us. I think Gemma thought that because Helen was quiet, it meant she was hiding the way she really felt about her. But that was rubbish."

"I can see why Helen would want to speak to Mr Jordan about it."

Sarah was quiet again for a minute or two.

"Do you think Gemma might have hurt Helen?" she asked.

"I don't know. Perhaps I'll have to ask Gemma that."

"Yes."

"Thanks for calling, Sarah. Can I reach you again if I need to ask you anything else?"

"Sure," she said and gave me her mobile number.

"Thanks again. I appreciate it."

I closed the phone.

So, I thought, it was more than just jealousy. Unrequited love, again. A boy and a girl. Helen must have been someone really special.

I dragged back my mind to the present and what I was in the office to do.

There was some mail on the mat, and for the two hours before my meeting with the solicitor I immersed myself in other business. At least there was some other business, so that was encouraging.

But first I had to clear the three messages which still lay on the desk, and they reminded me of the main things on my mind, the recent threats and a need to unravel some kind of mystery about the inheritance. I had almost convinced myself that the inheritance was linked to Helen's death, mainly because of where Ilse lived. Now, perhaps, I had to think again. There was Gemma to consider, and perhaps there was Stuart as well.

The offices of Grace, Swindle and Little were at the St Paul's end of Cheapside, so that meant a return to the Circle Line, at least as far as Barbican, and then a brisk walk down Aldersgate Street, through the wintery air.

Hemmed in between a Health Food Shop and a card emporium was a distinguished looking, although narrow, marble facade with a pair of glass doors. The firm's name was etched into the glass. I pulled open one of the doors, entered and went up to the security man who was ensconced behind his desk. He didn't seem interested in who I was to see, as long as I signed my name on his sheet and fastened a badge to my lapel.

Through more glass doors, the marble staircase was no doubt designed to portray an image of prosperity and importance. In fact it just reminded me of the thinly carpeted stairs to my own office.

A polished brass plaque on the wall of the first floor landing confirmed whose offices lay behind a pair of equally polished, heavy wooden doors. I pushed one open with some effort. Behind them the terrazzo flooring turned to thick carpet and the temperature rose by at least ten degrees. What was sensible clothing outside was unnecessary here and the first thing I did was to unfasten my coat and loosen my scarf.

The secretary, sitting in a booth marked "Enquiries", was clearly used to the situation and had dressed accordingly in clothes I normally associated with high summer.

"Yes?"

"I have an eleven o'clock appointment with Mr Swindle. My name is Mason."

She looked down and checked a list on her desk. Then pressed an intercom.

"Hi, Lisa. I have a Mr Mason to see Mr Swindle....OK, thanks."

Then to me, "Would you like to take a seat in the area over there?"

She indicated an open entrance opposite, through which I found a seated area of leather sofas interspersed with low tables. On the tables I found copies of every broadsheet, including the Financial Times. This was a distinct step up from the three year old Readers' Digests at my dentist's.

I didn't think I had enough time to start reading, so I took off my coat and scarf, sat down and spent a few minutes looking at the abstract pictures on the walls. Their meanings defeated me, as usual.

When ten minutes had passed I changed my mind, and picked up The Financial Times to see what it had to offer. It used to be my regular daily when I was at the bank, but I had rather lost touch since then.

I was just turning the page and wrestling with a large sheet of paper which refused to fold where it should, when someone appeared in the entrance and addressed me.

"Mr Mason?"

It would have been easy to conclude that he had been lying in wait before approaching, until I was in the most confused and embarrassing situation with my newspaper.

"Yes." I wrestled on. "I'm sorry. I always have trouble with these huge papers."

I rose to shake his hand, then forced the newspaper into some sort of order, replaced it on the table, grabbed my outdoor clothes and smiled with acute discomfort. Another good impression not made.

"If you would just follow me."

And off he went. I scuttled behind him and was led into a very distinguished looking conference room, as thickly carpeted as the entrance area and with an oval table surrounded by plush chairs.

"Would you like a coffee?"

"Yes, please."

"Milk and sugar?"

"No. Just as it comes, thanks."

"Good man. I like to taste my drinks, too."

He went to a phone on the wall and ordered two coffees and biscuits.

"Please, sit down," he said and I chose a chair in the middle of one of the long curves. He sat facing me and placed a large pad on the table. The fountain pen he produced looked expensive.

"Now, my secretary tells me this is about the will of Annie Glenn." He was writing as he spoke. "You must be aware that I am bound by client privilege not to reveal a great deal."

"I am aware of that, but the Hetherington family has been left in something of a dilemma since the death of their daughter."

His expression changed as he looked up.

"The death of which daughter?"

"Helen."

"Good God. I didn't know she was dead. How did that happen?"

"This is part of the dilemma."

The door opened and the secretary from the enquiries desk came in with a silver tray bearing cups and saucers, a small cafetière and a plate of biscuits.

When we were each settled with our cups, and I'd finally decided which chocolate biscuit to choose, we got down to business.

"How did she die? It doesn't seem like five minutes since she was here."

So she had been to see him. It occurred to me that if I was going to be able to reconstruct Helen's last day, this would be a good place to start.

"She died just over three weeks ago, and it was an accident on a railway line."

"You don't mean suicide."

"The police think it might have been."

He made some more notes on his pad.

"So does the family think it was caused in some way by the terms of Annie Glenn's will?"

"The family doesn't think she killed herself."

"Ah. I suppose it's not something they would want to think."

"In case it's worth anything, I don't think she killed herself either."

"Do you have any evidence to support that opinion?"

"Only circumstantial, which is why I'm here."

He put down his pen and looked at me. I had the impression he had decided to take me seriously.

"How can I help?"

"First of all, can you tell me exactly when it was that Helen came to see you."

He gave me the date and approximate time and I wrote them down in my notebook. It was the day she died.

"Now this is where the difficult bit starts, because you will no doubt start quoting client privilege reasons why you can't tell me things."

"Go on."

"I happen to know that you wrote to Helen, shortly before her death, pointing out that you were unable to give any details about the person who inherited. Were you able to be more forthcoming when she came to see you?"

He studied my face intently, as if working out how much he was prepared to say.

"She brought some photographs."

"Photographs of whom?"

He paused, considering some more.

"Photographs of the person who inherited."

"If I were to tell you that the person who inherited lives not more than a stone's throw from the place where Helen died, what would you think?"

"And how do you know this?"

"It wasn't difficult. Her name is Ilse Chambers?"

"Yes."

"If I were to tell you her address, would you be able to confirm or deny it without breaking any confidence?"

"If you were to tell me, rather than me telling you, I suppose I could confirm it."

He answered a little hesitantly, but I suppose that was only to be expected. He did have a moral and professional obligation to consider.

I looked directly at him.

"Orchard Cottages, Monks Colne, Essex. Does that sound right?"

"I'll need to look at the file to confirm, but yes, it sounds right."

"Thank you. The trouble is that the person living at that address is not called Ilse Chambers, but Ilse Lamont."

"Well that's easily explained. Some married people like to keep their maiden names."

"Have you met her?"

"Of course."

"Do you think it likely, having met her, that she has ever been married?"

"I see what you mean. So where are you going with this?"

"The question is why did Annie Glenn leave all of her considerable estate to Ilse Chambers/Lamont, a person of whom the family has no knowledge."

"I can't help you there. I drew up the will, and I remember being surprised by the sole beneficiary. But I have no knowledge of any reason behind it."

"Does the name Lamont mean anything to you in this context?"

He thought for a moment.

"No, it doesn't."

"Do you mind if I ask you how long you have handled Annie Glenn's affairs?"

"The firm has handled her late husband's affairs for a considerable period of time, through our Glasgow office, you understand."

"So you don't know much about them personally?"

"No."

I didn't feel there was very much further I could go with this, but there was one thing I could usefully find out.

"Would it be possible to enquire of your Glasgow office about the name Lamont, in relation to Annie Glenn?"

"Are you retaining my firm's services in this case?"

"I wasn't intending to, no. But you handled Annie's will, and a young person died not too far from where the beneficiary of that will lives. Now that could be a coincidence, but I intend to look into it, and it would be useful to know if the name that person is using has any relevance to the family. Call it tying up one last loose end of a case you must have been paid handsomely for already."

"It may take a few days."

"There's no rush, but if you could answer that question I know the whole family would be grateful. I certainly would be."

I fished in my pocket for a card and passed it across the table.

"You can reach me here. I shall look forward to your call."

I was hoping he was intrigued enough to make the enquiry for me, and I pushed back my chair to leave.

"Normally I would hesitate before doing what you ask," he said, "but I can see no harm in asking one simple question. After all the family have been our good clients for a long time."

That was all I wanted to hear. I leaned across the table and shook his hand.

"Thank you for your help."

I handed my identity clip back to the man on the desk downstairs and went back out into Cheapside.

Crossing the road I went into the new Paternoster complex, bought a coffee and took it into St Paul's churchyard where I found a bench that was free and not covered in pigeon droppings.

I needed Joyce to bounce some ideas off, but I didn't want to worry her unduly. I decided I could tell her about Gemma, but I wouldn't mention the note on my car or the motorbike, or Stuart.

"Hi Joyce. It's me. I'm in London."

"What are you doing there? You said you would stay away for a few days."

Not much point staying away now I've been tracked down at home, I thought.

"I've been to talk to your solicitor about the mysterious person who inherited."

"Any good?"

"To a certain extent, yes. Look, leave that with me for a while, will you? I'll let you know if and when I track down Ilse Chambers. No point in building up your hopes till then."

"I suppose not. So why did you call me? Not just to tell me you're in London?"

"No. I think I know who G is. Sarah, from Colbox, called me. Apparently the Gemma who works there fancied Helen."

"Oh my God!"

"Yes, I know. Who could have expected that?"

"No wonder Helen wanted to speak to her boss. What will you do?"

"I'm not sure. It makes Gemma a suspect, of course, although I can't see how she could have been involved in what happened to you up here. And to me those notes imply guilt."

Joyce didn't say anything.

"In one sense," I continued, "if Gemma has nothing to do with Helen's death, with Helen gone there is no G problem anymore. Do you think Mr. Jordan would like to know?"

"There's nothing to be gained by just telling him one of his employees is a lesbian. He might be homophobic. That could make life very difficult for Gemma."

"That's a good point. Perhaps I should just let him know that the mystery is solved and there's nothing for him to worry about."

"Yes, that would do, as long as you're sure Gemma isn't involved in what happened."

"I don't see how she could be."

I nearly said that everything hangs together with Ilse living so close to where Helen died, then realised that Joyce didn't know that.

"Be careful," she said, "won't you, up there in London."

"As careful as I can be. See you soon."

I closed the phone. There was nothing I could do now but wait to see what I could discover. Perhaps there was something else for me to do waiting at the office. At least that would take my mind off Helen and Joyce.

I set off back up towards Barbican station.

Chapter 9

I was feeling quite pleased with myself as I left the tube station at Euston Square, so much so that I called in at the little kiosk there to buy myself a large Danish pastry.

Things were beginning to fit together, at least in relation to the inheritance, and if the solicitor was able to discover the link to the Lamont name which I suspected, it should be possible to get some idea of the total picture in that jigsaw puzzle.

When I turned the corner I saw the black truck parked across the street from my office. As the man in the garden had suggested, it was a Mitsubishi truck with a double cab. I had no doubt it was the same one and why it was there, and I saw two occupants in a quick glance before pulling back around the corner to think.

There was little or no subtlety in parking there, which confirmed my earlier view that I was dealing with someone not quite in the Moriarty class.

What were my options? I could ignore the truck and walk into the office building as normal. That might work. Whoever it was had no way of knowing what I looked like. Or I could go away and come back later. That would achieve nothing. Or I could confront whoever was in the truck.

I realised I could not expect to continue in the detective business for long without facing the occasional confrontation, so I decided on the third option.

The truck had been facing me, so instead of entering the street in plain sight, I doubled back round the block and approached the vehicle directly from behind, trying to keep out of sight of its rear view mirrors.

I reached the back of the truck without being seen. Then, crouching, I made my way along the driver's side, keeping low and out of his mirror's view. Either my approach strategy was good or the driver was half asleep, because nothing had happened by the time I reached his door.

What needed to happen next was not my normal way of operating, so I took a deep breath before going ahead.

Yanking the door open with my right hand, I grabbed the collar of the driver with my left hand and pulled him out of the cab. He stumbled to the ground, half falling, with the inevitable, "What the...?"

I pulled him upright and round to face the truck, pinning his right arm behind him and pushing it upwards.

"Hey. That hurts!"

"That was the idea," and as his colleague opened his door I shouted, "And you stay where you are, or I'll break his arm."

It went very quiet. I pushed the arm a little higher.

"Do as he says," said the owner of the arm.

"Good move."

I waited till I was sure, all the time working out what to do and what to say. This situation required careful thought. And it was not a situation I was used to dealing with.

"Now. Did you want to talk to me?"

"Who are you?"

There was something about the way he said 'you' that reminded me of Ilse.

"Let's leave out the attempts at humour, shall we? You know who I am. That's why you're here. Do you think a perfect stranger would pull you out of the cab like that?"

"You're hurting my arm."

"I know, and you are the only one who can stop the pain. Tell me what's going on."

"I don't know what you mean."

I pushed a little harder, aware that I had no idea how far I could safely push.

"You've been pestering my sister."

"And who is your sister?"

Nothing, so I increased the pressure again.

"Ilse."

"Ilse what?"

"Ilse Chambers."

"You sure of that?"

"What do you mean?"

"Is that her real name?"

"'Course it is. It's the same as mine."

That, at least, was interesting.

"Look, let go of me," he said, a trace of panic in his voice. "I'm not going to do anything."

"You kidnapped a friend of mine."

"It wasn't me. It was 'im."

How many times had I heard that?

"But you were involved."

"The whole thing was stupid," he went on. "It was supposed to be you."

The tone of his voice had changed. He began to sound deflated, and if I was right he was not much of a danger, at least for the moment. I'd barely touched him and he hadn't fought back. Lucky for me, as I was no fighter.

I made a decision.

"Climb back into the cab and move along. I'm coming in after you. Try anything funny, and I will break your arm."

He went to climb in, so I let him go and followed him.

"What's going on, boss?"

"Just shut up."

I closed the door, partly to keep out the cold.

"OK. Talk to me," I said.

"About what?"

"You accused me of pestering your sister. Why would I do that?"

"I don't know."

"You're a joke you are. You kidnap innocent people from quiet gardens, lie in wait for people, then claim you have no idea what it's all about. Let's try this again. Why would I pester your sister?"

"That girl got herself killed. It was near Ilse's house. You came round asking questions and it frightened her."

"Is that all? You're taking things to extremes, aren't you? Writing obscure notes, kidnapping people. Just because I asked your sister some questions. I asked a lot of people questions. She's not the only person who lives round there."

The tone of my voice rose as my anger increased.

Silence.

"It all seems very suspicious to me. I gave my card to your sister, as I did to all her neighbours. She must have shown it to you. Why would you go to such lengths to stop me talking to your sister? Is she hiding something?"

"No."

"Or are you hiding something?"

"No." Even louder.

"What did she do?"

He turned and put his face closer to mine.

"She didn't do anything," he spat at me. "That's why you were wrong to bother her."

"So why the need to put the frightners on me here?"

This made no sense. There must be something I was missing. Some reason why it was so important to scare me off.

His shoulders slumped a little, but there was still a hint of defiance in his voice.

"I've always looked after her."

"Did your sister ask you to come after me?"

"No."

"So why did you?"

"I told you. I look after her."

"Why am I not convinced? A caring brother discovers that someone has been talking to his sister, asking questions no less." I couldn't keep the sarcasm out of my voice.

"Does she give you a list of all the people she speaks to, so you can scare them off?"

"Don't be stupid!"

"So why this time?"

More silence.

"Perhaps I should go to the local nick and identify this truck as the one used in the kidnapping of my friend. We have an independent witness, you know."

He turned to his partner.

"I told you. Bloody stupid, that was."

"But whose idea?" I chipped in.

His head fell forward again. I waited.

"All right," he said. "So what are you going to do?"

"I am tempted to go to the police, like I said. It's what you deserve. But I think perhaps I'll let your sister decide."

"You stay away from her."

"Oh. I've already called again. It was pissing down last time I went and she very kindly offered me a towel to dry off. I thought that was a very generous thing to do."

"She never told me."

"Why would she? She wasn't frightened. A little nervous, perhaps, but not frightened."

He was looking at me now, rather uncertainly. Perhaps he was not the sharpest knife in the drawer, but he could see that I now held a trump card, in fact two cards. I could tell his sister, and I could go to the police.

In point of fact he had done me a favour. I'd been wondering how to find an excuse to visit Ilse again, and now I had one. He had given it to me on a plate. But I was still left with the question, why scare me off?

"Whatever it is you're trying to hide, I'll find it," I told him with as much confidence as I could muster. "There must be something to make it worth your while going to these lengths."

I was watching to see if my words were making any impression.

"Now stay away from me. It's lucky for you my friend wasn't badly hurt. But she might still press charges. In fact she would if I asked her to. If I don't ever see you or your truck again, I shall leave you to get on with your life. Perhaps you should leave your sister to get on with hers."

He grunted. There was not a great deal he could say.

"Are we agreed?"

"I suppose."

"Just remember what'll happen if I so much as clap eyes on you again."

I looked across at his partner in crime, and as I did so my eyes caught sight of a crash helmet resting behind the cab seats.

"What's this?" I said, twisting round to reach it.

"It's mine," Ilse's brother shouted angrily, but I'd already seen half of the stencil on its back and knew I'd seen it before.

"Yours, is it?"

"Yeah! What of it?"

"So where were you first thing this morning?"

"What's that got to do with you?"

"Visiting your sister, were you?"

"So?"

"You must have stayed the night to have been outside my station early this morning."

"Who says I was outside your station?"

"I do. I recognise your helmet and I have the bruise to confirm your poor riding skills. If you wish to continue to be incognito as you ride, I would get rid of the skull and crossbones if I were you."

He was looking at me and I knew from his expression that I was right.

"So now I have two reasons to report you, attempted murder and kidnapping."

"I wasn't trying to kill you."

"It felt like it to me," I said, rubbing my arm. "And adding together the other things you've done - which reminds me."

"What now?"

"Who is it that writes your notes for you?"

"What do you mean?"

"Oh, come on. 'Look under the bench', 'You're next', 'I told you to leave it alone' - all those."

"It was 'im," he said, pointing with his thumb to his partner in crime.

"Not a good choice. Next time, choose someone who can spell."

The writer turned away to look out of the side window.

Ilse's brother made a sound which earlier generations would have described as "Hurrumph!"

"So, do we have a deal?" I asked him.

"If you leave my sister alone."

"Yeah, yeah, we've been through all that. No more threats. No more notes. I don't want to hear or read a dicky bird from you. Do you understand? If I do, well, you know what'll happen. The police will soon find you, and they'll have to go to your sister to get your address. So if you don't want your sister bothered, stay out of my life."

I hoped that my attempt at a threatening demeanour was having the required effect. I'm no Philip Marlow or Frank Cannon, just not the threatening type – not even subtly like Sydney Greenstreet in Maltese Falcon. And I'm no Jim Rockford, who could persuade anyone to do anything. But from his face I saw I'd made my point, so I climbed down from the cab, crossed the road and went up to my office.

The phone was ringing.

"Greg? Hi. Are you all right?" It was Joyce. "I've been trying to get back to you on your mobile, but I couldn't get through."

"I was in the tube for a while. What's up?"

"I was thinking. It can't be Gemma."

"What do you mean?"

"I agree that if someone caused Helen's death, it must be the same person who bundled me off in the garden. Did Gemma know where your office is?

"No. You're right. It can't be her. Anyway something else has happened since my last call?"

"What?"

Now it's a funny thing about honesty. It is undoubtedly the best policy most of the time, but sometimes it's kinder to be less forthcoming. And then again, at other times, things are not even as simple as that.

Knowing the threat was now contained would help put Joyce's mind at rest, but if she knew who had taken her from the garden, she might want to press charges, and I had made a deal, of sorts.

"Greg?"

"Yes, I'm here. I know who was making the threats."

"How on earth did you find them?"

"They found me. I told you they're not very bright."

"Should I come up so we can go to the police?"

"Just a minute. Can we think this thing through? Knowing who it was has given me a useful lead."

"What lead? What have you found out?"

"I haven't found out anything as such, I just said it was a lead. But it could well answer a lot of questions in the long term."

"What do you mean?"

"These guys can be a pain in the neck if they keep on harrassing me. And you. But I don't believe they are essentially dangerous. I have persuaded them to stay away from us, under threat of my going to the police and reporting what they did."

"Why can't we just report them and have done with it?"

"Because I think it might be in our best interests not to antagonise them. They're the sort of people who are likely to go off half-cocked, and come after us in revenge if we bring the police into this."

"I get the impression you're being rather evasive. Is there something you're not telling me?"

"Do you trust me?"

"Of course. I wouldn't have asked for your help if I didn't trust you."

"Good. Then bear with me for a while. I think I may have found a way forward, but I need to act cautiously so I don't mess the whole thing up. And I don't want to end up not being able to answer the question you want answered the most."

"You will be careful, won't you."

"Of course. Don't say anything to your parents. I don't want to build up their hopes, then not be able to deliver the goods."

"OK."

"Look. I'll see you tomorrow if you like. How about The Crown again, for lunch?"

"Lovely. One o'clock?"

"Yes. I'll see you then. Bye, Joyce."

I leaned back in my one comfortable chair and considered what I had so far.

The link between Essex and London; a brother trying to protect his sister; a sister who changes her name; the hint of an accent I couldn't put my finger on; an unexpected will; and always Helen's death. Why? Was it murder? Is that why Ilse's brother was protecting her? Was it an accident? But how could that have happened? Was it suicide all along? But, if it was, why was someone trying to warn me off?

I hoped it wasn't suicide. That would answer the question, but cause even more heartache for the Hetherington family.

Somehow or other, the whole will / death thing must hang together. The big question was how?

It seemed clear now that Stuart and Gemma were not involved, at least I thought it did. And I had no other leads. No other motive for murder except, perhaps, the inheritance.

The answer must lie with Ilse. And now I had another reason to visit her again. I also had a start to my reconstruction of Helen's last day.

When my return train pulled into my station I looked round for a member of the station staff. I had been using the station for so long that I knew most of them by their first names.

It was rare for a train to depart without someone being on the platform to signal to the driver. Although the rail company had installed mirrors through which the driver was supposed to check all doors were closed, I don't believe anyone thought the system was foolproof.

I saw Chris at the end of the platform and waited till he came back along to his office on the platform.

"Hi Chris,"

"Hello Greg," he said. He always made it sound as if he was surprised to see me.

"I wonder if you could help me."

"Try me."

"Can you remember the young woman who was found dead near here a few weeks ago?"

"Yes. Terrible case. And as I recall noone knew why. Must have been suicide. It happens more often than people like to think. Especially at stations."

"I know. Look could you have a look at this photo? It's the girl, Helen, who died that night."

I gave him the photograph and he looked at it closely, then back at me, then back at the photograph."

"What?" I said.

"Is this her?"

"Yes."

"Now that's a funny thing, because I did see her, and I think it was that day."

"Can you remember what sort of time it was?"

"It would have been late afternoon. But it was still light."

"Is there any particular reason why you remember seeing her?"

"That's the funny thing. I happened to notice her get off the train. Well you do, don't you, when they are young and attractive?"

"And?"

"She was walking along the platform and suddenly she looked across towards the car park and started to run."

"As if she'd seen someone, you mean?"

"Yes. It looked as if she'd seen someone she knew, and wanted to catch them before they drove off."

"And this was afternoon. Can you be more specific about the time?"

"Well, I said it was light and so it was, but only just. So four or five, I suppose."

"Thanks, Chris. That's very helpful."

I took the photo back and returned it to my pocket.

"Why are you asking these questions?"

"I'm helping Helen's family work out what happened to her. It looks as if you were one of the last people to see her alive."

"Streuth! Is that so?"

"What you've told me could be very useful. Thanks."

I left him standing on the platform, deep in thought.

Monks Colne was only a five minute drive from the station, so I drove straight there.

Ilse opened the door in the same cautious way.

"Oh. It's you."

"Yes. Can I come in?"

"I suppose so." Not the most welcoming of invitations.

I could see no point in beating about the bush.

"I met your brother," I said when I was facing her in the hall.

"Oh," she said again.

There was no question in her voice, I noticed. As if it had been inevitable.

"Can we talk?"

"What about?"

"I think you know."

She was looking at me closely, a mixture of fear and confusion in her expression.

"I haven't done anything."

"Then you have nothing to fear from me. But your brother seems to think you need protecting."

"What's he done now? Something stupid, no doubt."

"Can we sit down and talk about this?"

"I suppose I shall have to, eventually. You'd better come in here."

She indicated a room at the front of the house. It was sparsely furnished with an elderly three piece suite in a dark green chintz, which seemed to match the era of the kitchen.

"I'll make some tea," she said, and left me.

There was a little more sense of life in the living room, with pictures on the walls, various ornaments on the mantlepiece and a colourful rug in front of the fireplace. I wondered why there was no fire lit on such a cold day. Perhaps Ilse spent all her time in the kitchen. As she had inherited so much money, she certainly wouldn't be hard up. Another question to consider. Perhaps the money hadn't come through to her yet.

I looked at each picture in turn, but they were bland in the extreme and told me nothing, until I reached a calendar on the wall beyond the fireplace. It showed a Scottish scene of open moorland with mountains in the background. Interesting it should be Scotland, I thought.

There was so much I wanted to ask her, but I would have to tread very carefully, or I would risk losing my best lead to the truth, whatever that turned out to be.

Ilse returned with a plastic tray bearing a teapot and two mugs. As she busied herself pouring the tea, I sat down on one of the armchairs.

The hot mug she gave me came in sharp contrast to the ambience of the room.

"I think it's time I introduced myself," I said. "My name is Greg."

No reply. I sipped my tea.

"What should I call you?"

She looked at me.

"My name is Ilse."

"That's an unusual name."

"Is it? I haven't really thought about it."

"Your brother, he must be quite close, to want to protect you."

"We get on. What has he done?"

"He came to see me." Another case of complete honesty not necessarily being the best policy.

"Did he threaten you?"

"Why do you ask that?"

"Because he said he might."

As my tea had cooled a little, I was able to drink it properly rather than sip it. Useful thinking time.

"What does he think he's protecting you from?"

"From people asking questions."

"Any questions, or questions specifically about the accident?"

"Any questions. I don't know anything about the accident. I told you."

That was interesting. What did she have to hide besides a possible involvement in Helen's death? I didn't think for a minute it was simply a question of extreme shyness. Something, or things, were being hidden.

I looked round the room for inspiration as I drank my tea.

"These pictures came with the house, I suppose."

"They're not mine."

"I like the picture on the calendar. Was it sent by a friend in Scotland?"

There was a slight change in her expression, very slight, but it was there.

"My other brother sent it."

"Does he live in Scotland then?"

"Yes."

"What took him up there from London?"

The question clearly puzzled her.

"You said you were from London."

"Oh, yes. But I used to live in Scotland."

"Ah. I see."

I wasn't sure what it was I saw, but anything that linked Ilse to Scotland was potentially relevant, and certainly intriguing.

"So you and your brother moved south. In search of work, I suppose?"

"Yes. There weren't many jobs where we were living."

"Where was that?"

"Montrose."

I smiled.

"I only know of Montrose from Scottish football results. I couldn't tell you where it is."

"Dad was a fisherman."

"Was?"

"He's dead now."

"I'm sorry. Is your mother still up in Scotland."

"She's dead too."

"Oh." I didn't bother quoting Oscar Wilde on losing both parents. It would have been entirely inappropriate, and I don't think she would have understood anyway.

"How long have you been in London?"

"About twenty years."

"And did you find it easy when you first arrived, getting a job?"

She looked at me. Every one of her answers came after a short, but significant pause, as if she was weighing very carefully what she would or could tell me.

"Doug's a builder."

Ah, I thought. That explains the ladder.

"Dad gave him some money to buy somewhere he could live and do up."

"And you?"

"I came with him. We shared the house and I did things for him."

"Things?"

"Well, I helped him with the house to start with. Painting and things. Then he sold it and bought somewhere else, so he could do the same thing again."

"I see. He became a developer."

"I suppose you could call it that. He got people working for him. The business grew and I did the books for him. I've always been good with figures."

"So why did you decide to come and live out here, in the sticks?"

"I wanted a change."

I was watching her eyes, and they moved distinctly when she said that.

"But you don't like it, you said."

"No."

"So how long have you lived here?"

"About eighteen months, I suppose."

At least that fitted with her entry in the phone book.

"Have you made many friends here?"

"Not really. The neighbours speak, but that's all."

"You must feel very lonely."

"Yes."

"I think you've done very well to stay as long as you have. Has it been worth it, coming here?"

"What do you mean, worth it?" Distinct suspicion was back in her voice, so I decided to ease off and stick with what I had, not that it was a great deal.

"I mean are you glad you came? Most of us have dreams – things we would like to try. Sometimes the dreams work out, but sometimes they don't. The only way to discover if the dream is as you expected, is to try. You tried. Are you glad you tried?

My attempt at simple philosophy appeared lost on her.

"I preferred living in London."

A good detective, like a good gambler, must know when to stop. Now was the time.

I leaned forward to put my mug on the tray as I rose to leave.

"Well, thank you again for your hospitality."

"Why did you come?" she suddenly asked.

That threw me. She had never asked me a question before.

"You haven't asked me anything, except about the calendar and my brother."

I wondered how far I dare go with this. Was she involved with Helen's death or not? If she was, I knew I must give no indication that I suspected the fact, or she would clam up completely. I sat down again.

"You asked me earlier if your brother had threatened me. He told me today he's trying to protect you, but only from people worrying you with unnecessary questions. Is there another reason? Is there something you're not telling me?"

Her expression changed completely. I may not have hit the nail squarely on the head, but it was close. She turned away and spoke down towards her feet.

"I have no idea what happened to that girl. Her death was nothing to do with me."

"Good. Then I suppose I shall have to believe you."

She lifted her head and turned to look at me.

"Do you believe me?"

"I want to, Ilse. But this case is so complicated I'm not sure who I can believe."

I stood up again and nothing else was said as she showed me to the door. I thanked her and, once again, heard the door close abruptly behind me.

George Harrison was singing 'All things must pass' as I drove home and pondered what I had learned. A lot of things must pass, I thought, before I get to the bottom of this case.

Ilse was from Scotland. That's when the penny dropped. Her accent. Of course. And Annie had lived in Scotland. Ilse said her parents were dead. It would be interesting to know how long ago they had died.

She had moved to the country from London, to live quite close to where Annie had lived. Was that relevant or coincidence? Surely not another coincidence.

London is surrounded by open country. Why come to this particular corner?

Eighteen months ago Annie was still alive. Did something happen after Ilse arrived to cause Annie to make her sole beneficiary?

And always I was left with what I started with. How and why did Helen die?

Ilse didn't seem like a person who would push someone under a train. That left me with the same question. Was it an accident or suicide? In fact I was no further forward.

Chapter 10

Once again Joyce was at the pub before me. I glanced at my watch as I hate to be late, but I wasn't. Being early must reflect her concern.

She was nursing an orange juice at the bar. I ordered a pint of IPA and we moved away to find a table.

"What are you doing with yourself?" I asked her.

"Nothing much. I signed on again yesterday, and part of the deal with getting benefit is that you have to apply for work."

"I suppose teaching is out of the question now."

Her head fell.

"Yes. I was so stupid. I don't know what came over me."

"We're all allowed to make mistakes," I offered.

"Not as big as that one. What with dad losing his job, and now losing Helen. At least Mum and Dad thought I was OK and set on a good career for life. Then I go and screw everything up."

She noticed my expression.

"Don't look at me like that."

"I'm sorry, but it was an amusing choice of words."

"Let's just order, shall we?"

We made our choices, and I went to order the meals.

"Are you getting anywhere?" she asked when I sat down again.

"I don't know. I think so in some respects, but nothing makes complete sense yet."

"Perhaps this is going to be one of those mysteries that is never solved."

"I hope not. I have some ideas and I'm waiting for the answers to some enquiries."

"What enquiries?"

"Well, first of all I think we can eliminate Stuart and Gemma. If we do that, the only area of enquiry we're left with is the inheritance."

"But how can that have caused Helen's death?"

"I don't know at this stage. But I can find nothing else and no one else to link in any way with what happened."

What should I tell her? How fair would it be to build up her hopes and then see them all come crashing down again.

I had a geographical link between Ilse and the accident site, and a brother who was going out of his way to scare me off. That must mean something.

I knew where Helen had been during part of her last afternoon, but only as far as the station. Who did she see, I wondered.

"There's too much mystery surrounding the inheritance, I know. Too many unanswered questions. But there's nothing else that we know of that even hints at a reason for Helen's death. What I need to discover is more about the beneficiary."

"This Ilse Chambers person?" and she said it with real venom.

"Yes. And, of course, I still don't know the real cause of how Helen died. But I think I am making progress."

I hoped I was able to sound convincing, but I saw no sign of a smile on Joyce's face. She just looked at me.

"It's like I said," she said. "A mystery that is never solved. You should be spending time on other cases and earning some money. You know we can't afford to pay you."

I leaned across and took her hand.

"And I've told you I don't want any payment. I'm doing this for you."

As I said it, I realised that this was, in fact, the truth. Obviously I was working for the whole family, but deep down, I wanted things to work out for Joyce.

"This is neither the time nor the place to come on to me," she said, sounding very serious.

"I didn't come here intending to come on to you. But I just suddenly realised something. How long have we known each other?"

"Since Year Nine. That school trip, remember?"

"Oh, yes. What a disaster that was. I'm not even going to try to work out how long ago that was, but all that time we've been good friends, haven't we?"

She didn't say anything, clearly curious as to where I was going with this.

"You know we have," she said eventually.

"I think perhaps I've been scared to do anything, or say anything, which might have led to us being more than just friends."

"You are coming on to me." But at least, this time she said it with the hint of a smile on her face.

"I'm still scared. I don't want to do anything that might lead to losing you as a friend. And knowing that makes me realise how important you are to me. I think you always have been important to me."

I was still holding her hand when the waitress brought our food, and we smiled as we separated to make room for the plates.

We ate in silence for a short time, while I considered whether I should say anything further. I kept my eyes focussed on my plate, all the while aware that Joyce was observing me from across the table. She was waiting for me to say more, and I wasn't sure what more I should say.

"This isn't the time or place." I said eventually. "You're quite right. I have to get this mystery solved, and I believe I will solve it. But when it's done, perhaps we could go out."

"What do you think we're doing now?" she said.

"You know what I mean. A proper date, not just a meeting to hear an update of what I am doing."

Now she put down her knife and fork and looked at me hard.

"Do you have any idea how long I have waited for you to ask me out?"

I was stunned.

"Really?"

"Yes, really, you idiot."

Now it was time for me to go quiet.

"Why do you think I took a teaching post in the Midlands rather than staying round here to teach?"

"Not because of me?"

"Yes, because of you. I assumed you weren't interested, but I was crazy about you and I didn't want to risk us meeting constantly, feeling the way I did."

"I had no idea."

"Obviously."

"You could have gone out with anyone. Fellers were falling over each other to get close to you."

"I know, but I wasn't interested."

"This is so funny. Are you serious?"

"I don't joke about things like this."

I just looked at her, my fork now poised between plate and mouth.

"Well go on, then."

"What?"

"Ask me out."

I felt like a shy thirteen year old. This was so ridiculous. Or perhaps it wasn't.

"Will you go out with me?"

"Yes. Of course I will. At last."

We both laughed and gradually got back to eating our meals, although I didn't find it easy to eat with the silly grin which I knew was spreading across my face.

We said little more until the coffee was in front of us.

"What do we do now?" Joyce said.

"I have a lot more enquires to make until I can tie everything together, always assuming it can be tied together."

"I didn't mean about that. I meant about us."

"I owe it to your parents to solve this case and find out what happened to Helen. Perhaps it wouldn't be a good idea to get too involved just yet. I need to concentrate. You've already proved something of a distraction."

"How?"

"Just having you with me is a distraction. I find myself thinking about you rather than the case. I must try not to do that.

"So?"

"We know now how we feel about each other."

"At last," she said again, smiling.

"Once everything is sorted, we can spend as much time together as we like. Until then, can we just play it a little cool and keep things to ourselves?"

"That's not going to be easy, but I'll try."

"Why won't it be easy?"

"My mum will know something's up, just by looking at me. She always can."

It was my turn to smile.

"Just play it down for the time being. Hopefully it won't be for long."

"All right. I'll try."

I paid and we left for the car park, where our cars were parked about as far apart as they could have been.

Joyce turned towards me and I took her arms and drew her towards me and kissed her, for the very first time, on the lips.

When she finally eased away she said, "You expect me to play it cool when you kiss me like that?"

"I shan't find this any easier than you," I assured her. "Listen, let me get some more work done, then come round to mine later. What do you say?"

"I say 'Yes'," she said.

"Good."

Pecking her on the cheek I made my way across to my car.

"Don't take too long with your work," she called after me.

Later, we were sitting on my sofa, well half lying would be more accurate. Cold coffee was congealing in the bottom of two mugs on the floor.

"I've got to move," I said. "My left arm's gone to sleep."

We were so wrapped around each other it was difficult to get up, and when we did, we immediately fell back down side by side in fits of giggles.

I took her hand.

"Listen," I said to her. "Can I get something clear in my mind?"

"What?"

"When I take you out, I want us to do what you like doing most. So is it going to be a film, the theatre, a meal, a night club? What would you prefer?"

Joyce snuggled up to me and smiled.

"All of the above."

"That's going to be a long evening."

She kissed me again.

"Do you have a problem with that?"

"What do you think?"

The moments passed and my thoughts began to drift back to more serious things.

"Can I change the subject?"

"What is it?"

"If I tell you something, can you keep it from your parents till I can confirm things?"

"What is it? What have you found out?"

"Please don't say anything yet, but I've found the person who benefitted from your grandmother's will."

She sat up suddenly.

"Where? Who is she? You didn't tell me."

"Not yet. She doesn't know yet that I know, and I'm waiting for some confirmation in order to put two and two together. Can we go and see your parents? There is something I want to ask them."

"Of course. Do you want to go now?"

"No. Tomorrow will do. Now, I want you to tell me which day you are free to go out."

"You choose. I've waited this long and I have no other plans."

"OK. I'll set something up and let you know."

"Lovely."

We snuggled back down together and I forgot all about the case completely.

The following morning I drove back to Dedham.

It felt suddenly strange, coming into the house after what had just happened between us. When I was last there it was on business, although I had been before, of course. Now I felt oddly conspicuous and tried to shrug off the feeling, aware that I had to get back to business in order to solve the persistent mysteries that remained.

Joyce's mother appeared at the door to let me in, looking no happier than when I had last seen her.

"Hello, Greg. Do you have any news?"

Joyce, who had appeared alongside her mum, exchanged glances with me.

"What?" Joyce was right. Mothers don't miss a trick.

"I just wanted to ask you a few more questions," I said, hoping to avoid confusing the visit with personal matters.

She looked disappointed.

"Oh. All right then."

She gave Joyce a puzzled look and led us into the living room, where Oliver was reading the newspaper.

"Hello, Greg," he said half-heartedly.

Joyce and I sat on the sofa, but unnaturally apart, or so it seemed to me.

"Two things, really," I began. "And I'm sorry to return to distressing matters. After Helen was found, I assume that all she had with her was brought back here."

"Yes. Eventually. It was retained by the police, but then they returned it. I think they said it had no material connection with the case."

"Could I see what it was?"

Joyce's parents exchanged looks, then her mother said, "Yes. I'll get it for you."

She brought in Helen's handbag and I took it to the dining table and began to take things out. When I found the photographs I knew that another piece had fitted into place.

"Who is this?"

"We don't know, but we found the pictures in a trunk of Annie's things that was stored in the garage."

"You have a trunk of Annie's things here?"

"Oh, yes. Didn't we mention it?"

"No. Could I see it later?"

"Of course."

"Why do you think Helen had these photos with her?"

"I don't know. We think the person is the same in each picture. Helen was convinced the pictures meant something. Perhaps she just stored them in her bag so she would have them with her."

"Do you know if she tried to find out who this is?"

"No. It was only just before she died that we found the pictures."

Surely this was relevant. I had recognised Ilse immediately, but kept it to myself.

"Now. Before I look in the trunk, can you think of anything or anyone Annie mentioned? Think back as far as you can. Whoever this Ilse Chambers is, I'm sure she must have some link with Annie."

Joyce's mother sat down on a dining chair and stared at the photos still lying on the table.

"Annie once said something strange. It was the day of Alan's funeral."

"My grandad," Joyce added.

"She said that if she moved south she would be able to visit a friend in the Midlands more often. But when I asked about the friend, she changed the subject."

She looked at me.

"Do you think that is important?"

"It could be," I said. "Do you have any idea who this friend might be?"

"No. None at all."

"OK. Let's see what I can find in that trunk. Would you like to help?"

Joyce's parents looked at each other.

"We went through it before with Helen," her mother said, continuing to look at Oliver as she spoke. "It'll seem strange doing it again."

Oliver nodded, and she added, "But if you think it would help."

"Well it's likely that you'll make more sense out of some of the contents than me."

It took us ages to work our way through the whole trunk. We separated everything out into irrelevant, not likely to be relevant, and possibly relevant. Then we separated each of those piles into known or recognised and unknown items.

The floor had become strewn with empty coffee mugs and plates of crumbs from the biscuits and sandwiches we consumed. We sat round in a circle, faced by six collections of assorted material, all precious to Annie in one way or another. Most of it a mystery to us.

"What now?" Joyce asked me.

"I think it's likely that we need to start in the collection of unknown and possibly relevant. Something in there might give us an entirely new lead to sorting out what has happened."

I leaned forward and began to dig. After a few minutes I found a small pack of something wrapped in newspaper. I unfolded the paper and found a collection of photographs of a wooded area.

"Do you know where this is?"

The pictures were passed round.

"No idea," they all said.

"Then there's this one of a War Cemetery. Any idea where this is?"

No one had.

"Why would Granny have a picture of a War Cemetery?" Joyce said. "Look, it says Commonwealth War Graves Commission."

She turned to her mother.

"Was there anyone in our family killed during the war?"

"Not as far as I know."

"Could she have had a brother?" I asked.

"If she did, she never mentioned him."

"Perhaps she had a brother, who had a daughter, and that's the person in the photograph."

"Maybe," I said. "Can I keep these, at least for the time being? It would be interesting to know where this cemetery is."

I wrapped the photos up in the newspaper again and put the little package in my pocket.

We searched some more, and all we could find was an ageing print of a tall building of grey stone. It looked very stark and rather imposing, but there was no clue as to what or where it was.

"Look," I said. "I think it's possible that any number of things in this trunk could be useful in helping us answer questions. Can we put them back in some sort of order, so I can get at them again if I need to?"

"Why don't you take the whole trunk?" Oliver suggested. "It's no use to us, certainly not at present. If its contents can help you in your enquiries, you might as well have it with you."

He turned to his wife.

"No reason why not," she said.

"That would be helpful. Thanks."

We began to repack the trunk, while keeping each sorted group of items together. The ones I thought most likely to be useful were placed on top.

"Good," Oliver said as he got up from the floor and flopped into an armchair. "I'm getting too old for this game."

Joyce and I returned to the sofa, a little closer than before and exchanged glances.

"What's going on?" Joyce's mother said. I was aware that she had been observing us.

"What do you mean?" Joyce replied, as innocently as she could.

"You don't look the same."

She turned to me.

"Greg?"

"What? I don't know what you mean."

Joyce and I exchanged looks again and smiled.

"I must get off," I announced. "Things to do. Could someone give me a hand with this thing to the car?"

Oliver rose again.

"I'll do that."

We carried the trunk out to the car and placed it in the boot. Joyce followed, and when Oliver returned to the house we were left standing by the back of the car.

"Mum could tell," she said.

"I know," I smiled. "It's hard to keep that sort of thing a secret from someone who knows you that well."

"When you've gone, I'll go up to my room and try to avoid any more questions. It's a bit confusing, thinking about you now, at the same time as I'm thinking about what happened to Helen."

"I'll get off and see what I can dig up."

I kissed her on the cheek.

"Will that do for now?"

She smiled. "For now."

I drove off home, thinking about Joyce and the photographs and what they all meant.

Later, on the dining table, I spread out the pictures from my pocket, and then added the ones I had called unknown, but possibly relevant.

There was the cemetery, the wooded area and the stone building. The building appeared to be in a town, as the angle of the shot suggested quite narrow streets. But there was no transport visible in the street, and the faded colour of the print suggested the picture was taken a long time ago.

And then the cemetery. I had seen War Cemeteries in northern France and Belgium. There had been a school trip to visit sites from the First World War, and places like Thiepval, Ypres and Vimy had formed impressions it would be hard to lose. But the concept of a War Cemetery in England was different.

I supposed that a lot of people killed abroad during wars were brought home for burial, although I was not sure of that. It had certainly happened during recent conflicts. But why would Annie have such pictures? They must mean something.

My pad was lying next to the computer, and I picked it up to sort through the notes I'd jotted down before.

Threats in London - that was sorted out now. Ilse had a brother. A stupid brother, but a brother who said he wanted to protect her. But from what?

Ilse's connection with Annie - I knew she lived in Scotland, but no more than that.

Annie's maiden name - I was still waiting for the solicitor to reply, if he ever would.

What happened to Helen? - accident, suicide or murder? If murder, by whom?

Ilse - probably not.

Her brother - possibly.

Stuart - perhaps but probably not.

Gemma - perhaps but probably not.

I sat back and stared at it all. If Helen was killed, surely it must be by someone I'd already met. I ruled out a chance encounter as being highly implausible. Dickens and Shakespeare might fill their works with amazing coincidences, but those sorts of things didn't happen in real life. Helen had died near Ilse's house. That must mean something.

Yet the more I thought of Ilse, the less I could see her as a murderer.

Perhaps I was no good at this detective game. If I was a poor judge of character, I couldn't expect to solve anything. But she was so timid, it just didn't seem to fit. Or perhaps she was an excellent actress. What chance would I have if that were the case?

But if not Ilse, then who? Her brother? But why?

As my thoughts veered round in never-ending circles of possibility, I was brought back to the likelihood that it was an accident, or suicide.

No, not suicide, I suddenly decided. That didn't fit with the reason Helen was there in the first place. And she had so much going for her. Why should she suddenly take her own life?

She had the three photographs with her - photos of Ilse, and she died near Ilse's house. She must have found out who Ilse was.

And her brother said he always tried to protect her. Did that mean anything?

It could have been an accident. It was dark, after all. But Helen wasn't stupid. If there was a train coming she would have heard it. No, it had to be murder. And the answer surely lay with Ilse. I would have to go and see her again.

I was aware that whatever the facts were, the more often I visited Ilse, the more cagey she would be likely to get with her answers. This was another aspect of a detective's job I had to get right. How to elicit relevant information, which meant how to ask the right questions in the right order. And how to ask those questions while keeping the other person at their ease.

This last thing was difficult with Ilse as she was naturally nervous, definitely introverted and probably suspicious of my motives.

But she must know more than she had said so far, so I would have to see her again and try to piece together some sort of clear picture from what she said. But not today, there were other things to do, and certainly other things to think about.

Chapter 11

The next morning, armed with the cemetery photographs, I went back up to London, and headed straight for the Imperial War Museum.

I asked the man on the information desk if there was someone I could speak to about War Cemeteries in Britain; someone who might be able to identify one from photographs.

He picked up a phone and spoke to someone, then ushered me into a small conference room and told me to wait. I was soon joined by a man who introduced himself and asked how he could help.

"I have some photographs of a Commonwealth War Cemetery. I'm almost certain it's in this country. I wonder if you could tell me where it is."

"Interesting," he said, "but not necessarily easy. Let me see what I can do."

I spread the few pictures on a table and stood back while he examined each one for a few minutes.

"It's difficult, but I have some ideas. What's this about?"

"It's a bit of family history really. My girlfriend's grandmother died recently, and we found these pictures among her possessions. We're interested to know what they mean and if there's someone from the family buried there."

He looked a bit more.

"Can you leave these with me? I can't identify the place myself, but I am sure someone will be able to. Come back in a few days, and I hope I might have an answer by then."

I took out one of my cards and offered it to him.

"Would you be so good as to give me a call if you come up with a name? I should be very grateful."

"I'll see what I can do."

So I left the War Museum none the wiser, but with the possibility that there might be an answer in the near future.

I took the Northern Line up to Euston and pushed my way through the crowds in the covered walkway towards my office.

There was a fair amount of correspondence waiting for me which was encouraging, but as I opened it, I found it hard to concentrate on anything but Joyce and Helen and Ilse and all those unanswered questions.

I felt I was getting somewhere with the inheritance mystery, but was that relevant to what happened to Helen? Was I missing something important, perhaps to do with Stuart or Gemma? And was I getting fixated on something that would not, in the end, answer the most important question?

Stuart's story held together. He was not involved in Joyce's abduction and he had an alibi for the time Helen died.

Then there was Gemma. Perhaps I should try to discover more about her. Now I knew it was Ilse's brother who had caused all the aggro, the fact that Gemma didn't know my office address was irrelevant. Perhaps the inheritance and death were not linked, but that still left the fact that Helen had died near Ilse's house. Of all the coincidences I kept finding, if the inheritance did not cause her death, that was the greatest and weirdest.

I found Sarah's phone number and punched in the numbers.

"Hello?"

"Sarah. Hi. It's Greg Mason. Can you spare me a minute?"

She was quiet for a moment, then replied.

"Yes. Give me a minute to go outside where it's more private."

I waited, and listened to her footsteps and the sound of the door squeaking open and closed.

"OK," she said.

"Can you tell me more about Gemma? You said she couldn't take her eyes off Helen."

"That's right. She followed her about. When Helen went out for lunch, Gemma would leave at the same moment. Things like that."

"You seem to be saying that Gemma was stalking her."

"Well, I suppose, in a way she was. I hadn't thought of it like that."

"Let me ask you something very difficult. Do you think that Gemma would be capable of hurting someone?"

"You think she might have caused Helen's death? My God!"

"I don't think that, at least not yet, but I need to be clear whether it is worth spending any time asking her more questions. What do you think?"

"I don't know. I don't know what to say about that."

"OK. Perhaps it was unfair of me to ask. Thanks for your help, Sarah."

I closed the phone and sat there thinking once more.

Then my office phone rang.

"Mr Mason?"

"Yes."

"It's the Imperial War Museum. You are in luck. Someone has been able to identify your photographs. They show the Commonwealth War Cemetery at Brocton on Cannock Chase."

"Brocton?"

The name meant nothing to me.

"Yes, it's a few miles south of Stafford."

"Is there anything particular about the servicemen who are buried there? Are they from particular regiments perhaps, or were they killed during certain battles or wars?"

"Well, I know that a lot of them died during the Spanish 'flu epidemic after the First World War. And there are a lot of New Zealanders from the First War there as well. But I can't think of anything else."

"Thank you for that information. It was very kind of you to call, and so promptly. I shall call back soon to collect the photographs."

"You're most welcome. Goodbye."

I put the phone down and pondered on what I had just heard. It didn't seem to lead me anywhere useful. Except the fact that Cannock Chase is in the Midlands, and Joyce's mother had remembered Annie mentioning the chance to visit a friend in the Midlands.

But this was a cemetery. Could visiting a friend refer to visiting a friend's grave? But Spanish 'flu? That was 1918. Annie would hardly have been born then. She might know of someone in the family who was buried there, but she would be unlikely to call them a friend.

It was near to Stafford, he said, and I was across the road from Euston Station. I looked at my watch – just coming up to quarter to twelve.

On the spur of the moment I called Joyce.

"Hi," I said. "Do you fancy a trip this afternoon?"

"Where to?"

"Stafford."

"Where?"

"Stafford. I'm following up a hunch. Would you like to come with me? We can get there and back easily in a day. If you can catch the first train up to town, I'll meet you on Euston station concourse with a picnic lunch to eat on the train. What do you say?"

"This is not the kind of first date I had in mind."

"But will you come?"

"Of course I'll come. I'll be there as soon as I can."

She rang off.

It would take her an hour and a half to reach me, I reckoned, so I was able to get on with other things before walking back across to the station.

I bought two day return tickets from the automatic machine and made my way to the refreshment area to choose some snacks and drinks for the journey.

On the main concourse again, I was looking up at the destination board when Joyce ran up to me, red in the face and clearly excited.

"Here I am."

She put her arms round my neck and pulled me into a kiss.

"Hey! Watch out for your lunch."

"What time is the train?"

"In twenty minutes, up there, look."

I pointed up at the board.

"I made some enquiries, and we should be there in an hour and a quarter."

"But why are we going there?"

"Let's go and find the train, and I'll explain everything then."

Joyce bounced along beside me, her arm tucked into mine. I liked the closeness of her and couldn't help smiling at the memory of our conversation in the pub two days before, and later on my sofa. All those years wasted because I was too scared to ask and risk being let down and spoiling a friendship. But that was then. Now we had found each other and life would be altogether different.

Sitting on opposite sides of a table next to the train's window, I began to unpack two salads, a baguette filled with ham and lettuce, a packet of crisps and two bottles of Seven-Up which I had been carrying in my pockets.

"My word. You know how to give a girl a good time."

"I'll have you know this is cordon bleu British Rail food."

"That's an oxymoron."

We both laughed.

I broke the baguette into two sections, opened the salads and pushed Joyce's half of the lunch across to her. For the next ten minutes we ate and hardly spoke. Then the train pulled out.

"OK," Joyce said. "What's going on?"

"This is where I find out if I am a real detective, or just someone who keeps adding two and two together and making five."

"Go on then."

"Your mum said that Annie talked of visiting a friend in the Midlands. In her trunk there were pictures of a War Cemetery. This morning I've discovered that that cemetery is in the Midlands. That's where we are going."

"To a War Cemetery?"

"Yes. I reckon that if we go through the list of people buried there, we'll find a name with a link to your grandmother. I don't know why, but I'm sure there's an answer there."

"An answer to what?"

"To why Helen didn't get anything from the will. And perhaps to why she died."

"Are you sure, or are you guessing?"

"I suppose it's a sort of guess, or you could call it intuition, and there are those who say we should always follow our intuition. But anyway, even if nothing comes of it, we still get most of a day together. Doesn't that make the journey worthwhile?"

She smiled and I realised again how much I loved to see that smile. It took me back to school. I was always the joker, saying anything to get a laugh, often to the annoyance of my teachers.

It was Joyce who always saw the humour in my comments. She would turn round and smile at me, even while the teacher was telling me off, and that smile, almost on its own, made the jokey comment worth making, and any punishment worth taking.

So how had I come so far through life without letting Joyce know how I felt about her? I don't know. She looked far too beautiful ever to be interested in me. At school, at parties, at discos and later on in pubs, we were part of the same group of friends who did virtually everything together. Joyce was often the centre of attention, and most of the other blokes in the group had been out with her, sometimes often. But never me.

And there we were, sitting on a train, content just to look at each other.

"Shall I come and sit next to you?"

"No," she said. "I wouldn't be able to see you properly if you were sitting here. We can talk across the table."

"I don't want to talk," I told her.

"I know," and she smiled that smile again.

When the train pulled into Stafford station we made our way, hand in hand, to the exit, looking for the taxi rank. There were two white Skoda Octavias purring at the kerb. I approached the first driver.

"Can we go to the War Cemetery at Brocton?"

"Certainly."

"And can you wait for us there, to bring us back? We shouldn't be too long."

"OK."

We climbed in the back of the taxi and set off through the strange town and out into countryside. Initially we saw farmland, with dairy herds and occasional fields cleared for planting. However they soon gave way to wooded areas, and I remembered the name Cannock Chase that I'd heard in the phone call from the War Museum. It had sounded like heathland, and clearly it was.

It didn't take the taxi long to reach the place, and the driver stopped just before a corner in the lane. To our left we could see an area of gravestones with a tall cross dominating the scene. Brocton War Cemetery.

Joyce and I looked at each other.

"Can you wait, please, driver?"

"Right, guv."

We left the vehicle and stood side by side looking at the scene.

A neat hedge at the roadside was separated by three stone flagged steps leading up to a wrought iron gateway set between brick pillars, topped with white stone. Simple, yet imposing.

Behind the entrance was an area of grass, interspersed with shrubs and trees. I recognised a rhododendron, but I am not very good at plant names and I could only describe a bush of deep red winter foliage and several slender trees.

Set back on the lawn were rows of white stone memorials, with a cross of what looked like white marble standing in the centre. The whole scene was simple yet dramatic, peaceful and moving at the same time – in fact intensely powerful.

"Why are we here?" Joyce asked me.

"We need to find the record of all those buried here. There has to be a connection with your grandmother. I suspect this may be her friend in the Midlands."

We looked round, made enquiries and were shown to a memorial book in which were listed all the names and their causes of death. It seemed that most were young men in training, a mixture of British and New Zealanders, who died of the Spanish 'flu. I started to search through the names.

"What are we looking for?"

"Any name linked to your family. Glenn, Lamont perhaps, anything that catches your eye."

"Lamont?"

Her query reminded me that so far I had no proof related to Ilse's surname.

"Well, any Scottish sounding name. Annie was from Scotland, after all."

We looked in silence through the pages recording such a tragic loss in such an unexpected way. When the 'flu hit the camp that was there during the First World War, with so many men living in such close proximity, they wouldn't have had a chance to avoid contagion.

It's bad enough for a New Zealand parent to hear of their son's death at the battle front so many miles from home, but to come so far and die of 'flu seemed totally unreasonable.

We could find no names that told us anything. There were a few Scottish sounding names and I wrote them down, but none had a known link to Annie. I closed the book and looked at Joyce.

"I was so sure."

"Never mind," she said and put her arm through mine. "It was a good idea."

We retraced our steps to the taxi and I went to speak to the driver.

"Is there anything else out here? Another cemetery perhaps, or is this the only one?"

"There is a German cemetery up there," he said, pointing to a side road. "We do get a few German visitors who want to go up there."

"Can you drive us up there?"

"If you like."

We got in, he started the car again, moved off and immediately turned left to head along a narrow lane, bordered by a grass verge and quite young looking trees. Looking to right and left I could see only scrubland. They appeared to have put this German cemetery a long way along the lane, well back from the Commonwealth one. Tactfulness, I assumed.

Eventually we reached a parking area, beyond which the lane was blocked with wooden posts. But we could see a paved entrance area beyond the posts and made our way there.

The person we spoke to said that every German who died in Britain during the two world wars was eventually brought here for burial. Some from a Prisoner of War Camp, some shot down in German airships during WW1, and any others. He pointed out the separate areas for First and Second World War memorials.

We walked round for a few minutes and it was interesting, but hardly relevant to us, so I thanked the man for his help and we returned to the taxi.

"Back to the station, please."

"What now?" Joyce said.

"I don't know. There must be something here, or your grandmother wouldn't have had photos of the place. What we don't know is the name of the person she came to see, or to remember."

"Perhaps someone else took the pictures."

"That's possible, of course. But why?"

I leaned forward toward the driver.

"If a person wanted an overnight break in Stafford, where would they stay? Somewhere within walking distance of the station, perhaps."

"There's a couple of old inns there. Most of the modern places are further out, like your Travel Lodges and the like."

"OK. Take us to one of those inns, if you would. You can leave us there."

"Whatever you want."

"So do I detect an unplanned dirty weekend?" Joyce said coyly. "I haven't brought anything with me, you know."

"We could always find a chemists"

"What?" and she punched me hard on the arm.

"Just kidding."

The driver dropped us outside the Stafford Knot and I paid him, adding a generous tip for his time.

"Thanks, guv."

We went inside and straight up to the desk.

"I wonder if you could help us. We're looking for the place my girl friend's grandmother used to stay when she came here. She's doing her family history and we're trying to fill in as many details as we can."

The young woman behind the desk looked from me to Joyce and back again.

"We don't usually give out the names of our guests to all and sundry."

"Her name was Glenn. Mrs Annie Glenn."

"Mrs Glenn?" her attitude changed immediately. "Oh, yes. We know Mrs Glenn well. How is she?"

"I'm afraid she died," Joyce said.

"Hence the family search," I added.

"I'm sorry to hear that." She seemed genuinely upset at the news.

"Did she stay here often?" I asked her.

"Well, let me see, I've been working here for five, no nearly six years, and she probably came at least once a year during that time. In fact she has been more frequently recently."

"As often as that?" Joyce's voice reflected her surprise.

"Would you like me to check the registers?"

"No, thanks. It was just the name of the hotel we wanted. We'll take a few photos outside as a record, then see what else we can discover about her."

Then an idea struck.

"You wouldn't happen to know who Mrs Glenn visited when she stayed here. As she came so often, you would think if she had a friend in the town she would stay with them, yet she stayed here."

"I'm afraid I have no idea."

"If she wanted to call a taxi from here, would she use the same number each time?"

"If she asked at the desk, they would probably call Staffcabs for her. We have an arrangement with them."

"Could you give me their number?"

"You can take one of their cards."

"Thank you. You've been very helpful."

"You're welcome, sir, and madam" she added.

We turned and headed back out into the street and I could not hide my elation.

"Yes!" I exclaimed and hugged Joyce.

"This calls for a celebration. The tea's on me."

We walked off, arms around each other, looking for a teashop.

"So your grandmother did have a friend here. Perhaps it's a daughter, or niece, or someone related to a distant part of the family your mother didn't know about."

"Seems like it," Joyce said.

Rejecting Starbucks and similar establishments, we eventually found an elderly shop front, outside of which a blackboard enticed potential customers with words like scone, cream and jam.

We were served at our table, and soon sat surveying a pile of scones, a large bowl of double cream and two pottery containers of different jams. The tea proved to be strong and good.

"They look after you in Staffordshire, it seems."

"I found all the people I came across in this area very friendly."

"Oh, I forgot. You used to teach up here."

"Not here exactly, but not far away, in Derbyshire."

We ate and drank until I felt stuffed.

"When I first mentioned a date, I never thought it would be a teashop in Stafford."

"That's like the questions TV interviewers ask," Joyce said. "When you were a child, did you ever think that one day you would grow up to be a private detective?'"

She held her teaspoon across to me like a microphone.

"There are still times," I said, "when I'm not sure if I'm justified in calling myself a private detective."

"You've done very well today. Don't demean yourself. You might prove to be the best in the business."

I laughed.

"As long as I can solve the mysteries bothering your family, I shall be content. I shall take the rest as it comes. But you've reminded me. There's something else I need to do while we're here."

I took out my mobile and dialled the number of the taxi company.

"Staffcabs."

"Hello. I wonder if you could help me. We're making enquiries about our late grandmother."

"Oh yes?"

I realised it must have sounded strange.

"We know she used to come to Stafford a lot, and stay at the Stafford Knot. What we don't know is where she used to go when she was here."

"Don't ask me for private information about clients, because I can't give it to you, even if you say she is your grandmother."

"Was."

"All right, was."

"What harm can there be in telling me where someone, now deceased, used to visit?"

"It may be that the person she visited doesn't want people to know about it."

"What if it was not a person, but a place?"

"Ah, well, I suppose that might be different."

"Listen. Her name was Mrs Glenn. Could you ask your drivers if they remember taking a Mrs Glenn anywhere? I'm in the teashop opposite Boots in the High Street. If anyone comes up with useful information, I shall make it worth their while. My name's Greg."

"I'll see what I can do."

"Thanks."

I ordered more tea.

"What will you do next?" Joyce asked me.

"Take you back home and spend a lot of time remembering how much I enjoyed being with you."

"Me too," she said.

We continued to sit in companionable silence while we sipped our tea.

After a while the teashop door opened and a woman came in and looked round. There were few customers for her to see and her eyes rested on us. A waitress came down to greet her and I heard the woman mention my name.

"I'm Greg," I said, and stood up.

The woman came towards me and I asked if she would like a cup of tea.

"Oh, yes. Thanks."

I looked at the waitress who had clearly heard the exchange, then I held out a chair so the woman could join us at the table.

"I'm told you've been enquiring about Mrs Glenn."

"Yes. Thanks for coming. Did she ever use your cab?"

"Several times. Not exactly as a regular, you understand. But we're a small firm, and it was often me who picked her up."

"Did you always take her to the same place?"

"Yes. The German cemetery."

"The German cemetery?" Joyce and I said together.

"You sound surprised."

"Just a bit. Did she tell you why she visited there?"

"I remember her saying she was visiting a friend. Someone very special to her."

"You've no idea who or why?"

"No. None at all."

We didn't say much else. She drank her tea and I gave her a generous tip for coming. Then we set off back to the station.

On the train we considered what we had to go on now.

"So we know Granny knew someone German who died. How would she know a German?"

"I have no idea," I said. "But it must have been a member of the German military, if he was buried at Brocton. You remember what the guy told us. All Germans who died on British soil during both World Wars were taken there for burial."

"That doesn't make any sense."

"Neither does leaving her inheritance to Ilse Chambers. Wait a minute." A penny had just dropped. "Ilse is a German name."

"So she could be related to this friend."

"That certainly seems likely. Perhaps Annie was her godmother."

"That might give her a reason to leave her something, but not everything, surely."

"There has to be a very close connection," I said.

"Well I can't think what it might be. She was married to Alan, that doesn't sound very German, and she had two sons with Scottish names. There was nobody else."

The journey continued and we both fell silent, eventually collapsing against each other in a rather undignified, exhausted heap.

When the train arrived at Euston I had that tell tale horrible taste in my mouth that happens after a daytime sleep.

As we set off for the tube together I couldn't stop thinking of the German link. What could it be?

"Penny for them," Joyce said from opposite me in the tube train.

"Oh I can't get this German thing out of my mind. Perhaps there is something obvious we're missing."

"Let's not think about it any more. Let's think about other things."

She smiled that smile.

"And don't get me excited. It's too distracting."

But the smile didn't go away.

Chapter 12

I persuaded Joyce that we should go our separate ways from the station, and later I flopped down on my sofa and considered the need for another visit to Ilse. If I could make it the last visit, so much the better, as every one got harder, in particular the thinking of excuses for going.

Perhaps I should phone ahead and warn her of my visit? But I realised that would give her the chance to plan what to say, and hide anything that might need hiding. Far better to stick to the surprise principle and hope.

But during the evening I discovered something which made a visit even more necessary.

I'd called the office to check my answerphone messages. I had no idea how the system worked, but it was very useful and I'd come to depend on it.

Jocelyn Swindle's PA had called to tell me that Annie's maiden name was Lamont. So that explained Ilse's name, and confirmed what I felt I was beginning to realise anyway.

The next morning I drove out there, armed with the photos Helen had with her and what I now knew. It was time for a bit of bluffing. Somehow I had to flush out the missing facts, preferably by getting her to tell me things, rather than just by asking questions.

"I'm sorry. It's me again," I said when the door opened. "Could you spare me another few minutes of your time?"

There was a resigned look on her face, an appearance of extreme world-weariness. It occurred to me that I may not need to push very hard to find what I needed.

She showed me into the living room, which was as cold as before.

"You'd better sit down," she said.

"Thank you."

She was watching me very cautiously.

"I went to Stafford yesterday."

Her eyebrows creased, just a little.

"There is a war cemetery near there."

"Why are you telling me this?"

"Because I suspect it's all part of the story you haven't told me."

"I haven't done anything."

"No, I don't think you have, intentionally."

I was watching her very carefully.

"There are two cemeteries there," I continued, "one for the British and their allies and one for the Germans."

No real response, except that her eyes never left mine and I sensed a slight look of concern.

"I thought it was unusual," I added incidentally, "that there should be a cemetery for Germans in this country. There can't have been many Germans killed in Britain during the two world wars."

She began to wring her hands in a very distressed way.

"What's the matter?"

"Nothing."

"Ilse," I said, trying to inject some extra patience into my voice. "your reaction to my mentioning the German cemetery was clear. What does it mean?"

"I can't tell you. My brother." Her voice tailed off.

"Your brother what?"

"How much do you know?"

"Not very much. I know your name. I know you inherited a fortune. But I have no idea why. And I don't know why Helen Hetherington died so close to your house."

She was now wringing her hands so hard I thought she might wear off the skin.

"I don't know what to do," she said and turned and walked away from me across the room.

"Look," I said to her back, "if you're finding this as difficult as that, why don't we go and make some tea, while you think about things."

What I didn't add was that we could then sit in the kitchen where the temperature had previously been considerably higher.

"All right."

She moved to the door and I followed her along the hall to the kitchen. I was right. It was warmer.

What would the British do without tea, I thought? The panacea for all problems and sources of distress.

I sat back in the same chair I'd used before, while Ilse began the ritual of kettle and pot.

When she was seated across the table from me, I knew I had to get the next bit right.

"Ilse. I've told you what I know, and that is all I know. Can you fill in any gaps for me? I think it might take a weight off your mind. And it will also make Helen's parents feel a lot better. I can then go away and leave you alone."

I paused.

"No one should lose a daughter," she said. "But sometimes it can't be helped."

"Are you saying that what happened to Helen couldn't be helped?"

"No." She came back so suddenly and loudly it made me jump. "I didn't mean her. What happened to her was terrible. I was thinking of somebody else."

"What do you mean? Who?"

She visibly collected herself, drawing her knees together and clasping her hands tightly, as one waiting for a dentist's needle to enter the gum.

"Ask me what you want to know."

"Good. Thank you."

So, one thing at a time, I thought, and chose my next words with great care. I didn't want to lose her co-operation now.

"I know you are the person who inherited the fortune Mrs Glenn left when she died."

"Did that solicitor tell you? He said he wouldn't."

"No. I worked that out for myself. But it is you, isn't it?"

"Yes. But I never wanted her money."

She said that very quickly, but with a sense of conviction. Could it be true?

I placed the three pictures of her on a low table.

"This is you, isn't it?"

She picked up the picture of herself as a child, and looked at it as if looking at a stranger.

"Yes. She brought these pictures here."

"Who did?"

"The young lady who died."

"I thought she must have done. How did she find you?"

"I'd been up to London, to the flat to get some things. She recognised me at the station and followed me home."

"What happened?"

"She came to the door and showed me the photos. I asked her to come in."

"What did you tell her?"

"Everything. It wouldn't have been fair not to. She should have had that money, not me. It was all wrong."

"Then?"

"She left. I never saw her again."

"When she left, did you see anyone else about?"

"It was dark by then. I watched her walk down the path, then I closed the door. I didn't do anything."

"No, Ilse. I don't believe you did."

I would leave Helen's death for now, I thought. It might be easier to start with Ilse's link with Annie and leave any blame for the death till later.

"Can you tell me why these photographs were found among Mrs Glenn's belongings?"

"Oh dear. No one was supposed to know."

"Know what?"

"I told that girl. I suppose I might as well tell you. She was my mother."

"What?" I couldn't help myself.

So that was it. She looked straight at me as she said it. I had no doubt she was telling me the truth.

"Yet, no one else in the family had heard of you."

"No. They wouldn't have."

"Why? What happened?"

"I was adopted. My mother told me I was born in Aberdeen, in a special place where she was able to have me in secret. Then she let me go to a couple who wanted a daughter. That's why I went to school in Aberdeen."

"But why should your mother want to have you in secret?"

"Because of who my father was."

I waited. Her expression had changed and I could see she was considering something very difficult for her.

"Obviously, then, your father was not the man Mrs Glenn married."

"No."

I waited some more.

"He was a German."

"A German?"

"Yes."

"That's why you reacted when I mentioned the German cemetery."

"She took me there."

"She took you to Brocton? So your father is buried there?"

"Yes."

I couldn't make this out.

"Excuse my asking, but were you born during the war?"

"Yes." Her head fell forward.

"But that cemetery is for servicemen. Your father must have been a prisoner of war."

"No."

"But how come he's buried there, then? There were no Germans fighting in this country, except the Channel Isles. Ah!"

Another penny dropped.

"Was he a pilot during the Battle of Britain?"

"He was a pilot, but not during the Battle of Britain."

"What happened?"

"She knew him from before the war."

"Knew him?"

"Yes. They had met, quite by chance. Then he came to Scotland on a secret mission. I don't know anything about it, but she said he was very brave."

"What happened to him?"

"He was killed."

"I'm sorry. That must have been devastating for her."

We continued to sip at our mugs of tea. I felt the conversation becoming a little easier and the atmosphere rather less tense.

"So how did you find her? Is that why you came to live out here? To be near her?"

"Yes." Then the flood gates came open, as if it was a relief to share things she had kept trapped inside. It occurred to me that Annie must have felt similarly when they met, as she had never before been able to share anything about her daughter with anyone.

Ilse told me about her adoptive father becoming ill. She went up to Montrose with her brother, and it was during his last few days that Andrew finally told Ilse the story of how she came to be adopted.

Eleanor and Andrew Chambers had lived a difficult life in the George Street area of Aberdeen. Andrew was a fisherman and often away from home, leaving Eleanor to care for their two sons, bearing the ever present threat that her husband might not return from sea.

She longed for a daughter, but the doctor had told her, after the birth of her second son, that no more children would be possible. Whenever she saw little girls playing in the street, or walking with their mothers, the yearning returned, and try as she might she could not let the longing go.

One day, when her husband was at home for a couple of days, she broached the subject of adoption. He listened as patiently as he could, but didn't share her wish for a third child.

"Anyway," he told her, "no one would consider us for adoption, with me being away at sea. They look for settled families, with mother and father there most of the time."

158

"But you could get another job."

"Another job? Are you mad? If I wasna in a reserved occupation I'd be conscripted straight into the army."

"But you could work in the docks. That's still a reserved job. Then you could be at home every night and we would be like other families."

These discussions went on day after day, whenever Andrew was at home, and gradually Eleanor wore down her husband's defences until he agreed to look into the possibility of work in Aberdeen docks.

The move was not easy to arrange, but it was possible, and eventually Eleanor began to get used to having her husband at home every night. It changed her life.

The agreement with Andrew had been that he would change his job, and she would look into the possibility of adopting a little girl. This she did with great enthusiasm, and when she discovered an institution in the city which was always on the lookout for good families, she immediately began to make enquiries and, eventually, applied.

There followed several visits to assess the suitability of the Chambers family. Eleanor worked hard to ensure that the house was always tidy and clean when they came and, although very nervous, she tried her best to give a good impression.

Andrew had agreed to adoption rather grudgingly. He felt that war time was no time to be adding to their burden. What with rationing and the increasingly difficult food shortages, things were hard enough for them anyway, without adding to it.

He blamed the Germans for all the privations of war, and there were days when he felt like joining up, simply to get his own back at the people who were causing so much hardship. But he stuck to his bargain, tried his best to adjust to a life on shore and bit his tongue when the resentment began to overwhelm him.

Their baby daughter arrived when she was only a few days old. Being convinced of Eleanor's previous experience with her two sons, the institution had no qualms about releasing Ilse to her care at such an early age, and arranging for her formal adoption.

Never having had any inkling of this before, Ilse was understandably shocked and asked Andrew why he had waited till now to tell her.

He told her he was never one for emotions and didn't know how to. He said that if his wife had lived, he was sure she would have done the right thing and told Ilse much sooner. There had been times when he felt he should, but he could never find the words, and then she was grown up and it didn't seem to make any difference. She called him Dad, so what did it matter?

In the end he realised that it did matter, and that it was right to set the record straight, so he gave Ilse her birth certificate.

"I looked at my birth certificate," she said, "but all it showed was my name and the date I was born. So I went to the library and asked some questions. They told me to write to the Registrar General's office, because they would have a copy of the original birth certificate.

"It was all very complicated after that. I thought it would be easy to find my real mother. After all, I'm her daughter, I'm entitled. But they told me I would have to be prepared. I would have to see someone for counselling. It made no sense to me, but I had no choice."

"Did your full birth certificate give you the information you wanted?"

"It told me I was born in Aberdeen and gave my mother's name, Annie Lamont. But it said father unknown. I suppose that makes me a bastard."

"Well, in a manner of speaking, but that sort of thing doesn't matter so much these days."

She looked at me.

"Perhaps."

She didn't sound convinced.

"Did the counselling help?"

"It made me realise that I was running a risk."

"What sort of risk?"

160

"Well, for a start, my mother might not want to see me. I don't know what I would have done if she hadn't. They kept asking if I still wanted to find her. I don't know how many times I told them. In the end they told me that some sort of agency would look for my mother. It took quite a long time."

"That must have been nerve wracking for you."

"In the end, I didn't know what would happen; whether I would find her or not. Then I had a letter from the agency saying they had found my mother and that she was prepared to see me. They gave me her new name, Annie Glenn, and her address. Then it was up to me."

She took a sip of her tea and I just waited. I was getting quite good at that.

Ilse said it was difficult, meeting her mother for the first time, but that Annie was really pleased to see her. She had written and been invited to visit.

"I went out on the train from London to meet her. She was so glad to see me. I couldn't quite believe it.

"She said she thought she'd never see me again. How she could still remember my face when I was born, and how she felt when I was taken away.

"I wanted to ask her why she gave me away in the first place, but it was too soon and she told me all about that later on. We got on really well. I couldn't believe it. She was lovely.

"On my way back home I decided to move nearer to her, so we could meet more often and more easily. We wanted to get to know each other after so long. I thought it was going to be really difficult. But it was easy."

"You must have been so excited," I suggested, rather feebly.

"She took me up to Scotland and showed me where she used to live. It was a farm, not far from Glasgow. She described how my father came down by parachute and landed in her back yard."

"And she had no idea he was coming?"

"No. He was supposed to have flown back to Germany after his mission, but something happened to the plane and he had to jump out."

"So it was pure chance that he happened to land where he did."

"Oh yes. It was like a love story."

Her expression changed.

"My mother said she always had mixed feelings about it all. She felt that if he hadn't landed on her farm, he might still be alive. But she said that once she found me again, she realised that if he hadn't landed there, I would not be here."

She smiled a very embarrassed smile and I realised that compliments like that must have been rare in her life.

"I'm glad you found her and were able to spend some time with her before she died. Unfortunately I never met her, but her daughter-in-law speaks very highly of her. I get the impression she was a very special lady."

She nodded.

"She took me to see my father's grave."

"That explains your reaction when I mentioned it."

She almost smiled at me, but her natural reserve was strong.

"I am so embarrassed about the money," she said.

"It was quite natural for your mother to leave everything to her only living child. You have heard about her sons, I suppose."

"Yes. She told me all that. But it's not as if I'm hard up or anything."

"I am sure the Hetheringtons will understand when I explain the situation. They had no idea your mother had another child."

"I never thought about her leaving me anything. It was never mentioned."

"She clearly changed her will when she got to know you. It's a real compliment to you that she wanted you to have everything."

"I know, but I don't really want it. I don't know what to do with it."

"Well, it's legally yours to do with as you please."

"I shall have to think about that."

"Why don't you ask the solicitor for some advice? He knows all the details of the case. I'm sure he will advise on what is possible."

We finished our second cups of tea and I began to feel a little easing in the atmosphere.

"Were you happy with your adopted family? It's none of my business, I know, but I would like to think they looked after you well."

"My mother died when I was small."

"Oh, that must have been terrible."

"It was. There were three of us. They already had the two boys before they adopted me."

"It must have been hard for your father."

"Yes. He told me what happened. He said the Germans had targeted Aberdeen's shipyard and harbour. Apparently the east coast of Scotland was in easy reach of the Luftwaffe's aircraft from their bases in Norway. He said the beach area was strafed a number of times by machine gun fire. There were anti-aircraft guns on the esplanade and where Dad worked was more like a war zone.

"A lot of families in the city built air raid shelters in their gardens, and there were large concrete public shelters too. They called it the Aberdeen blitz and it was on the night of the heaviest bombing that Mum was killed.

"Dad said he never understood how Mum was the only one killed. His experiences at the docks had made him really angry at the Germans and this gradually increased to hatred. He said he did all he could to insist that his family took all precautions at all times.

"My brother told me that Dad used to say: 'I'll not let the bloody Bosch destroy my family. Make sure, as soon as the siren sounds, you get to that shelter'."

"And we did, although I can't remember anything about it. I was too small. But apparently we all went with neighbours and friends to a nearby school to take shelter.

"Dad said I was crying a lot, and Mum realised I had lost the piece of towel I always had clamped in my mouth. My comforter, I suppose.

"Anyway Mum rushed out to find it. And that's when the bomb fell.

"From then on, Dad's fury at what the Germans had done knew no bounds. He swore vengeance, but knew there was nothing he could do. I suppose that made him frustrated as well as angry. It was now down to him to raise a family of three, and the realisation of how difficult this would be only made his anger even worse."

"Didn't you tell me he was a fisherman?"

"He was, till he went to work in Aberdeen docks so he could be around the family more. Then, in Montrose, he went back to fishing. It was what he preferred."

"Do you know exactly where it was you were born?"

"Only that it was in Aberdeen."

I fumbled in my inside pocket and produced the picture of the stone, city building.

"Is it possible that this is the place?"

"I don't know. When I lived in Aberdeen I didn't know I was adopted. I never went back. There never seemed any reason to. There were so many bad memories there."

That comment gave me pause. What bad memories? The implication was that her childhood had not been happy. But that was not something I needed to explore, so I let that rest.

"I have a difficult question for you now."

I saw her fists clench again as she tensed to hear what I might say.

"The Hetheringtons will ask me if I have found you, or at least found the person who inherited. Can I say I have, without telling them who you are? If I'm able to tell them you are Annie's daughter, they will at least know there was a good reason for what she wrote in her will."

"I told you. I don't want that money."

"But you are entitled to it. She was your birth mother."

"I know, but still. I've got an income. I'm still working for Doug. He's been bringing work out for me to do since I moved."

"Do you still share the same house?"

"No." She smiled. "I couldn't live with him, he's so unpredictable. But he's a good businessman. I live in one of his flats, so that doesn't cost me anything."

"Look. Think about what I asked. Let's meet again soon. Would you like to go somewhere to eat, perhaps? I would like to show my gratitude. You have been very helpful and this has all been very difficult for you."

"I don't know if I should."

"I'll phone you in a couple of days. See how you feel then. OK?" and I moved to get up.

"All right," she said.

"Good."

We walked together down the hall, and this time she didn't close the front door right behind me, but waited a while.

Chapter 13

I came downstairs the following morning to find nothing for breakfast. No eggs, no bacon, no cereals, no milk. Somehow during the past week I had turned into Old Mother Hubbard. My cupboard was bare except, I was relieved to discover, for coffee. So I made some.

Counting the days since this whole business started and Joyce had been grabbed, I realised I had done no shopping in that time. So today would have to be the day.

It was not something I enjoyed, but it would be a change from twisting my brain around seemingly insuperable problems, trying to estimate someone's honesty from their expression, and trying even harder to elicit information from someone without them realising it.

I sat on the sofa with my coffee in one hand and my notebook in the other.

So, what did I know? Ilse was Annie's daughter. Her father was a German airman, in Britain for some sort of secret mission. He was killed and buried at Brocton. The reason for the inheritance was now clear. All that was left was how Helen died. Did Ilse know anything about that, or not? I thought that was the one thing I still had to discover. I was wrong. Something much more extraordinary was waiting round the corner.

Finishing the coffee, I put the cup down, turned the notebook upside down and began to compile a shopping list, trying to push other things to the back of my mind.

In the car I chose a CD that would take my mind off Helen and Ilse, and Eric Clapton soon began to fill the car with Border Song, track one from the Two Rooms compilation of Elton John songs. The bouncy blues rhythm soon had my left foot tapping as I immersed myself in the music.

By the time I reached the supermarket, all I could think of was my groceries and whether or not I preferred the Phil Collins version of Burn Down the Mission.

Half an hour later, when I realised how full my trolley had become, I decided it was time to join the check out queue. But this was fatal to someone trying not to think. There was nothing else to do while standing and edging forwards gradually towards the cashier.

It occurred to me that I should not leave any loose ends to my investigation. That meant checking up some more on Gemma to see if it was possible she was involved in Helen's death. I thought long and hard about the possibility of being wrong about Stuart, but he had cleared himself in London, as well as helping save my life. Gemma did not fit in with the fact that Helen died near Ilse's cottage, but perhaps there were things still to discover.

But if Ilse was to be believed, and she was not involved in Helen's death, why was her brother going to so much trouble to protect her in his own bizarre way? Perhaps he was more deeply involved himself, and perhaps Ilse suspected this herself. That would explain her unwillingness to talk when I first met her.

I found myself hoping it was an accidental cause of death. That would be easier all round.

The only other loose ends involved Joyce's family, telling them about Ilse and, eventually I hoped, how Helen had died. They would have to wait till I had spent more time with Ilse, and eventually persuaded her to let them into Annie's family secret.

I drove home, unpacked the car and made myself a late breakfast. Then I picked up the phone.

"Ilse? It's Greg."

"Oh hello." Not a great deal of enthusiasm there.

"Would you like to go out for lunch? I know a nice quiet place where we could chat and have a good meal. What do you think?"

"I don't know. I'm old enough to be your mother."

"Oh Ilse, it isn't that kind of taking out. It's a favour for helping me."

"But what will people think?"

"Who cares what people think? Perhaps they'll think you are my aunt and it's your birthday treat. That really doesn't matter."

"I don't know," she said again.

"How often do you go out? It will be a real treat for you. Come on. It's on me."

There was a pause.

"My brother won't like it."

"Does that matter? And anyway how will he know? I certainly won't tell him."

Another pause. I was getting quite used to them.

"Oh, all right then."

"Good. I'll pick you up at twelve thirty, shall I?"

"If you like."

"Excellent. I'll see you then."

I breathed a deep sigh. I'd never really expected her to agree, but I was glad. At least it probably meant she was beginning to trust me.

My car pulled up outside her house at twelve thirty on the dot. When she opened the door I hardly recognised her. She had done something entirely different with her hair, and her clothes didn't look as if they had been found at a jumble sale.

"You look nice."

Again, she almost smiled.

"The neighbours will be watching."

"Good. It will do them good to see you looking so smart and attractive."

"I'm not attractive."

"It's all in the eye of the beholder," I said, for want of any better response. "What's that you're carrying?"

"This is my mother's journal. She gave it to me shortly before she died. Look."

She handed me a hard backed note book. It was nearly an inch thick and so old and frail that the spine had broken and pages were loose.

"Be careful with it," she said.

I smiled.

"You'd better look after it while I drive."

We went to a pub I knew in Suffolk, far enough away from Monks Colne to put her mind at rest about neighbours.

It was clear and fresh and we were both well wrapped up, so it took a few minutes to unravel scarves and hang up coats and hats before we settled at our table.

I could tell this was an unfamiliar experience for her. She looked rather uncomfortable and didn't seem sure what to do. It was also clear that she was hanging on to her mother's journal as if her life depended on it.

"Now," I said as I settled into the deep cushion on my chair, "would you like a drink?"

"Oh. Perhaps I could have some fruit juice?"

"Certainly. What would you prefer, orange, grapefruit, pineapple?"

"Ooh pineapple. That would be lovely."

She sounded like a little girl at her first party. The change in her was so great that I began to feel a little more confident about getting all my remaining questions answered.

I bought our drinks and we spent some time studying the blackboard suspended over the bar. There were so many specials that day, it was hard to choose, but eventually we placed our orders and settled back to wait.

She saw my eyes settle on the journal.

"Would you like to see it?"

"I don't want to pry, but I'm certainly interested."

"It tells how my mother met my father. Look."

She opened the notebook very carefully, found a page near the beginning and passed it for me to read. It was in a very firm, but clear script, with rounded letters which made it easy to read.

"There, look, on the left hand page."

I read:

12 August 1935:

Travelled to Luxembourg with my parents. The channel crossing was rough, but the train was comfortable.

We are staying in a hotel in Echternach. It is by a river and there are wooded hills nearby for walking. They call it the Petit Suisse as it is supposed to be like a miniature Switzerland.

14 August 1935:

Went walking with my parents. Fell over a tree root and twisted my ankle. A young German man came to help, but my father sent him away.

15 August 1935:

Met the young German in the town. His name is Hans Jurgen. He is very kind and would like to meet me again. We must be very careful in case my father finds out.

16 August 1935:

Walked with Hans by the river. He speaks good English. He is fun and I like him.

17 August 1935:

Met Hans secretly again. We walked through the trees and he kissed me. My first real kiss.

19 August 1935:

Took a bus to Luxembourg City and caught the train for Calais. This time the channel was calm. The train to Scotland was slow. It is good to be home but I miss Hans already.

"So Hans was your father."

"Yes," she said and her face lit up. "My mother said he was the love of her life. He was tall and handsome and had dark blue eyes."

"I can tell he made an impression on her," I said as I passed the notebook back.

"The next pages are about her life in Scotland and the man she was going to marry. His name was Alan."

"I'm told they were almost childhood sweethearts."

"Yes, their parents' farms were close together and they had known each other since they were children."

"So how did she meet Hans again? You said he landed in her back yard."

"Yes. One night during the war. Look"

She very carefully turned more pages in the note book and then handed it back to me.

"Look at 10th May."

10 May 1941:

The most wonderful and horrible things have happened. Hans came, but then he was killed. Can't write anymore now. Too upset.

13 May 1941:

I can't believe what happened. I heard a noise and went outside with the shotgun. There was Hans lying on the ground with a twisted ankle and a parachute drifting all over the place.

We just stared at each other. Then he said it was my turn to help his twisted ankle, and I remembered Luxembourg and we laughed.

He told me he was on a secret mission and had only jumped from his plane as it was going to crash. I had heard the crash and everyone was talking about it the next day.

It was incredible because he did not know where he was going to land, and he had no idea that I live here.

I thought again of coincidences and how many there had been in this case. Are things meant to happen, I wondered, or do they just happen by chance? And how often do those chance happenings mean something?

I read on as Ilse watched.

I took him into the house and made some soup. He said he must get back to Germany. He was convinced Germany will win the war and knew that if he was found, and he had disobeyed orders, they might shoot him.

He agreed it would be easiest to get to Northern Ireland, then try to cross to the south. I had just enough petrol to get the car to Kilmarnock and back. From there he could catch a train to Stranraer for the ferry.

On the way we stopped for a rest and fell asleep in a barn. It was wonderful. He was so gentle and kept telling me how much he loved me.

Then I took him into Kilmarnock and dropped him off. As he was crossing a road, he turned to wave and a lorry hit him.

I ran and ran, but they told me he was dead. Someone asked me if I knew him, and I said 'No' and went back to the car and drove home.

I can't believe what has happened. Hans came, but now he is dead.

"That's an awful thing to happen," I said and Ilse just nodded.

"It was so sad."

At that moment the waitress arrived with our food, so I closed the book and put it on the edge of the table.

"This looks good," Ilse said, but I knew her thoughts were really elsewhere.

We ate together in silence for a while.

"Tell me about your childhood," I said eventually. "It sounded hard."

"It was not happy," she said after another pause. "Dad was always angry, and my brothers were always getting into trouble."

"I imagine it was difficult for your dad, having three children and having to work as well."

"It wasn't so bad when my aunt came to stay. She was nice, I remember. Kind, and..." her voice tailed off and a glazed look came into her eyes. "I suppose she was like another mother, when she was there. When she wasn't, there were friends in the area. Some we liked and some we didn't."

"And they helped look after you?"

"We went there in the morning, and I stayed while my brothers went to school. Then, afterwards, we stayed till Dad came home from work. They used to give us supper sometimes. I was very small, of course."

As she described the situation during her childhood, I began to realise what a different world it was then. She spoke in short sentences and I often had to prompt her with questions before she would continue.

I began to see reasons for the harrassed looking person I had seen on my first visit. An unhappy childhood followed by teenage years that were not much better. The move to Montrose when they were older, that allowed her father to go back to fishing. She described her brothers as tearaways, and having met one of them, that sounded about right.

It seemed the only good things that had happened in her life were meeting her real mother and the inheritance, and she said over and over again that she didn't want the inheritance; that she had never wanted it.

The plates were cleared away and we turned our attention to the list of desserts on another blackboard which stood on a low easel to the side of us.

"What would you like?" I asked her. "As far as I'm concerned, on a day like this Sticky Toffee Pudding and Custard sounds ideal."

"It does sound good."

"I'll order two then," and I went to the bar before she could change her mind.

The meal and the glow from the wood fire had brought colour to her cheeks. She was beginning to look almost comfortable, but there was always something there in the background, I thought. A sense of worry about something.

"You said your dad was always angry. I suppose the situation he found himself in, with three small children, would be enough to make any man angry."

"It wasn't that."

"Oh?"

"He never forgave the Germans for killing my mum. He used to swear about them all the time. Blamed them for taking his wife away and for making our lives so hard."

I didn't know what to say.

"My brothers were the same. Even when they were older they would pull a coin along the side of any German car they saw. They said it served them right for buying a car from Mum's murderers."

"And how did you feel about that?"

"I suppose I didn't know any different when I was small. It was the way we were. And as I got older, I suppose the thoughts stuck in the back of my mind. I don't know."

"So when you discovered your father was German...?"

"I didn't want to believe it at first. It was like the worst thing possible. There was no way I could tell my brothers, I thought. I had found my mother, only to find out that my father was a German. How do you think I felt?"

"I'm sure you were shocked."

"But when my mother took me to the cemetery and talked to me about how they were only young men who were buried there – that they were just like the British soldiers in the cemetery down the road – that they were only doing what they were told, and that they had mothers and fathers just like everybody else."

It was the most I had ever heard her say at once. This was something which affected her deeply. I felt even more sorry for her, but wondered if it all meant anything so far as Joyce and her family were concerned.

"So she managed to put your mind at rest, did she?"

"Yes, she did about that, but it was hard. To know I had lost my mum because of my real father's country."

I hadn't thought of it like that, but I could see what she meant.

Our puddings arrived and we didn't say much for a while. Sticky toffee does not make conversation any easier.

"So you told your brothers about your real father eventually?"

"Yes. I wish I hadn't."

"Were they angry."

"My brother in Scotland won't speak to me now. Doug, that's the one in London, was furious. He said it was a disgrace, to discover I was fathered by one of them bastards. I told him it wasn't my fault."

"That's true enough," I said unnecessarily.

"He said he was ashamed. Told me no one must know. I said it made no difference now. The war was a long time ago. I try to tell him what my mother had said, but he won't listen."

"Doug said he feels ashamed, but it's me who's ashamed of him, for feeling like that. How can I be ashamed of my own father? My mother said she loved him very much. Said he was the love of her life."

She had used that phrase before. It obviously meant a lot to her.

"So that was why..." I stopped myself just in time. I was about to mention what happened to Joyce in London, but there was no reason for Ilse to know about that. She already found her brother difficult to deal with. There was no point in causing her extra worry.

"Why your brother was upset at me coming to see you?" I continued.

"Yes. He said no one must know. Told me not to tell anyone. You can't imagine what he gets like when the subject of Germany comes up."

"But your brothers can't have been very old when their mother was killed."

"It wasn't so much that. It was Dad poisoning their minds like he did."

"I'm really sorry you've had such a rough time. I suppose in one sense it could hardly have been worse. For your mother to have you adopted, and then to lose your new mother and have to live in an atmosphere of hatred and bitterness. And how sad for your birth mother, Annie. All that time with her husband, two sons to bring up, all the sadness she had, and at the same time harbouring memories of the man she loved the most. I'm glad you found her. I'm sure you did the right thing in trying to find her. You obviously got on very well. She must have been very glad you managed to discover where she was."

"Yes. She said she was. She said it made everything worthwhile. All that time, not able to say anything about having a daughter and about, well, you know, my father."

Our coffee arrived and we sat silently looking at our cups for a while.

Then I asked her, "What will you do when you go back to London?"

"I don't know."

"Do you have somewhere to live?"

"Yes. I still have my flat."

"You could buy somewhere new now. Live wherever you like."

"I don't know. It doesn't seem right to have all that money."

"Your mother obviously wanted you to have it. She would want it to make you comfortable, I'm sure."

"I've got to think about it."

"When will you leave Monks Colne?"

"Soon, I think. There's no reason to stay now. Just more bad memories. That poor girl."

"But good memories too, surely, of spending time with your mother in the time she had left."

She didn't answer that, and I went up to the bar to pay the bill. When I returned to the table she was still staring at her empty cup.

"Are you OK?"

She looked up and tried to smile.

"Yes."

I knew there was one more question to ask, and I hesitated as I didn't want to hear her refuse.

"Ilse. I need to ask you again if you would mind if I tell the Hetheringtons your relationship with the family. It will set the record straight for them and they will understand why your mother did what she did."

"I suppose it's all right. I told the young lady, after all. There's no reason to keep it secret, is there?"

I assumed the question was rhetorical and didn't comment. It was her decision to make.

There seemed no point in prolonging the conversation and her discomfort.

"Are you ready to go?"

She pushed back her chair and stood straightening her clothes. I went to retrieve our coats and scarves.

When we were sitting in the car again she said, "Thank you for bringing me here. It was a lovely meal."

"You're very welcome."

"Would you like to read more of my mother's journal," Ilse asked.

"Yes I would, if you trust me to look after it. " I smiled across at her. "I suspect Helen's mother might like to see it later on as well."

We drove on in silence through the lanes. I couldn't call it companionable silence, but I felt more comfortable with Ilse than I had before and I was glad to have been able to thank her for her help.

As I pulled up outside Ilse's cottage another car went by, and I glanced at it and did a double take, but the car was gone. Was I seeing things, or was that Gemma at the wheel?

No, it can't be, I told myself. Don't be ridiculous. You're imagining things.

Chapter 14

Back home I went through my notes, crossing out what was no longer applicable to Helen's death.

Stuart was in the clear and so was Ilse. Doug and Gemma were still possibilities, in fact they were the only people I knew of who may have had a motive.

Gemma had been stalking Helen and I had heard of cases where this led to murder. Doug carried with him an abhorrence of anyone discovering his sister had a German father. This may be considered a bizarre motive for murder, but if he had discovered, somehow or other, that Helen had met and talked to Ilse, who knows what a person like that might do. I knew him to be violent, and Ilse had confirmed this.

Annie's journal lay alongside me, and I wondered what information it might contain that could help. But all I could find were personal details of discovering she was pregnant, going to Aberdeen to have her baby and then, later on, her marriage and family life. This would be interesting for Joyce's mother, no doubt, but it couldn't help explain why Helen died.

I'd convinced myself that the inheritance issue would solve all aspects of the case. Perhaps it was such an intriguing and unusual story that it begged to be investigated and drew me in, distracting me from the main mystery related to Helen. This was something else I would have to watch out for if I was to make a successful investigator, distractions, red herrings and anything which took my eye off the ball, so to speak.

But even so, I thought it was most likely that Doug had caused Helen's death. He may not have actually killed her on purpose, but by an exposed railway line in the dark, all sorts of things are possible. She might have tripped during a struggle. He might have threatened her and things got out of hand.

There didn't seem to be any other possibility, other than, but no, I was not going back to accident and suicide again. I didn't really believe it was either of those.

A couple of hours later the phone rang. It was Joyce's mother.

"Greg?"

"Hello. How can I help?"

"Would you like to come over for dinner this evening?"

Ah, I thought. She wants to find out what's going on, probably in more ways than one. Fair enough.

"Thank you. Any excuse not to have to cook."

"Good. Shall we expect you at about seven?"

I wondered if she'd already spoken to Joyce. One way to find out.

Joyce answered after one ring.

"Hi. I've been invited to eat at yours tonight."

"So I've heard."

"What's been said then? Are we expected to make an official announcement about how we feel about each other?"

"Very possibly."

"Ah. Just as long as I know. Are you OK about this? Has your mother been hassling you with questions?"

"No questions, just meaningful looks. She knows me very well."

"I expect she does."

"So what's going on with the investigation?"

"I'm nearly there."

"Really?" Her voice rose, perhaps a mix of surprise and pleasure.

"I shall have some interesting news for you tonight."

"Interesting? Not good?"

"Quite good. But not the best, yet."

"That's something anyway."

"See you tonight then."

There was a slight pause.

"I love you."

"I know, and I can't quite believe it."

Joyce opened the door before the sound of the bell had died away.

"Hi."

"Are you ready for this?" She smiled her welcome.

"Is it going to be like the inquisition?"

"Oh no. Far worse than that."

Oliver came out and greeted me.

"Let me take your coat." He smiled knowingly at me. "Then I can get you a drink.

"Pam's in the kitchen," he said over his shoulder.

I went straight in there and found her working at something on a wooden board.

"In answer to your questions," I said, "the answers are yes, no and yes."

"What?" She spun round. "Do you know something?"

"Yes, about the inheritance. That's the first one. I'll tell you everything when we are all together."

"Are we going to like what you tell us?"

"Only you can decide that, but I hope at least I can put your minds at rest to a certain extent."

"What's the no?"

"There are some things I still don't know, particularly, I'm afraid, about Helen. I've only been able to piece together part of what happened to her."

Oliver came in.

"Drink?"

"Red wine, please," and I moved to follow him into the living room.

"Just a minute," came from the kitchen.

I turned back to my hostess, who was standing with her arms out clumsily, holding her flour-covered hands away from herself.

"And what's the other yes for?"

"Yes, I'm in love with your daughter."

She took a step towards me.

"And don't try anything with that flour on your hands."

She beamed at me.

"I'm delighted. I really am."

Well that was good to hear, I thought. At least that might temper the effect of the other things I have to say.

I found Joyce in the living room, loading a CD. I took her arm, turned her towards me and kissed her.

"Is this something I have to get used to?" Oliver asked. I hadn't realised he was there.

"I'm afraid so," I assured him.

Joyce's mother came into the room, quickly wiping her hands on a towel.

"What?" Oliver asked her.

"Greg has some news."

"I know." He smiled knowingly.

"Not about that. About Helen."

He turned to me.

"Do you know what happened?"

Joyce took a step back and I sensed Oliver looking at me.

"Well, not quite all of it," I said. "but some of it. Shall we all sit down."

I looked from one to the other and decided to plunge straight in.

"Ilse Chambers is Annie's daughter."

"What?" they all said together.

I took them through the whole story, as I understood it. How Annie had met a German airman she referred to as the love of her life.

"Poor Alan," from Joyce's mother.

How Ilse had been born in secret and given away for adoption. How she had been brought up in Aberdeen, but her mother had been killed in an air raid. How her father and brothers hated all Germans for killing her.

I mentioned the move to Montrose, that Ilse and her brother had come to London and how Ilse had finally decided to try to trace her birth mother and found Annie. I told them how Annie had been delighted to find her daughter and had told her the story of how she met her father. She had taken her to Scotland and to see his grave at the German cemetery on Cannock Chase.

"So that was Annie's friend in the Midlands?"

"Exactly."

"But I knew none of this."

"I know. That's why it seemed such a mystery."

"So Annie left everything to her only surviving child," Oliver said. "I suppose we can hardly complain about that."

"Of course we can't," his wife chastised him.

"Look," I said, holding out Annie's journal. "Ilse has let me borrow this. It's Annie's journal. You can read her own account of what happened."

I took the journal across to Joyce's mother. She looked from Joyce to Oliver, then back to the book, and gingerly opened one of the pages.

"You need to be careful," I warned. "It's become rather fragile."

She was reading and turning pages as if it was an important historical document. But then, I suppose, for them it was.

"Listen," she said and read out loud:

'28th June 1964

Archie brought a lovely girl to see us today. Her name is Pamela.'

Joyce's mother smiled.

"That was me."

'She is staying with the Johnstones. Perhaps we will be seeing more of her in the future.'

She turned more pages.

"It's all here. All about Fergus and me, that was Helen's father," she said to me. "How she tried to help me when she could see things were not working out for us.

"Listen."

'4th September 1969

'Pam has gone off to see her parents. I hope the change does her good. She certainly isn't happy, and now she is pregnant she needs a husband who will look after her.'

"It was on that journey to my parents' that I met you," she said to Oliver. "Do you remember?"

"Do I remember?" And then to me, "I got on the train and there was this beautiful woman sitting across from me. She was fast asleep. I couldn't take my eyes off her."

He smiled across at his wife.

"Stop it," she said. "You're embarrassing me."

A few pages further on she stopped, and her expression changed.

"What is it, Mum?"

"I've found the piece about Helen's father being killed, and poor old Archie. Do you know, I think I was more upset about Archie than I was about Fergus. His brother always gave him such a hard time. I thought things had worked out for him when he moved away. But then he came back to visit, and suddenly he was gone, they were both gone."

Tears began to roll down her cheeks.

"Darling."

Oliver moved across to sit next to her and put his arm round her.

"Don't be upset. It was such a long time ago."

"I know. But the memory is still there, and being reminded like that, it brought it all back."

Joyce's mother was still thumbing carefully through the journal.

"Poor old Annie," she said. "Listen to this."

'3rd July 1941

'Visited the doctor today. He told me I am pregnant. Hans' child.

I asked him if he was sure. He said the blood test confirmed it.

What shall I do? I can't tell Alan. Thank goodness my parents are abroad.'

"Then there's this:

'8th July 1941

'Alan knows something's wrong. Every day he asks me how I am.

I tell him I'm just a little tired, but I don't think he believes me.

I told him the doctor said I've been working too hard. That perhaps my commercial course is harder and more demanding than I expected.

He told me I don't have to continue with it if it tires me out.

He is so kind. I can tell he loves me and I feel so ashamed. I don't know what to do.

13th July

I have an idea. If I can make up some secret war work and pretend to be recruited through my college, I could go away somewhere and have the baby in secret. I can't think of anything else. I must work out how I could do this.

16th July

I have heard of a place in Aberdeen where I might be able to go to have my baby. I have telephoned for an appointment and I go in two days.

20th July

It is all arranged. I can go to Aberdeen. It will be funny being there, and it is like a large institution, but if it means I can have my baby safely, it is what I must do. But I shall have to give up the baby for adoption afterwards. At least Alan and my parents won't know.'

"What a terrible thing to have to do," Joyce's mother said. "To have a baby in secret and have to give it away."

"Alan can't have known anything about it," Oliver said. "She must have kept the secret to herself for all those years."

"Yes, all about her German, and the baby. It must have been like having a secret life. I had no idea."

She was still turning pages and reading.

"Oh, listen," she said.

'15th February 1942

I have a daughter and I've called her Ilse. I've had to agree to have 'father unknown' on the Birth Certificate. That's why I decided she should have a German name. She should have something of Hans.'

"That's so sad. She must have been devastated to have to give away her child like that. I can't begin to imagine what that would feel like."

She closed the book and looked up at me, wiping her eyes with the back of her hand.

"I'm sorry Greg. None of this concerns you."

"It's part of your story," I said. "And therefore it's part of Joyce's story. So I'm interested."

Joyce was beaming at me.

"What a lovely man you are. Thank goodness we've found each other at last."

I cleared my throat in a very embarrassed sort of way.

"Enough of this. We have other things to think about."

"Yes," said Joyce's mother, who then blew her nose very loudly, causing us all to laugh.

"The thing is, that Ilse is very embarrassed about the inheritance. She says she never wanted it, and I believe her. I don't think she has any idea what to do with it, and I think it makes her life much more complicated than it was before."

"I know how she could use it."

"Oh, Oliver, stop it. She was her daughter. She's entitled."

"I know."

Oliver shrank back into his chair.

"But what about Helen?" Joyce asked. "Do you know what happened?"

"Not yet. I have a theory, but it's rather an odd one."

"Tell us," Oliver said.

I told them that Ilse lived near where Helen had died, and described how Helen had traced Ilse and how it was possible that Doug had found her there. How he had perhaps followed her along the track and being so determined in his own weird way that no one should know of Ilse's German father, he pushed her in front of the train.

"It all makes sense in a way," I said. "Ilse has described him as impetuous."

Joyce, probably remembering what had happened to her in London, nodded.

"No wonder he wanted to scare you off."

"I thought he was protecting his sister, which is what he told me. But perhaps, all the time, he was trying to protect himself."

"How can anyone bear a grudge for all that time?" Joyce's mother said.

"I suppose, for some people, the thoughts just never go away, and the longer they stay, the more they fester and grow."

"Have you told the police?"

"No. Because it's only a theory, but I think it is likely that Ilse suspects something of the sort. The question is how do we confirm everything?"

"How do we pin it on him?" Oliver added.

"Ilse is desperately embarrassed by the whole situation," I said. "I sense she feels that if she hadn't tried to find her birth mother, Helen would still be alive to receive the inheritance you expected her to get."

"Oh dear."

"Bloody war!" Oliver exclaimed. "Once again, greedy, senseless, warmongering politicians have affected the lives of far more people than the soldiers and civilians killed in battles and air raids."

He had stood up and was facing the window, tension visibly pulsing through his body.

"Because of the war, Annie met this man and had a child. Because of the war her child's adopted mother was killed in a raid. Because of the war a man's hatred for the enemy caused our daughter to die over fifty years later. It's all insane. And so unnecessary."

He threw the remains of his drink into his mouth before turning round again.

"And where does it all leave us? Still broke and without a daughter. Bloody Hitler!"

There was nothing anyone could say to that.

Joyce's mother got up and went to Oliver.

"Oliver, we can get through this. I know what you said is true, but we have to look ahead. We still have Joyce, and now we have Greg as well."

Joyce and I exchanged looks and smiled.

"Hey," she said suddenly. "We're supposed to be celebrating."

"I shall feel more like celebrating when that thug is behind bars," Oliver said.

"Come on, Dad," she cajoled. "Do this for me. Greg will sort it all, won't you, Greg?"

"I hope so," I said. "I certainly hope so.

The meal was excellent and over coffee we listened to Joyce's mother read more extracts from Annie's journal.

"What a sad life she had," Joyce said, her voice beginning to blur after all the wine.

"I know," her mother said. "Found love and lost love, never being able to tell Alan anything, or us for that matter. Sons who never got on. She blamed herself for that, you know. But I think Alan blamed himself as well. That's no basis for a happy marriage.

"Then she lost them both together and then her husband. She must have been delighted when her daughter managed to trace her."

She turned more pages in the journal.

"Listen to this."

'13th February 2003

Ilse came to see me today. I stood on the platform at Ipswich station, staring at the tunnel where her train would eventually appear. It seemed strangely symbolic, as if she was somehow being born again.'

"Isn't that amazing? It must have been so moving."

"Then I had to check myself and my excitement, ready for potential disappointment."

"How strange it must feel," Joyce said, "to meet someone you have not seen since they were born, over fifty years before."

"You know," Joyce's mother said. "I'm beginning to feel as sorry for Ilse as I was for Annie. What an awful life she had, and none of it was her fault. And to have a brother who could do such a thing."

"That is still only a possibility," I reminded her, "although I think it's likely."

"The sooner you prove it, the better," Oliver said.

"Do you remember," I asked Joyce's mother, "telling me that Annie had looked younger during the last year or so of her life? That would be because she'd met Ilse. She had a new interest in her life. She'd found the daughter she thought she'd lost, and she must have felt awful having to give her up for adoption."

The conversation went on, interspersed by extracts from the journal, until we realised we were all falling asleep.

"Look," I said eventually. "There's no way I could drive in this state. Would it be OK to doss down on your sofa for tonight?"

"Of course. It is late, isn't it. It's time we all turned in. It's been a good evening."

I would have drunk to that, but I couldn't possibly drink anymore.

Joyce came across to the sofa to join me, while her parents began to clear up.

"You don't have to sleep down here, you know."

"I might as well. You wouldn't want our first night together to be in a drunken stupor."

"Well, if you put it that way."

She smiled and I pulled her towards me into a kiss.

"I probably don't even taste very good. I certainly don't to me."

Joyce got up and began untying my shoe laces. Then she lifted my legs onto the sofa.

"I'll get you a blanket," she said.

"Don't look after me too well. I might start to get used to it."

And that's all I can remember of the evening. I certainly don't recall the blanket arriving.

There are some nights when I don't dream at all, and others when I find myself involved in the most complex of situations. No doubt some therapists would put this down to my state of mind at the time, or a deep subconscious condition of some sort. It seems to me that alcohol can also play a not unimportant part in the process.

I was alone in a country lane and vehicles kept whizzing past. All I could see of their occupants was a passing glance each time. Doug in his truck, then someone on a motorbike, then Gemma in a car, then Stuart on a tube train, then someone in a taxi, perhaps it was Annie, then two more guys on a motorbike, and then I was left wondering where they'd all gone.

In the dream Joyce came up and took my hand.

"I can't find it," I said to her.

"You will," she said, "Just keep looking."

"But where?"

I was turning my head from side to side, but I couldn't see anywhere to look.

"Bloody Germans!" Oliver shouted suddenly.

"Yeah! Too right!" Doug joined in. "Look what they did."

"But I couldn't help it," Ilse whined in the voice of a pathetic little child."

"You should have been more careful," said a voice. Whose voice, I couldn't tell, but it sounded familiar.

"It was her fault." Another voice. I looked around, but couldn't see anyone.

"It wasn't my fault. All I wanted was to love her."

I sat up, suddenly wide awake. I knew whose voice it was.

The room was pitch black, but when I looked at my watch I discovered it was seven thirty. More sleep than I had expected. I had to move and go somewhere. I knew now how Helen had died.

I went up to the bathroom, splashed some cold water over my face and used some of the mouthwash behind the wash basin.

The flushing of the loo must have woken Joyce, because when I left the bathroom she was standing on the landing waiting for me.

"Are you all right?"

"Yes. And I think I know what happened. I have to go. Things to do."

I kissed her and made my way down the stairs with her following right behind me.

"Tell me," she said by the front door.

"I can't, till I am sure. I'll call you."

The crunching pebbles in front of the house sounded like gunfire as I made my way to the car. I didn't care who I woke now. I knew what to do and drove home.

Thank goodness I'd done some shopping. I came down from the shower dripping wet and poured a glass of orange juice while I waited for the kettle to boil.

I put the television on to pass the time till nine o'clock, but the programme was so boring, I soon turned it off again.

It was important to get this morning right, or I might lose any chance of proving what happened to Helen.

Chapter 15

When I arrived at Colbox it was barely light. Another of those days when the sun had apparently given up the struggle without really trying.

There were few cars in the parking area and I pulled in, as I often did, with a vacant space on either side of me. This was a habit begun on a very windy day when I opened my car door to have it snatched from my hand and into the wing mirror of the car alongside. Needless to say the other car was bigger than mine and remained unmarked, while mine still carried the scar of impact.

Today however it was calm, but still cold. I fumbled for my gloves and got out of the car, wrapping my scarf tightly round my neck.

Sarah greeted me with the same smile.

"I wonder if Mr J. is free," I said, unwrapping my scarf and opening my coat. "I came early in the hope that he would not be busy."

"He's not here yet," she told me. "Is it about," she paused, "you know who?" and she looked cautiously over her shoulder.

"Yes, and I am not going to see 'you know who' again without Mr J. being here to say he doesn't mind."

"Well you won't have to wait long. He's coming in now."

I turned and saw someone not in shirtsleeves this time, but encased in a long, woollen overcoat with an Astrakhan hat on his head.

"Mr Jordan."

"Hello. Greg, isn't it? You're bright and early."

"Yes. I should have made an appointment, but something occurred to me, and I was hoping you might be free for a few minutes."

"Certainly. Sarah, two coffees, please."

I followed him to his office and waited while he removed his winter cocoon. I left mine on. It took me a long time to get warm.

Sarah brought in the drinks, put them on the desk and left again. Frank went to take his usual chair.

"Now," he said.

"This is a little difficult, and I need to say at the outset that I'm only working on a theory."

"All right," he said cautiously.

"I understand that Helen was not as unknown to Gemma as Gemma would like us to think."

He shuffled in his chair.

"How do you mean?"

"Not to put too fine a point on it, I am told that Gemma had her eye on Helen, but Helen wasn't interested."

"You mean she's.?" He stopped.

"Yes. Apparently she colours outside the lines."

"What?"

"Oh, sorry. It's an expression I heard. She prefers other girls."

"Are you sure?"

"I'm going on what I've been told. Is this a problem for you, discovering that one of your employees is gay?"

"I hadn't ever thought about it. I suppose it can't be a problem, can it? We're an equal opportunity employer. Any race, any colour, any religion, any preference."

"Right."

Frank appeared to be having difficulty taking in the implications of what I had said, so I waited a minute.

"Would you mind if I talk to Gemma again?" I said. "And could I have someone else in the room with us, to be on the safe side?"

"Someone like?"

"Well, you, if you like, but perhaps Sarah as well, so both sexes are on an equal footing, so to speak. And would it be possible before we speak to Gemma to pull her file and look up her address. Then perhaps check if she was at work on the afternoon in question. She didn't seem sure before."

He continued to look at me while he depressed his intercom.

"Sarah. Could you come in please? And could you bring Gemma's file with you?"

"Are you sure of all this?" Frank asked me. "If you start making allegations which are unfounded, Gemma could cause a problem for you."

"I know. I'll be careful."

"And if you think Gemma is involved in Helen's death, shouldn't the police be involved?"

"I shall tell the police what I know when I'm certain about it. As far as I know they still think it was either an accident or suicide."

There was a knock at the door and Sarah came in with a file in her hand.

"Is the coffee all right?"

That's when we both realised we hadn't touched our cups yet, and I jumped from my chair to retrieve mine, swallowing a large mouthful rather too quickly.

"Yes, it's good, thanks." I said.

Sarah placed the file in front of Frank and then went to stand in the middle of the office, looking backwards and forwards between Frank and me.

"Do you want to ask her, or should I?" Frank said.

"You are the one with authority here. Perhaps it better be you."

"OK. Sarah, Greg here has the idea that our Gemma is a lesbian and had her eye on Helen."

Sarah spun round to stare at me.

"Who told you that?"

"Who told me doesn't matter."

Sarah's expression softened when I said that.

"But it does open a possibility," I went on, "and the more I think of the possibility the more likely it feels."

"Oh," she said.

"I need to speak to Gemma again, and it would be helpful if you could be here when I do. I don't want to be accused of something I have not done or said."

"I shall stay too," Frank said. "I have a vested interest in knowing if one of my employees has done something stupid."

Sarah looked back at me and then at Frank.

"All right," she said.

"Good," said Frank. "Pull another chair over and I'll send for Gemma after I've looked in this file. What was it you wanted to know, Greg?"

"Her address for a start," I said.

He looked at the paper in front of him.

"Barn Lane, Monks Colne."

So it could have been her in the car I saw. She couldn't live far from where Helen died. My thoughts began to race, and I tried hard to keep my expression unchanged as I felt a surge of excitement at hearing this unexpected news.

"Is there anything more you want before I send for Gemma?"

"No thanks. Let's see what she has to say for herself."

Frank sent for Gemma and there was soon another tap on the door.

"Come," Frank called.

The door opened and Gemma began to come in, then stopped.

"What's going on?" she said, looking at me.

"I don't know," Frank replied. "Come in and tell us."

She was clearly not sure what to do and I could see her thinking. This, in itself, made me suspicious of what was going through her mind, about what she had done and what we might already know.

"Come in and sit down, Gemma," Frank repeated. "Greg here has some more questions for you."

"Do I have to answer them in front of you and Sarah?"

"Yes, if you would," he said. "If you have nothing to hide, that should not present a problem for you."

Gemma was clearly undecided what to do, but in the end she closed the door and came and sat between Sarah and I.

Never had I been more aware of the need to get the next few minutes right. To ask the right questions in the right order and not cause Gemma to panic.

"Gemma. You told me when we last spoke, that you didn't know Helen Hetherington very well."

"I didn't."

"How many were working in your department when Helen was there with you?"

"Three, I suppose."

"You suppose. Three is not very many. Did the three of you always work separately?"

"Not always."

"Were there times when you and Helen were working on the same thing at the same time?"

"I suppose."

"And when you were working with her, you never chatted with her, or got to know her at all?"

"No. She wasn't interested in chatting. She just wanted to get on with her work."

"Yes you told me before, she was rather quiet, and you were more, what was it you said? Chatty?"

"Yes."

"What was she like?"

"How do you mean?"

"How do you think she looked? Was she attractive? Did she dress well? What did you think of her?"

Gemma turned to Frank.

"What is this?"

"Would you mind answering Greg's questions, Gemma? They seem quite straight forward to me."

She turned back to me, rather at a loss for words.

"I suppose she was all right."

"She was all right?"

"Yes."

"Was she the sort of girl you felt you wanted to get to know better?"

"I told you. She wasn't interested."

"Wasn't interested in what?"

"In me."

"And did that make you disappointed?"

"How do you mean?"

"Did you feel let down, or upset, or did it not bother you at all?"

Her face began to colour and I noticed that she didn't answer immediately. That must mean something, I thought.

"OK. Let's move on," I said. "You told me before that you couldn't remember the exact day Helen died, and that you couldn't therefore tell me whether or not you were at work that day."

"That's right."

"And you still can't recall the exact day Helen died?"

"No."

"Gemma, where do you live?"

"What has that got to do with anything?"

"What's your address?"

"I live in Monks Colne."

"Where in Monks Colne?"

"Barn Lane."

"Interesting. The place where Helen died was very near Barn Lane. The police would have made enquiries at all the houses in the area. Yet you don't know when it happened. You must have been out."

"I don't remember."

"Do you live alone?"

"No, with my parents."

"Didn't they mention that the police had been?"

"Not that I remember."

"And I came along your road a week or two ago. Perhaps I spoke to someone where you live. Your parents perhaps. But they didn't mention anything to you?"

"No. I don't actually live with them. I have a flat over the garage."

"So no one came to your flat, and you don't recall any mention of people coming to the house asking for information about Helen's death."

Silence.

"So when did you learn what had happened to Helen?"

"The following day, at work. Everyone was talking about it."

Gemma looked across at Frank, then back at me.

"Why are you asking these questions?"

"Because no one knows what happened to Helen, or why. And no one seems prepared to say anything."

"But why are you asking me?"

"Because you worked closely with Helen for a time. And now we also know that you live not far from where she died."

She looked away from me, but clearly didn't know where else to look, and her eyes slowly returned to mine.

"You say you worked with Helen for several months, yet you didn't get to know her. You live near to where she died, yet you claim to be unaware of the considerable number of enquiries made in the area. What are you not telling us?"

"I can't tell you what I don't know."

"But what is it you do know, but are not prepared to tell us?"

More silence.

"Gemma?" Frank joined in.

"I don't know anything."

Frank looked across at me and I shrugged my shoulders.

"All right, Gemma," he said. "You can go."

Sarah looked embarrassed. I was staring at my notebook. Out of the corner of my eye I saw Frank look at his watch.

"Do you think that achieved anything?" he said with an edge to his voice.

"I think she knows something, but isn't prepared to tell us what it is. The fact that she was so evasive is suspicious in itself as far as I'm concerned."

"Well," he said. "I have business to attend to. Sarah you had better get back to work. Greg, is there anything else you want?"

"I don't think so. I'm grateful for your help."

"In that case, if you'll excuse us all."

His attitude had changed distinctly and I wasn't prepared to push and risk causing annoyance.

"Of course," I said.

I collected my things together and left.

On my way across the entrance lobby I exchanged glances with Sarah, but she turned away quickly. It appeared I'd lost what support I needed there.

Damn, I thought. What a waste of time. And I'd been so sure. Perhaps the dream meant nothing.

I retraced my steps to the car, started the engine and turned on the fan to generate some heat. Then I phoned Joyce.

"Hi. Where are you?...Can I come round? I need to bounce some ideas off you...Thanks...Ten minutes."

She answered the door when I arrived and greeted me with a kiss. Even that didn't make me feel any better.

"Let's go up to my room," she offered.

"OK," and I followed her up the stairs and into the room immediately behind Helen's.

She closed the door behind me and pulled me into a passionate embrace. I succumbed, but only so far, and when I was once again able to take breath, I attempted to clarify the real reason for my visit.

"Just a minute."

"What?"

"I need to share some thoughts with you before I forget all the salient points."

She gave me a look.

"Oh, all right," she said and steered me across to sit next to her on the bed. "But don't expect always to get away as easily as that."

"Put that smile away and let me concentrate."

She did so, to a certain extent.

"This is all between you and me. Right?"

"Right. If you say so."

She looked at me as I tried to work out where to start and what I dared say.

"I'm stuck," I told her. "There are two possibilities and I can't work out how to proceed with either of them.

"When I left here this morning I thought I knew what had happened, but now I'm not so sure again and I'm back where I started."

"OK."

"One. Ilse's brother may have caused Helen's death somehow. As I said last night I suspect Ilse might think that is a possibility. He has this bizarre motive to do with not wanting anyone to discover that Ilse's father was German. He certainly has a temper and we both know he is capable of doing really stupid things. It would explain why he was so keen to put me off with all those notes. But I have no actual evidence at all. So how do I prove it?"

Joyce put her head down in thought.

"So, what's number two?"

"Two. Gemma caused Helen's death, somehow or other. It seems she had become infatuated with Helen, but Helen wasn't interested.

"I've just been up to Colbox to ask her some more questions, and I did it in front of her boss and the girl from reception. But she said nothing. And now I fear I may have lost the level of co-operation I thought I had up there."

There were so many thoughts rushing through my mind. Should I tell Joyce how close to the death scene Gemma lives? Was I sure it was Gemma? It could still be Doug. Is there still an outside chance it could be Ilse herself. But surely not. If I was that bad a judge of character I might as well go back to work at the bank.

I had hoped to introduce Ilse to the Hetheringtons, perhaps idealistically thinking she and Joyce's mother might become friends, making up for losing Annie somehow. But I'd have to be absolutely sure of Ilse's innocence before introducing her to them. I realised that meant there were still three possibilities, but deep down I still wanted to give Ilse the benefit of the doubt.

I might like to think the case whittled down to Gemma or Doug, but there was still the possibility that Ilse knew more than she was saying. That would account for her reticence when she first met me.

Joyce tucked her arm into mine and gave it a little squeeze.

"Do you think we should go to the police?"

"I don't see what they can do. We're no nearer to solving the mystery than when we started, except that we've whittled it down to fewer possibilities. I can't give them any proof of anything. There's no hard evidence. It could still be an accident or suicide as far as they are concerned.

"There is still the outside chance that it was an accident, although I don't think it was. And neither of us thinks it was suicide. But in order to persuade the police it was murder, or at least that someone caused her death in one way or another, they would expect some evidence on which to proceed. I can't give them any."

"Perhaps there is something we are missing."

"I keep thinking that, but I don't know what it could be."

"Is there anything you haven't told me that might give me the germ of an idea?"

I looked at her.

"What?"

"Apparently Gemma lives down Barn Lane in Monks Colne."

"So she lives as close as Ilse to where it happened?"

"Yes. I must have gone to her house asking questions, but Gemma says she can't remember anyone coming at all."

"It sounds as if she was hiding something from you this morning."

"Oh, I'm sure she knows more than she's saying. But how to get to that knowledge, that's the problem."

"Do you trust that Ilse is telling you the truth?"

"I believe all she has told me about her background, and the fact she gave me the journal to show your mother means that she trusts me. In terms of the inheritance, I think she has been honest and straight with me. She has admitted that Helen did come to see her on the evening she died, but claims that the last she saw of her was from her front door as she left."

"So it sounds as if you don't think she had anything to do with it."

"No, I don't. The trouble is, if she's lying, after your parents have come to feel a little sympathy for her and her difficult life, the disclosure that she had something to do with Helen's death would be shattering."

"Yes, I see that. But aren't there times when you have to follow your instinct, and your instinct seems to be telling you that Ilse has nothing more to hide."

"It took her a long time and a lot of persuasion to be able to tell me about her life and her connection to Annie. It does seem likely that she is now being open and we can trust her."

"OK. I think that her brother, this stupid Doug character, is a much more likely candidate, and certainly Gemma appears to be hiding something, which is suspicious."

"So we are back with wondering what to do next. How do I find out which one it is, and how do I get the truth out of them?"

"Isn't your best way to Doug through Ilse?"

"Yes, but I don't think she's sure. She suspects he might have done something, but once she closed the door when Helen had left, that was it as far as her knowledge of what happened is concerned. He may have told me he tries to protect her, but I sense Ilse's a little scared of his temper. To ask her to challenge him would not be fair to her, and it may do no good anyway, as she wants to believe he is innocent, so he could tell her anything and she'd believe him."

"That leaves Gemma."

"Yes."

"Does she live on her own?"

"No, with her parents. She said she has a flat over the garage."

"How many houses down Barn Lane have a flat over the garage?"

I looked at her, impressed and feeling stupid that I hadn't thought of that.

"Not many, I'm thinking," she said.

"I sense a search coming on. Get your coat."

We leapt to our feet, the possibility of a lead providing a resurgence of energy.

As we came downstairs, Joyce called to her parents.

"I'm going out with Greg."

We both got into my car, that was a first, and I gunned the engine and crunched across the gravel to the road and away.

I had the sudden feeling that we were homing in on something important and I began to feel like a detective again.

The lanes between Dedham and Monks Colne are not wide and I had to control my urge to drive quickly. As it was I took the bends quite hard, and Joyce made a comment about me wanting to be Nigel Mansell.

We entered the lane from the end nearest to our local railway station, and I became aware that Helen must have driven down this way on that fatal night. I hoped Joyce was not thinking the same thing.

I crawled along. There were high hedges on both sides of the road and some of the houses were well hidden. However, most were old cottages, with no entrance other than a small garden gate like Ilse's, certainly no entrance for a car and therefore no garage.

We considered every house, but there were no possibilities at all until we reached the entrance of the lane to the railway line. There was the house where the dog had leapt at me in the doorway. I stopped the car.

"Look at that. Lots of outbuildings with space for garages and flats all over the place. I came here twice asking questions. Surely this can't be the place."

"I think we should go on. This may not be the only house with a garage."

So I inched the car forward and we continued our slow progress to the other end of the lane.

The only other candidate was a relatively new barn conversion with a garage set back to the right in a landscaped garden. Above the garage there was a high, steeply pitched roof with windows set into it.

"There is enough room for a flat there," Joyce said. "I'll go and ask."

And before I could reply she'd left the car and was pushing open the gate.

At the front door I saw her talking to a middle aged women dressed in jeans and a brightly coloured smock. The woman was shaking her head and soon Joyce returned to the car.

"Gemma doesn't live there," she said.

"What did you say?"

"I asked her if Gemma lived there. Told her I was a friend who was expected, but I had lost the precise directions to the house."

"You could be good at this game."

"So it must be the other place. Do you want to try the same thing there?"

"If you like. But watch out for the dog if you go to the door."

She smiled.

"I will."

We drove back and I parked in the entrance to the lane, much where Helen must have parked, I thought.

Joyce went to the door again, and I waited in the car.

"Any trouble with the dog?" I asked when she returned.

"No. I didn't see a dog. Gemma's at work."

"So she does live here. Right at the entrance to the lane and right across the road from Ilse. How extraordinary."

"What do you want to do now?"

"Could you bear it if we walked down to the railway line?"

She looked away and through the windscreen.

"I think I'd rather stay here, if you don't mind."

"I don't mind at all. I shall only be a few minutes."

The lane was poorly surfaced, but dry. I pulled my scarf more tightly round my neck and set off for the accident site, if that is what it was.

Along and to my right ran the boundary of Gemma's parents' garden. I kept my eye on it, and as I rounded the bend which brought the railway into view, I noticed a small garden gate, overgrown with brambles and looking as if it was rarely used.

My thoughts went back to reading The Secret Garden. I'd always had a fascination for garden gates set in brick walls. This one was set in a thick whitethorn hedge, but it still looked intriguing.

I looked from the railway to the gate, and walked on to the crossing. An idea began to form in my mind, but once again I came up against the need for proof and I had no idea how to find any.

Chapter 16

I am a firm believer in not spending time trying to think of something just beyond my reach. It never works and just generates frustration.

If I can't think of a name, or which movie someone was in, I consciously try to think of something else. The more we push our conscious minds to retrieve something, the more it won't.

Someone once wrote that the best way to think of something is to stop thinking about it, to say three nursery rhymes one after the other, and then see what happens. Remarkably, very often this method works.

Based on this sound principle, having tried and failed with the nursery rhymes while walking back to the car, I took Joyce home and drove into Colchester with my car radio playing loud. I heard it on the Grapevine, Marvin Gaye was singing and I wished I could hear something useful on mine.

The lyrics of songs can be relevant so often to what is going on in life, or is that just my wishful thinking?

In town I parked my car and went to raid the shopping centre for a new shirt, trying hard not to think of the one thing which kept annoying me and demanding my attention.

Then on to the music store to look at CDs. Finally, in desperation, I bought a newspaper, then a take away meal, took them home and settled down to eat and then to read the paper from cover to cover before doing the crossword.

The net result of this was sleep in a very uncomfortable position on the sofa, with an empty wine bottle on the carpet beside me, and the same old furry taste in my mouth.

At that point I gave up, cleared everything away, had a very hot shower and turned on the television. There I stayed till it was time for proper sleep.

The next morning, still determined to distract my brain into action, I took my usual train, my usual tube, and bought my usual coffee on my way to the office. It occurred to me that if I was not careful I would soon fall into the same rut generated by my city work.

During my last visit I'd left correspondence distributed in some sort of order on the desk. The notes from Doug were also still there. I picked them up, read them again and put them in my pocket. If he was the culprit, and the police made an arrest, I would not need to show the notes to anyone else.

There was one new letter to open and I added its contents to the collection in front of me, then perused the cases I had pending.

A teenage boy who had gone missing and was thought to be in London; an elderly woman trying to find her sister; a man suspecting his wife of having an affair. I picked up two messages relating to that one and recalled one of my first cases, which was similar.

Some city high flier claimed his wife was having an affair, and when I looked into it I discovered she was coming up to London to do some temping work each day as her husband never gave her any money for herself.

I read through the cases I had, wondering which to follow up first, trying to keep thoughts of Joyce and Helen out of my head, but failing.

Eventually I opened up my laptop and began work on tracing the missing sister, using all the family search sites I knew. My pad became covered in possibilities as I traced, checked and cross checked and the time passed quite quickly.

At just after midday I closed up my computer, locked the office door and made my way down to an Indian restaurant in the street for one of my favourite buffet lunches. Coming out of the doorway I bumped into Ilse.

"Hello," I said with a mixture of confusion and surprise.

It was odd to see her so suddenly, and out of context. She looked smartly turned out and more like the woman I had taken to lunch than the dowdy hermit I had first encountered.

"What a surprise."

She was clearly embarrassed and rather at a loss.

"I was just coming to see you."

"Oh?"

"Can I talk to you?"

"Would you rather do it upstairs in my office?"

"Yes, please."

"Come on then," and I held my arm out into the open doorway and let her climb the stairs ahead of me.

Back in the office I was aware again of how bare it looked as I took her coat and proffered a chair.

"Not very impressive, I'm afraid. I haven't been here long."

I sat facing her and waited for her to speak. She smiled her embarrassment before plunging in.

"I've been to see the solicitor who did my mother's will."

I felt a slight tremor of potential excitement, and immediately squashed it for fear of disappointment.

"I told him I didn't want the inheritance."

She clearly still found it easier speaking one sentence at a time.

"And what did he say?"

"He said the inheritance is mine to do with as I wish."

"Quite right."

"But that he would be prepared to help me if there was anything particular I wanted to do."

"Yes he would, for a considerable cost, no doubt."

Always the cynic, and it was me who had suggested she see him in the first place. Not helpful, Greg, I chided myself.

She looked at me, and frowned as if she hadn't thought of costs.

"Well, if you use his professional services, he will expect you to pay for them. He won't exactly do things as a favour."

"I see."

I tried to ignore my rumbling stomach and thoughts of the buffet curry which awaited me downstairs.

"He told me there are ways of using the money to save on Inheritance Tax and gave me some suggestions. But that's all."

"And?" I let it hang.

"I have decided what I want to do."

She paused again. The words blood and stone came to mind.

"And I would like you to help me."

"I will help in any way I can. Just tell me what I can do. And I will not be charging you for my services."

I don't know why I said that. I suppose I felt sorry for her. There was certainly reason to.

"Thank you. Only I wouldn't know how to go about things."

"I understand."

I gave into my stomach's demands.

"Look, have you had any lunch? Do you like curry? I was just on my way to eat."

"I don't mind curry if it's not too hot. But you mustn't pay for me again."

"OK. Let's go downstairs for lunch and you can pay this time. You can probably afford it," I added with a tentative smile.

"Yes. I suppose I can."

I took her back down to the street, along to my favoured eating place and showed her how the buffet system worked, walking round with her and telling her what was what. We sat opposite each other after a few minutes, and she began to make cautious inroads into the variety on her plate.

She ate without speaking and this only fuelled my curiosity as I was fairly sure what she was going to say.

"Do you like the curry?"

"Yes. I wasn't sure, but yes, I do."

"So what have you decided?" I could wait no longer.

"I want the young lady's family to have it."

"Wow! All of it?"

"Yes. I just don't want it. It wouldn't be fair."

I looked at her over my fork of Lamb Pasanda.

"Do you not think your mother would like you to keep some of the money?"

"I don't know."

"Think about it. I've got to know Helen's family quite well. Although it's true they were confused and, OK, angry when they discovered the inheritance came to you, now they know who you are, that you are Annie's daughter, they are not going to want all the money for themselves."

"This is so difficult."

"I know and I understand."

We ate on for a while and I asked if she would like to return to the buffet.

"Oh, no. I couldn't eat any more."

"Do you mind if I do?"

"No."

Call it lack of self control, call it greed, I don't care. When faced with a buffet - eat as much as you can - lunch, one plateful just doesn't seem to do the offer justice. I could see she was thinking when I returned to the table.

"I should like to meet them," she said suddenly.

I smiled.

"And I am sure they would love to meet you. Would you like me to ask them?"

"If you would."

No time like the present, I thought, as I fished out my mobile phone.

"Joyce, hi, it's me."

"What a lovely surprise. I was just thinking about you."

"Good thoughts, I hope."

"What do you think?"

"Listen. Ilse would like to meet you all."

"Really?"

"She has something to ask, and I gather she would rather do it to your faces."

"Oh. I see. This sounds very mysterious."

"Yes, well, I don't want to say anything. In a way it's not for me to say. I'm just the go-between, as it were."

"When does she want to meet us?"

"I think the sooner the better."

"Can I call you back? Dad's out and I don't know where Mum is. I shall need to ask them both."

"Of course. I'll look forward to your call."

I put the phone away, aware that Ilse was watching me. She looked her question at me.

"They will call back. But I've no doubt they will meet you. They'll be too intrigued not to want to meet Annie's daughter."

We chose our dessert and soon left the restaurant. In the street I wasn't too sure what to do for the best.

"Are you on your way home now?"

"Yes."

"I'll call you there, later on. Will that be all right?"

"Yes. Thank you."

She held out her hand to shake mine, and I took it. It was soft, but a little firmer than I remembered.

"I'm grateful for what you have done."

I could see that saying it had taken some effort.

"This has all been very difficult," I said. "As much for you as for anyone else. I hope something can be sorted out that makes everyone happy."

"Yes," she said, and turned and walked away. I returned to the office, convinced now that Ilse had nothing to do with Helen's death.

My phone rang before I could begin anymore work.

"Hi Greg. Listen, Mum says she would love to meet Annie's daughter. Can you bring her round?"

"When would be a good time?"

"How about this evening? Mum and Dad say they are not doing anything else."

"I'll call Ilse later, when she has had time to get home, and let you know."

We rattled on a bit longer. Personal stuff – you wouldn't be interested.

At half past seven I found myself, once again, at Ilse's door. When she opened it I could see she had dressed exactly as she had for our pub lunch. I remembered complimenting her, and wondered if that was part of the reason.

I didn't have to say anything. She smiled, locked the door and followed me along the pathway.

There were several ways to get from Ilse's cottage to Joyce's. I favoured the rural route and it took us about twenty-five minutes, but very few words were exchanged during the journey.

As I turned into the drive I thought, as I had thought before, that there was little need for a burglar alarm with a gravel approach like theirs.

I walked round the car and opened Ilse's door as if I was her official chauffeur. She looked up at the house, and then at me, and I realised it was far beyond anything she had ever lived in.

"They don't need any money," she said suddenly.

"Things are not quite as they seem," I replied carefully. "Oliver, Helen's father, lost a very good job about a year ago. They've been struggling ever since."

"I see. I didn't know."

We walked up to the door and Joyce got there first. I must have been right about the gravel.

"Hello," I said with a certain amount of restraint. "This is Ilse."

"Ilse. This is Joyce – Helen's sister."

"I'm delighted to meet you," Joyce came forward to greet her, which rather took Ilse by surprise.

"And you," Joyce said, turning to me and kissing me on the cheek.

"Come inside, please."

We stepped into the hall and Joyce's mother came out of the living room to greet us.

"You must be Ilse. I'm so glad to meet you. Oh my, you have your mother's eyes."

Why is it that women can always tell these things, when men never notice? She shook her hand.

Ilse seemed likely to retract into her embarrassed shell.

"Come on in," Joyce's mother went on, "and make yourself at home. Hello, Greg," she added, almost as an afterthought.

Joyce had taken my hand and we were hanging back together. Oliver was standing with his back to the fire. A very masculine pose, I thought.

"Oliver, come and meet Ilse."

He did so with great courtesy.

"I am delighted to meet you," he said.

"Now," said Joyce's mother, in full hostess mode, "shall I make some tea, or shall we get to know each other first?"

"I suspect," I said, "that Ilse would rather say what she's come to say first. Wouldn't you?"

I turned to her and was met with a grateful nod.

"All right then. Let's all sit down."

We did so and it suddenly went quiet. I was getting used to the need to prompt by now.

"Ilse? It's up to you now."

"Oh dear," she began. "This is so difficult."

Everyone had their eyes on her, which can't have made it any easier.

"Can I say first how sorry I am about your daughter. It was a terrible thing to happen."

I saw Joyce's mother's head fall forward a little, but she recovered graciously and quickly.

"Then I want to tell you that I never wanted my mother's inheritance. You might think I got to know her so she would leave me all her money. But I just wanted to find my real mother. I never knew she had money. I never wanted any money, I just wanted to find my mother."

She was looking straight at Joyce's mother, as if it helped her concentrate and maintain her nerve.

"Now, because of me, you've lost your daughter and the inheritance I think you should have had. Well that's not fair and it's not right. It's bad enough losing your daughter. I want you to have the money."

"What, all of it?" This from Oliver.

"Just a minute," Joyce's mother said. "This is incredibly generous, and more than we ever expected, but we can't let you do that."

"But I want to. I think my brother might have something to do with your daughter. The least I can do is make amends."

Everyone looked at me and I nodded.

"He may be your brother in a way," Joyce's mother said, "but he's not your flesh and blood, as I understand it. I suppose we're not really, but I feel as if I was Annie's daughter too. So in a way, we are like sisters, or at least sisters in law."

I could see from her face that Ilse didn't know what to do with this comment.

"Anyway," she resumed, "I would never know what to do with all the money my mother left me."

It went quiet again, and I felt it might be my turn.

"Ilse. Would you agree to sharing the money, rather than giving it all away?"

She looked at me, a lack of certainty in her expression.

"I suppose I could."

"Oliver. Would you be prepared to advise Ilse on her best course of action in relation to Inheritance Tax, trusts or anything else that might be relevant?"

"Of course."

Then I looked at Joyce's mother and played my final card.

"Was Annie's house ever sold?"

"I don't think so."

"So that will form part of the inheritance."

"The solicitor told me there was a house," Ilse added.

"OK. Ilse you have a flat in London, and no immediate family who needs it. Why not rent out your flat or sell it, and move into Annie's house? As I understand, it's in Ipswich, which is a very convenient place to live. You could get to know Joyce's parents a little better. You are virtually in-laws, after all, as she said."

She was still looking at me with that wondering expression of hers.

"If you want to, you could give some of the inheritance money to Oliver to help him set up a new business, and keep the rest for yourself. That way you will have a bigger place to live in, Oliver could advise on how to save your money so you would have plenty to look after the house, have nice holidays, nice clothes and whatever else you want. What do you think?"

Ilse was now looking round at everyone. Oliver was controlling his excitement very well. His wife's face radiated a mixture of love and hope and Joyce was holding my hand so hard her nails were digging in.

"All right. I'll do that."

"Excellent. You can make that tea now," I said to Joyce's mother, "and kill any fatted calf you may come across in the kitchen. We need to celebrate."

It turned into a long evening, and I don't think anyone wanted it to end. Oliver promised to visit Ilse the following day to begin making plans. Pam, as I had been told I should call her, agreed to visit Mr Swindle with Ilse, to talk through what had been decided. Joyce and I receded into the distance onto the sofa, and discussed our own future together.

In the end, everything related to the inheritance sorted itself out. It was such a pity about Helen, but I couldn't help thinking that Ilse and Annie had lost so many people between them, in a way it put the loss of one into perspective.

I took Ilse home and as we approached her house I could see the black truck parked outside. She saw it at the same moment.

"Oh no!"

"What's the matter?"

"It's Doug. He'll cause trouble when he sees you."

"I don't think so," I said, with more confidence than I felt.

Doug got out of his truck and was waiting when we reached Ilse's gate.

"What's he doing here?" he asked his sister.

"He took me out."

"He what?"

"We've been to see friends. Now don't get angry again."

"What friends? What have you told him?"

"Nothing."

"I don't believe you," he shouted and grabbed her by the arm.

"Hey! None of that."

I tried to pull off his arm, but he had a very tight grip and Ilse was trying to push him away.

"And you can mind your own business."

I took out my mobile phone and held it towards him.

"Let her go, or I call the police."

No reaction.

"We had a deal," I added more loudly. "Do you want me to tell them what happened in London?"

"Bloody hell!" he shouted and threw off Ilse's arm as if it was stinging him. "Have you told him anything?"

"I told you," she said pleadingly.

He came up to me and stood very close.

"Stay out of my life. Or you'll get what's coming to you."

"Like Helen?" I said back into his face.

"What do you mean?"

"As if you don't know."

"What is he talking about?" he asked Ilse.

"The girl who died."

"Oh, her."

He took a step back and looked from me to Ilse.

"Doug. What did you do?"

"Nothing!"

"Can we go inside and talk about this before an audience gathers?" I suggested.

Ilse silently led the way, and I ushered Doug ahead of me.

"Let's go in here," Ilse said, leading the way into the living room. It was still persisting with its impersonation of an ice box.

"Sit down, Doug" Ilse said, and it sounded strange to hear her giving him instructions. But he sat as requested, but I stayed on my feet.

"OK," I said, determined to get to the bottom of at least one thing. "Doug. Can you persuade yourself to be honest with us? Ilse is terrified at the thought that you did something really stupid on the night Helen came here. I know about you and stupidity from London. So now is your chance to tell Ilse she needn't worry anymore."

He looked from me to Ilse and then let his head drop.

"I came on my motorbike," he said in a low voice to Ilse. "I was just getting off when I saw this girl come down your garden. I knew she'd been to see you, and I knew why. And I guessed you would have told her about......well, you know."

"My father?"

"Yes. I watched her and she walked down that lane across the road, so I followed her. I didn't do anything."

"You followed her," I said, "but you didn't do anything?"

"Yes."

"So why did you follow her?"

"I suppose I had some idea about shutting her up, or threatening her, but I didn't get the chance."

"What do you mean?"

"She was with somebody else, down by the railway."

"Who?"

"I don't know, do I? It was dark."

"You have no idea at all?"

"No. They were just like shapes. But I could see they were arguing. Then I heard a dog bark, and there was a scream and I heard the train's brakes squealing."

"What did you do?"

"I went back to the bike and rode off. I wasn't going to get involved in anything like that."

"So you abandoned her."

"There wasn't anything I could do."

"Yes there was. You could have helped. At least by doing that we might have discovered by now who the other person was. As it is you ran off. Cowardly. Stupid."

"Don't call me stupid."

"He's right, Doug. You could have helped."

"You can't blame me for what happened to her."

"We can blame you for running off and not finding out what had happened. And for not seeing if there was any way you could help. In a sense you are to blame for all the mystery. For all the pain and agony that Helen's parents and sister have been through, and are still going through, not knowing the truth of what happened."

"It wasn't my fault. You can't blame me."

"I'm not sure Helen's parents would agree with that. And I would guess the police might want to ask some awkward questions."

"Keep the police out of this."

"I'm not sure we can do that. They have this down as an open verdict, meaning no one is sure what happened. You can tell them there was someone else involved, and a dog."

"You have to tell the police," Ilse said quietly. "It's only right."

"But I didn't do anything."

"That's the whole point," I told him. "And there was a lot you could have done."

His head fell forward again.

"All those stupid threats in London. And just because you didn't want Ilse to tell me about her father. I hate to think what you might have done if you had caused Helen's death."

"What are you going to do?"

"Well, it just so happens that I'm almost sure who the other person was. The dog just about clinches it. So I have to work out how to bring that other person to justice, but that will involve telling the police, and you will need to tell them your story. There's no getting out of that."

Silence from Doug, but Ilse was becoming more firm with him now.

"Doug, you have no choice. It's the only way to get this settled."

Doug grunted and I took his grunt for assent, but it made no difference. I would have given his name to the police anyway.

It was Ilse who gave me Doug's details after he had left, still sounding very disgruntled.

"The police will come to talk to you, you know," I told her. "They need to know the details of what led Helen to be in this area in the first place."

"I know."

"Will you be able to manage that?"

"I shall have to."

I figured if I could convince the police about Ilse's brother's story, they might be persuaded to reopen the case. At that moment that seemed far from certain, but I had to tell them what I knew.

When I left Ilse I felt a huge sense of relief. Most of the questions were answered, but I didn't feel it was my doing entirely. In the end everything had come together in a way I could never have expected.

I had hoped that if I could solve a case as complicated as this, it would prove I could make it as a detective. As it was, I felt no more like a detective than I had before Joyce first called me.

Chapter 17

The approach to Colchester Police Station involved a short journey round a one-way system, but this gave me the chance to work out what to say.

"Good afternoon, sir. Can I help you?"

The desk officer looked tired, although he greeted me civilly enough.

"I have some information about the death of Helen Hetherington. Are you familiar with the case? It was October, this year."

"Yes. I remember that. Sad case."

"Yes, it was. Very sad, for all concerned."

He looked at me as if I was one of a series of nutters who came in off the street to confess to crimes they had not committed.

"And who might you be, sir?"

I felt that his politeness had become a little more forced.

"My name is Greg Mason. I'm a friend of the family."

"Which family would that be, sir?"

"The Hetheringtons."

"I see." He still seemed unconvinced that I was worth taking seriously.

"Could I speak to the officer in charge of the investigation?"

"As far as my memory serves," he said, "there is no ongoing investigation."

"But didn't the coroner return an Open Verdict? Doesn't that mean he wasn't sure what happened?"

"I suppose you could interpret it like that."

"How else could you interpret it? If he'd thought it was suicide, he would have said so. Similarly with an accident. Why should the case be closed if it is not clear how Helen died?"

"That's not for me to say."

A brick wall would have been more forthcoming.

"Let me try again. Could I please speak with an officer who was dealing with the case at the time?"

"I shall have to ask my superior."

"Fine. Ask away."

He picked up a phone and pressed a button.

"Guv. There is someone here who claims to have information pertaining to the Hetherington death in October. Can someone speak to him?"

We watched each other as he spoke. He wouldn't have trusted me less if I was a mass murderer revving a chain saw.

"Yes, guv. He says he's a friend of the family."

Long pause while he listened.

"Right, guv."

Do all lower ranks call their superiors 'guv'? It never sounded appropriate to me. I couldn't imagine a corporal in the army calling his sergeant major 'guv' and getting away with it. He put down the phone without taking his eyes off me.

"A sergeant will be coming along to take your statement. You can wait over there."

He pointed to a bank of wooden chairs at the entrance to a doorway.

"Thank you."

I held his gaze for a moment, then slowly moved towards the chairs. What was it they used to tell children? If you ever have a problem, you can always ask a policeman. I wondered if children were trusted anymore than I appeared to be.

It wasn't long before a plain clothes officer came briskly through the door, carrying a cardboard file.

"You here about the Hetherington case?"

"Yes."

"Come with me, please."

He led me along a sterile corridor to an even more sterile interview room, the like of which I had seen many times in television drama. There was a bare table and three chairs of moulded plastic. A small, barred window let in just enough light. The officer offered me a chair and then sat opposite me, placing his file, a pad and pen on the table.

"Name?"

I told him.

"Address?"

I told him that, too.

"Haven't you been here before?"

"Yes. About a fortnight ago."

"And someone told you then that we have no new information about the case?"

"I know. But this time I have some information for you."

"Have you now?" I had caught his interest at last. "What can you tell me?"

"I've been investigating what happened for the Hetherington family."

"Yes it says in the file. Some sort of private eye are you?"

"Some sort, yes."

It would be good to be taken seriously. Perhaps that will come.

"I've spoken to a woman who lives near the scene, and from what she's told me, I think Helen's death was not an accident. I'm not sure I would call it murder, but I think there was someone else involved."

"I see." He was writing it all down. "So who is this other person who lives near the scene?"

I gave him Ilse's name and address.

"I hope you will go and interview her. Could I ask you to go gently, though. She is rather highly strung, and it's her adoptive brother who was a witness to what happened. She's upset about the whole situation, particularly as Helen had been to visit her immediately before the incident."

He stopped writing and looked up at me.

"Let me get this straight, the girl," he looked down at the file in front of him, "Helen, was visiting someone near the scene, and this person's brother saw what happened later."

"That's it, yes. He's her adoptive brother, but otherwise, that is what happened."

"So why didn't he come forward at the time?"

"Because he doesn't live locally. And his sister wasn't aware that he saw anything until very recently."

"He hadn't told her?"

"No."

He wrote some more.

"As I recall," he said, "we found no evidence of anyone else being at the scene."

"I know, but the ground was frozen hard, so therefore there were no footprints. Added to which it was dark."

"Both true enough."

"What he saw was very vague, because it was so dark, but he did make out figures. I hope you'll agree, when you've spoken to his sister, and to him, that there is now sufficient circumstantial evidence to merit making further enquiries."

"Why are you telling me this? Why hasn't the witness himself come forward?"

"I don't think he is very keen to talk to the force. Perhaps he has some previous, I don't know. It wouldn't surprise me."

"You don't sound very impressed with this man."

"I'm not particularly, he's a bit stupid and impetuous perhaps, but I believe his story."

More writing, then he looked up at me again.

"We interviewed all the local people on the evening of the incident. Why was nothing said then?"

"As I said, his sister, Ilse, was not aware anything had happened at all until your colleagues called making enquiries."

"She didn't mention that the girl," he looked down again. Poor memory, I thought, or was it lack of interest. "Helen, had been to visit her that evening."

"You can put that down to her being highly strung. But there is no way she could have known for sure that the girl who died was the girl who had visited her."

"Interesting." He had written everything down now.

"So do you happen to know where this brother can be found?"

I gave him Doug's name and address and he wrote them down.

"And your interest in the case?"

"As I said, I've been looking into things for the Hetheringtons. I've been a family friend for a long time."

"I see. Well this is all very interesting. Thank you for coming in. I shall speak to my DI, and I think it likely that we will be going out to speak to this," he consulted his pad again, "Ilse Lamont."

"Thank you. That's all I wanted."

"Good."

He pushed back his chair and I rose to follow him from the room. The two of us retraced our steps to the desk officer and he left me at the door.

"Thanks again for coming in."

"And thank you so much for your help," I said to the officer at the desk as I walked past.

Sarcasm is not to be recommended, but sometimes it is just too hard to resist.

I went home and showered, then sat with a towel round my waist, listening to music, just letting the thoughts drift through my brain as the strings and brass of Rachmaninov filled the room. Soon I would have to see about Gemma, I thought, and try and sort out what actually happened and why.

If this was a Miss Marple or Poirot mystery I knew what would happen next. I would collect all the suspects together in one room and relate exactly what happened. The police would be present, of course, and they would be blinded by the obvious logic which they had so clearly lacked. The guilty party would be so ashamed when faced with the truth, that an admission would be immediately forthcoming, and yours truly, our hero, would move on to his next, even more challenging case.

That was not going to happen, and it couldn't happen anyway as I was not yet certain of the final details of Helen's life. Most, but not all.

She had been to see Ilse, Doug had seen her leave the house and followed her down the lane where he had seen her talking, perhaps arguing, with someone else. He heard a dog and the train's brakes. They were the facts, all the rest, so far, was conjecture.

Adjoining the lane is the garden of a house where a young woman lives, a young woman who had fallen for Helen, but been rejected. A dog also lives there, a large dog that likes to throw its weight around and isn't always easy to control.

Perhaps Gemma and Monty the dog had gone through the gate for a walk, Gemma had seen Helen and gone to speak to her. Helen didn't want to know, and perhaps raised her voice, whereupon the dog went for her. It would be most likely to jump up facing her, and if Helen had her back to the railway track at that moment, and the train was approaching, I could see how it might be possible for her to stumble backwards under the dog's weight, too late to recover before the train hit her.

But that didn't make sense. If she'd fallen backwards onto the track, and that's how her body was found, the police would have recognised from the body's position that it couldn't have been suicide. No one jumps backwards in front of a train, do they? Perhaps the train turned the body over on impact.

I began to consider all the possibilities. Perhaps the dog jumped up at her back. But if she was arguing with Gemma, she would have been facing her.

This was all good, clear conjecture, but only that. Gemma was the only person who could clarify what really happened, but would she be prepared to talk? How would I persuade her? How could I make her talk? Not easily, I thought.

Did her parents know or suspect what had happened? Could I approach Gemma through them? Only one thing was certain. Monty was not going to tell me anything.

After lunch I decided I must do something, anything to move things forward. There was no point in waiting for Gemma to have a sudden rush of conscience to the head and come to talk to me. I would have to make the first move.

Gemma would be at work, and I wasn't going to try talking to her there again, so I would go to see her parents. At least that way I might discover what they knew and if they were helping to cover things up.

I rang the doorbell, then stood back to prepare myself for Monty's onslaught. The woman I had spoken to before, who I now took to be Gemma's mother, opened the door.

"Yes?"

I saw the signs of recognition in her face, so I thought I'd get the usual comment in first.

"Yes, it's me. Again."

"How can I help? I thought I told you before that I know nothing about that girl's accident."

"I know. You did. But there have been some developments and I was wondering if I could share them with you to see if it might jog your memory."

"As far as I know, there is no memory of that evening to jog. But, if it would help. Come in."

This all sounded very innocent, and I wondered how long that would continue.

She led me into a large living room stuffed with furniture. A heavy three piece suite made three sides of a square in front of a large open fire with a distinguished stone surround. There were coffee tables, occasional tables, stools, pouffes and so many objets d'art on the mantlepiece and around the room, it was like stepping into a Victorian stage set.

"Please," she said. "Sit down."

"Thank you."

I chose one of the armchairs closest to the fire. It was still freezing outside.

"Perhaps I could tell you what I know, and see if any of it means anything to you."

"All right."

Once again it was important to get the words right and in the right order, but suddenly I felt more at ease than on previous occasions. Perhaps this detective thing was growing on me.

"The night that Helen died, she had been to visit someone along Barn Lane. In fact a near neighbour of yours. When she left the house it seems she walked along the track towards the railway. I have no idea why, but I suspect she wanted time to think about what she had just learned."

"This is all very intriguing, but I can't see what it has to do with us."

"Bear with me, if you would."

She gestured for me to continue.

"Helen was followed down the track by someone who was not pleased to see her there. The identity of that person is of no concern, except for what he saw, because if his story is accurate, he saw how Helen died."

I was watching my listener very carefully, and I could see no sign of concern or anything which would suggest she knew what was coming next.

"The witness says he saw someone go up to speak to Helen, and this person had a dog with them. It seems that words were exchanged and the dog was heard to bark, after which the train braked very suddenly and loudly."

It was when I said 'dog' that her expression changed, but only ever so slightly.

"Now I happen to know, from first hand experience if you remember, that you have a dog. A large dog, called Monty, I think. And when I walked along the track recently I noticed a gate leading from your garden."

"Are you suggesting that it was someone from this house, with Monty, who caused the girl's death?

"I am not suggesting it, I am telling you what I've been told and pointing out what could be deduced from that."

Her brow was now furrowed and she was thinking.

"Can you please think back to that night?" I said. "You told me before that you and your husband had been in the house and you had neither seen nor heard anything. Is that correct?"

"That's right."

"You were at the back of the house, you said."

"Yes."

"But can you recall where your daughter was that evening, and where Monty was. Was the dog in the house with you?"

"My God! You don't think...but you can't. It's impossible. Why would Gemma want to do any harm to that girl?"

"Has Gemma spoken to you about the incident?"

"No. I don't think so. I can't remember. She lives in the flat over the garage, and she lives her own life. We're not always aware of her comings and goings. In fact we often don't know where she is. But she's a grown woman. She has her own life to lead."

"Does she have a job?"

"Yes. She works at Colbox in Colchester."

"Did you know that Helen, the girl who died, also worked at Colbox?"

"No."

"Gemma didn't tell you?"

"No, she didn't. Why should she?"

"No reason other than interest. I would have thought that if a work colleague died in strange circumstances next to someone's garden, they might mention it. Don't you?"

The question was left hanging and the woman was now looking rather worried.

"Let me ask you again about your dog. Was it in the house that night?"

"I can't be certain. He often goes out into the garden for, well, you know what. He could easily have been outside that night. But that doesn't mean he got out through the gate."

"Could he get out through the gate, or would the gate have to be opened for him?"

"It would have to be opened."

"And you don't know where Gemma was that night."

"No. I have no idea."

She appeared to be considering possibilities, and not liking what she came up with.

"I take it Gemma is at work at present."

"Yes."

"Could I come and have a word with her later on, do you think? If she knows nothing, at least that will mean I can cross her off my list of possibles."

"Possibles for what?"

"Possibles for being in the lane with Helen just before she died."

It was interesting. She made no loud declarations of Gemma's obvious innocence. I would have expected at least that from a suspect's mother. Sometimes people's reactions are very surprising and rather revealing.

"I shall come back this evening, if you don't mind. Perhaps you would tell Gemma that I called and that I would like to speak to her later."

I got up and offered another of my cards. I know she already had one, but just to be sure.

She said goodbye to me a little wistfully and I wondered what Gemma's reaction would be when her mother told her I had been. If she told her what I had said about the dog, and if my theory was correct, Gemma would know the game was up. But that, of course, didn't mean she would admit to anything.

Closing the gate behind me I decided there was nothing else I could do immediately, so I went to call on Ilse.

"Hello," she said brightly when she opened the door.

"I was in the area so I thought I'd call to see you."

"Come inside."

This time we went straight to the kitchen, but unlike my first two visits there, now I felt more at ease and conversation was not a struggle. Ilse had gone straight to the kettle to make tea.

"Pam gave me a trunk which belonged to your mother. Most of the contents are a collection of memorabilia which, I suppose, must have meant something to Annie during her life. We did find a few photos in there which gave us some clues, before we knew who you were, but it should all be yours, I think."

She was looking at me occasionally over her shoulder as I spoke, and I thought how different this was from the first time, when I stood with the towel, dripping all over her floor.

"It's sitting in my living room at present, but I should be glad to bring it here. Or why don't we drive over to Annie's bungalow and take it with us? When were you thinking of moving in?"

"I'm not sure. Everything happened rather fast yesterday. I'm still trying to catch up."

She poured the boiling water into the pot and came to join me at the table. I noticed that she had returned to her less fetching clothes, but somehow she now looked more comfortable. The change was entirely in her face. Having everything settled must have taken a load off her mind, and it showed.

"The rent is paid up to the end of the month," she said, "so I could move anytime, I suppose."

"You know that Pam and Oliver will help, if you ask them," I said. "and I know Pam would like to take you to meet her parents."

"Oh dear. All these new people to meet. It's not what I'm used to at all."

"You'll get used to it, I'm sure."

She smiled a half smile, and once again I began to see how much different she would look once all the worries and uncertainties were behind her.

"Let's fix a date," I said. "I'll take you over to Ipswich with the trunk and help you find your way around."

I set a date a few days in the future, hoping that would give me time to see Gemma, sort out what really happened and tie up the remaining loose ends.

On the way home in the car I had the radio on, and there was a report of more cold weather to come with high winds blowing in off the North Sea. Just what we need, I thought. It would be warmer in London.

That set me thinking how good it would be to get back to the office and work on other things, while trying to earn some money. Having finally told Joyce how I felt about her, I sensed that we would have a future together before too long, which added to the urgent need I was beginning to feel about earning a living.

The case about Helen was not over yet, and I could never have imagined when Joyce first called where investigations would lead. But I felt I had at least begun to persuade myself that I was a detective. Perhaps an admission from Gemma would finally convince me.

I hoped the police would follow up those enquiries and go to see Ilse and Doug. That thought brought Ilse back to my mind. What a sad life. In some respects she'd lost more than Joyce and her family. I hoped the police would be easy on her and not make things worse.

Chapter 18

On the way back to see Gemma my mobile phone chirruped at me, so I pulled over to answer it.

"Is that Greg Mason?"

"Yes."

"This is Mrs Hughes, Gemma's mother."

I could tell by the tone of her voice that something was wrong.

"She's gone."

"What do you mean?"

"Gemma. She came home from work and I told her you had been and would be back this evening. She said she wouldn't talk to you and rushed out of the house. I thought she had just gone to her flat, but the next thing I heard was her car rushing out of the drive."

"I'm on my way," I told her, put the car back into gear and shot off down the road towards Monks Colne.

She opened the door as I was walking along the garden path and I could see her husband standing behind her.

"Come in," she said, but then her husband took over.

"What's all this rubbish about Gemma being the cause of that young woman's death? How dare you come to my house and make accusations about my daughter? What right do you have? Who do you think you are?"

"Geoffrey," his wife said mildly.

"Don't Geoffrey me," he shouted and then turned back to me.

"If anything happens to my daughter as a result of unfounded allegations made by you, I'll.."

But I never heard what he was threatening to do, as his wife shut him up and guided us all back into the living room.

"What have you got to say for yourself?" Mr Hughes was immediately back on the attack.

"Has your wife told you what I said earlier?" I asked him.

"Of course she has," he shouted.

"Then you will know I am not making allegations, but following up enquiries, and particularly the story told by someone else."

"You said that Gemma and Monty caused that girl's death."

"No, I didn't. I told your wife what I had been told, and asked her where Gemma and the dog were that evening."

"That's right, Geoffrey," his wife told him.

"And now it seems that Gemma has taken herself off," I went on. "Does that strike you as the action of someone not involved? I'm not saying how she might have been involved. But if she had no connection at all with what happened, why would she react like that?"

"He's right, Geoffrey."

Mr Hughes looked from me to his wife and back again, as if searching for the explanation he desperately wanted to find.

He was a big man in every sense, tall and broad shouldered with a thick neck and florid cheeks. Drinker, I thought, with a potential heart problem, which he is certainly not helping when he behaves like this.

"I could have gone straight to the police," I said. I had done, of course, but I wasn't going to tell them that. "Would you rather I told them what I know and left them to sort it out? Or would you rather I did it a little, shall we say, more quietly and discreetly?"

He was continuing to wrestle with his temper, apparently unable to consider that his daughter could be at fault.

"Geoffrey." She said it in a cajoling voice which I guessed she had used many times in the past.

He looked at her.

"Oh, all right," he said and flopped down into an armchair.

"Please," his wife said. "Sit down."

But I decided to stay on my feet. I thought it might generate a bit of authority, not that I really had any. At least it made me feel better with Mr. Hughes sitting down.

"So," I said. "do you have any idea where Gemma would have gone?"

"No," Mr. Hughes said, and his wife shook her head.

"Is the dog with her?"

"No, he's in the garden."

"Good. I don't mind going after Gemma, but I might have thought twice about a dog that size."

"Monty's all right. He wouldn't hurt a fly."

"I'm not sure the average fly would agree with you. He may be well behaved, but he is big and very heavy, and, I imagine, very defensive of Gemma."

Mr Hughes' head fell forward and he pushed his hands through his hair. I took this as a subtle sign of acceptance.

Mrs Hughes sat down on the arm of her husband's chair. She was beginning to find the likelihood of what happened very difficult.

"Now, can you think where she might have gone? Is there anywhere she likes to go particularly? Does she have any friends she might go to see? Anything you could tell me would be useful."

Mrs Hughes looked at her husband.

"She doesn't have many real friends," she said. "She spends so much time on her own. I don't know what to make of her."

"She's never had boy friends," her husband said towards his feet. "I don't know why. She's not unattractive."

That answered one question at least. I looked at his wife, and her expression told me she knew more than him. Or perhaps it was that she accepted, while he didn't, or couldn't.

"Where might she go if she wanted to be on her own?"

"I don't know," Mrs Hughes said. "There's the caravan."

"Where's that?"

"Seawick. Down by the coast. We often spend weekends there and the odd week during the summer. The dog loves it there. We walk for hours on the beach."

"Does Gemma have a key to the caravan?"

"Oh, yes. We all have."

"Is the caravan park open at this time of the year? I would have thought it would close down for the winter."

"All the facilities close, but owners can always get in if they want to."

"Can you think of anywhere else she might go, or do you think the caravan is the most likely place?"

"I can't think of anywhere else."

"Then I'd better go and look for her," I said as I got up.

"I'll come with you," Mr Hughes said, to my surprise. It was clearly not a suggestion.

"If you like." No point in arguing, although I didn't exactly relish the thought of his company.

He went in search of outdoor clothing and I met him in the hall.

As we made our way to the front door, Mrs Hughes was fussing round her husband.

"You won't be angry, will you dear?"

He hurrumphed his reply.

"Let's just find Gemma first," I suggested. "And bring a torch. I have one in the car, but we may need one each."

He ducked back into a cupboard below the stairs, and then we went out together, back into the cold, where the wind was beginning to pick up. Great, I thought. A wind chill factor on top of the cold. Just what we need.

I went straight to my car, determined to maintain some sort of authority and control over this journey. It looked as if Mr Hughes had expected to use his Land Rover, but he didn't argue and joined me in the Honda.

"Comfortable," was the first thing he said, as he reached for his seat belt.

"What the hell's that?" was the second thing he said as the CD player kicked in as I turned on the engine. I simply turned it off without reply. This was not the time for a detailed discussion on the finer points of Queen's later music.

"Which is the quickest way?" I asked him.

"I usually use the 120 right along to Clacton, then turn back to St. Osyth and down to the coast.

"OK."

I drove out along the lanes as fast as I dared in the wind, and we were soon on the A12 and flying north towards Colchester's northern by-pass.

"Tell me about Gemma," I said carefully.

"A funny girl," he said after a pause. "Always a loner at school. Got on with her work. Quite bright, but not brilliant, you know what I mean?"

I could see out of the corner of my eye that his face was fixed forward. He didn't want to look at me, or he was too scared of what might have happened to relax.

"Had several jobs before she landed the one at Colbox. She seems to like it there. She's been there a while. Speaks highly of her boss."

"Did you know that the girl who died also worked at Colbox?"

"Yes. My wife told me you'd mentioned it. But that could be a coincidence."

"It could be, but there have been too many coincidences in this case. And when there are too many, I start to consider that they are not mere coincidences, but actually mean something."

He was quiet for a while, then turned towards me.

"What do you know for sure that happened that night?" he asked.

Once again I was up against the honesty problem. What does he need to know, I thought. Let's stick to that.

"Helen, the girl in question, worked at Colbox. So does Gemma, and for several months they worked in the same department."

I waited for a response, but there was none.

"Rumour has it there was a little unfinished business between Gemma and Helen."

"What kind of unfinished business?"

"I'm not sure exactly. But I sense there was a bit of bad feeling between them."

"All right. It happens. What else?"

"I know that Helen visited someone living down Barn Lane. Quite close to you, actually. I also know that when she left the house she walked down towards the railway, because she was seen. And the person who saw her claims to have seen her by the railway line talking to someone else, and a dog barked just before he heard the train braking."

"And you assume, therefore, that it must be Gemma."

"It does seem likely. Think about it. Your garden is next to the lane. There is a gate. Gemma could have gone through the gate to walk your dog, and met Helen totally by surprise. Unfriendly words could have been exchanged on a not too friendly basis. Your dog could have reacted to what was happening by jumping up at Helen, by a railway line with a train coming."

"I asked you what you know. You are telling me what you think."

"One thing leads to the other. I know there was a connection between the two at Colbox. I know there was a problem between them. I know where your garden is in relation to the railway line. I know you have a large dog. Two and two usually make four. It's not rocket science."

"But even if what you say is true, it sounds like an accident to me."

"I tend to agree. But then why has Gemma taken off? We have to find out exactly what happened. Helen's parents have a right to know how their daughter died. Thoughts of suicide or murder are not what parents want to think. It's bad enough losing a daughter, without losing one like that. If it was a genuine accident, then it's going to be a little easier for them to deal with."

"If what you say is true, will Gemma get into trouble?"

"That is not for me to say, but I shouldn't think so. She didn't do anything wrong, although it looks as if she did leave the scene of a fatal accident, and the police might want to speak to her about that.

"I can hardly blame the dog either, for protecting its owner if it thought she was being attacked. But, as I said, that is not my decision to make. I just want to get at the truth."

"Why didn't Gemma just say what happened?" her father asked.

"Who knows? No doubt she was embarrassed. It was a pretty awful thing to witness. And if I'm right, she did walk away and leave Helen lying there, which doesn't show her up in a good light. She feels she has something to hide. We need to persuade her to tell the truth."

It went quiet again then. The road was dry, which was a blessing in the darkness, and once we left the A12 and began to head towards the coast, the traffic began to thin. I raced on, keeping to a steady seventy miles an hour.

There was a bright moon right in front of us, almost beckoning us on, but there were also large clouds. The speed of the wind rushing in from the sea carried successive clouds in front of the moon, each one casting the evening into sudden, but short lived, darkness. It was like driving from sunshine into shade. One minute everything was clear, the next all I could see was the road immediately ahead in my headlights.

At the end of the by-pass I swung straight round to the left onto the single carriageway road, glad there was little traffic about to hamper our progress.

Neither of us spoke. Gemma's father had run out of questions and there was nothing I wanted to say. I just wanted to find Gemma and get this over with. But I could sense his tension next to me. The words coiled spring came to mind.

At the roundabout in Clacton we turned right and headed west, parallel to the coast. As soon as we left the buildings behind us I could feel the wind pushing at the car from the left, making it difficult to maintain a straight line at the speed I wanted to drive.

We passed a garage and the road went down into a dip.

"There's a left turn soon," my passenger said.

"Yes. I know, although I haven't been along here for years."

Sure enough, as the road rose in front of us, there was the turning, and I left the main road and drove along into the middle of St. Osyth. At the crossroads I manoeuvred carefully to the left, the old buildings on the corner blocking my vision. The darkness now confirmed that I had a clear road ahead and I drove more carefully along a narrow, twisting lane.

There were no buildings and the road was flat, an area of reclaimed marshland used for arable farming and, along the coast itself, caravans and chalets. The American phrase 'trailer park' came to mind, but these were not permanent homes for the less well off, they were hired out, a week or fortnight at a time, for summer holidays.

At this time of the year they were largely deserted. There are few places in Britain more depressing than a holiday resort in winter. Everywhere is closed and boarded up. Nowhere to buy a drink, in fact little reason to be there at all, especially with a cold wind blowing off the North Sea.

The fields gave way on one side to a long fence, picked out in the headlights. On the opposite side I could see the effect of the wind in the trees, a dark swaying mass with branches swinging out over the road and then lurching back again.

"You'll have to tell me where to go. This is all strange to me."

"OK. Keep going, bear left where the road divides and watch for a parking area on your left."

I turned as instructed and we passed some sort of amusement area, the force of the wind hitting us head on as we approached the sea.

"There," he shouted, pointing ahead to an area of asphalt at the side of the road, "Now slow down, and when I say, you can park on the verge by these caravans."

A vast area of mobile homes had materialised to our left. They were so closely packed together, I wondered at the lack of privacy for people who chose to come here for their holidays. Not the sort of place for peace and quiet, I thought. It must be hell in high summer with every caravan taken and children rushing about.

"Here," he shouted again, and I pulled over and turned off the engine.

Getting out of the car was not easy as the wind was pushing against the door, but I managed to retrieve my torch from under the driving seat and followed my companion who was already making his way into the holiday park.

The clouds had thickened by now, completely obliterating the moon and making it impossible to see without the torch. Please let the battery last, I remember thinking. The spare ones are in the car.

I was able to follow Mr Hughes by the beam of his torch, although it sometimes disappeared behind a caravan. I tried to run to catch up, but I couldn't see far enough ahead to run safely.

The wind was whipping at my clothes and I could smell the salt and a faint whiff of fish on the air as it rushed past.

"Wait," I shouted, but the wind carried my voice away and I knew he hadn't heard me.

Right and left we went, twisting and turning through the vehicles until I was suddenly aware that he had stopped at a door.

"It's locked," he said as I came up behind him. "She can't be here."

"Why don't you open the door to see if there's any sign that she has been here?"

He fumbled for his keys and almost dropped his torch. I shone mine onto the lock on the door and eventually he managed to get it open and switched on the light.

Inside smelled a little musty. Not surprising, I thought, if no one has been here for months.

We were in a small living area with a kitchenette to our right and a short passage leading, I imagined, to the bedrooms. I could see nothing unusual as I looked round. There was not much to see.

He moved away along the passageway and I was just about to follow when I heard him say, "What's this?"

I caught up with him in a cramped bedroom. He had a piece of paper in his hand.

Throwing his torch down onto the bed he opened up the paper and began to read.

Not another note, I thought. I had hoped we had done with those. But this was not a threat. It was a message and Gemma had been there ahead of us.

"Look at this," he said, handing me the paper.

I read it out loud.

"I've had enough. I can't cope anymore. What happened was not my fault. I can't help the way I am."

"What the hell does that mean? I can't help the way I am?"

Gemma's father looked bemused. So she hadn't told her parents, although I had the impression her mother had guessed. No wonder she couldn't cope anymore.

"We have to find her," I said. "She sounds desperate to me."

"But where do we look? She could be anywhere."

"I think I know. Come with me."

I went back outside and immediately the wind hit me again, almost throwing the torch out of my hand. At least it still worked.

"Which way to the beach?" I shouted to be heard.

"Oh my God!" he shouted back, realising the implication. "This way."

I hurried along with him through the caravans and back to the road.

"Come on," I said, pushing my way into the wind.

The road was straight, which was a help, but I had to lean into the wind really hard to make any progress. Mr Hughes hurried alongside me, our two torches piercing the utter darkness.

After a while I could feel the ground begin to rise beneath my feet and I stopped, shining my torch to right and left ahead of us.

"It's the sea wall," he said, and I could make out a concrete barrier about four feet high, all there was to prevent the sea flooding the whole area.

We could hear the sea now. The North Sea, normally placid along the east coast, was being whipped up by the onshore wind into storm waves. Suddenly we saw one, crashing as it broke over the sea wall, its water running down onto a parking area below.

I hoped Gemma had not gone down to the beach. She would have no chance if she had.

We looked at each other and inched our way forward and upwards towards the wall. Another wave broke, and we jumped back as the spray hit us hard in the face.

"She can't be down here," he said.

"I don't know where else she would be. She sounded desperate in the note."

I shone my torch to right and left, but all I could see was sea wall and the footpath behind it, now soaked by successive waves.

"I'm going along here," I said, and I forced my way up to the footpath and began walking along to the left.

Another wave approached. I could hear it roaring up the beach and I steeled myself, bending down for as much shelter as the sea wall could provide.

It broke right over me. I could smell the salt, and my clothes were immediately soaked, but I stood up again and tried to continue walking, the power of the wind from my right making it increasingly difficult.

I sensed Mr Hughes coming up behind me.

"This is bloody stupid," he shouted.

"She has to be somewhere," I shouted back.

Pushing on, I heard another wave approaching, and I dipped down just in time to avoid being washed down the bank to my left. I shivered involuntarily and shook the moisture out of my trousers. It was bad enough the night I went to Ilse's, but that was nothing compared to this.

On I went, avoiding the crashing waves as best I could, the light from Mr Hughes' torch telling me he was still there behind me.

I didn't so much find Gemma as almost fall over her. She was sitting behind the sea wall, facing inland, hugging her knees. Her hair was plastered to her head and her clothes looked saturated.

She looked up.

"You," she said, and then she looked behind me. "Dad?" It sounded like complete disbelief, but mixed with gratitude.

"What are you doing here?" Not the most helpful of questions, but I guessed that by now, her father didn't know what to ask or to think.

Chapter 19

"Come here," he said, and bent down to pick her up as if she was five years old.

It was not easy getting back along that footpath. We still had to avoid the waves as best we could, but eventually we made it back to the road and on towards the caravans.

"Dad, I think I can walk now." Gemma spoke in a pathetic voice as if pleading for a return of lost dignity.

"Are you sure?"

"Mmm."

He put her down gingerly and she looked a bedraggled sight, rather like an unwanted kitten that had somehow escaped drowning.

"What's he doing here? How did you find me?"

"If it wasn't for Greg, we perhaps wouldn't have found you," he told her. "What were you doing here anyway?"

"Didn't you see my note?"

"Yes and I don't understand. But let's get back to the warmth of the caravan before we all die of exposure."

It is strange how it's just as hard to walk with a gale blowing behind you as it is when walking into its teeth. The wind was pulling at our wet clothes, adding a severe chill to the soaking we had all experienced.

Back at the caravan, Mr Hughes turned on the heating and then went in search of towels. Gemma perched on the edge of one of the banquette sofas and I stood there like a lemon, not knowing where to look, what to do or what to say.

What was going to happen next was something I didn't need to be part of. It was a father and daughter thing and really had nothing to do with me or Helen. I didn't want to leave in the state I was in, but I had little choice.

The towels arrived and Gemma took herself into her bedroom to get out of her wet clothes. I rubbed my hair with my towel, wiped my face and then dabbed uselessly at my wet clothes. The sooner I got home the better.

"Look," I said to Gemma's father, "you have Gemma's car to get home in. I need to get out of these wet clothes, but I can't do it here. So why don't I just leave you two to sort things out between you. I can speak to you again tomorrow, perhaps?"

He looked confused. Something was happening which he clearly had no idea how to cope with or to understand. His expression when he looked at me suggested helplessness and despair, but I couldn't help with what he had to do. This was all way beyond my experience or capacity to solve.

It seemed clear that I had to make the decision for him.

"I'll push off home then and be in touch. Will you be OK?"

"I don't know," he said, more honestly than I expected.

I dropped the towel on the kitchenette sink and went back out into the storm. It had begun to rain, but I could hardly get any wetter. I was starting to get quite used to it.

My only clue as to how to find the car was the direction of the wind, and it seemed to take ages before I reached the road. Without my torch it would have been impossible. I opened the car door with a struggle against the onslaught, threw my torch onto the passenger seat, started the car and switched the demister fan as far up as it would go.

Even with the wipers going at full speed it was impossible to get the windscreen clear enough to see, so I just sat for a while, watching the inside of the screen mist up. Then, as the air temperature rose the misting began to clear slowly, and it was only the rain blurring my vision.

I had two choices, stay there and wait for the rain to ease, or set off straight away and hope I could see well enough. The second choice seemed the most positive so I did a careful three point turn and set off slowly for home.

It was the slowest journey I can remember. Even with the headlights on full and fog lamps to help, visibility was poor and I had to crawl along, stopping from time to time as unexpected bends suddenly appeared.

Fortunately I was the only person stupid enough to be out driving, and there were no oncoming vehicle lights to dazzle me.

I was grateful to reach St Osyth village and the main road just beyond it. This provided a driving space considerably wider and the extra benefit of white lines for me to follow. I have no idea how long it took me to reach home, but as soon as I was in the house I threw off my clothes and went to stand in a very hot shower.

Sleep came eventually, after a hot drink. Getting under the quilt was like crawling into a warm hole of safety after the earlier experience with the storm and the sea, but it was hard to relax. Thoughts were chasing each other round my head, and it was hard to persuade myself that the case was solved after the two weeks of puzzle and confusion.

By her actions Gemma had confirmed my theory of what happened by the railway line. It only remained for me to hear her say it. Then I could decide, with her parents' help, how to proceed with the police.

I woke the next morning feeling a mixture of relief and exhaustion. The last few days had taken their toll, and as often happened, I had managed to keep going with little sleep until I allowed myself to stop and relax. Now my body was telling me enough was enough. It was time to take it easy.

Breakfast could wait. I made coffee and took it back to bed with my notebook, which I rescued from a still very wet jacket pocket. There was little more to do and I decided not to call Gemma or her parents, but to wait in the hope that they would call me. They could hardly leave things as they were, knowing what I suspected, especially after what had happened down at the coast.

My mobile rang. It was Joyce.

"Where are you? I was worried about you."

"I'm in bed and there's no need to worry. It's all over now."

"What's all over? Where have you been? Why are you still in bed?"

"I'm supposed to ask all the questions." I smiled to myself. I would have to get used to someone caring about me so much. "I'm in bed because I'm exhausted and I got soaked again last night. It's a long story, but I'll tell you everything very soon."

"You weren't out in that storm?"

"Just a bit. Listen, I'm waiting for a call." I hoped the call I was waiting for would materialise soon. "I'll come over and see you later on. Will you be there?"

"Of course I'll be here, waiting for you."

"OK. See you soon."

I closed the phone and let my head fall back against the pillow. What a change. A fortnight ago I was alone and trying to find things to do to earn a living as a detective. Here I was, with the woman of my dreams telling me she loves me, and my first, difficult case apparently solved. I could get quite used to success, I thought, and returned to drink my coffee.

It was Mrs Hughes who called and woke me up again, just before noon.

"We would like to talk to you." she said. There was little more she needed to say.

"When would be convenient?"

"Now, if you can. Gemma is here and her father."

"Give me half an hour," I said.

In fact I reached the house twenty minutes later. I only had to shave and throw some clothes on.

Before I left the car I took a deep breath, hoping this would be the end of the trail.

Mrs Hughes opened the door and asked me in. Gemma and her father were already sitting in the living room.

"Would you like any coffee?"

"No thanks. I've already had my share this morning."

"Sit down," Mr Hughes said.

His tone had softened considerably and he was less sure of himself, but he seemed to be putting a brave face on all that was happening.

"Gemma has something she wants to tell you."

He said it looking at Gemma rather than me, and his voice carried a measure of encouragement. But I knew she wasn't going to find it easy.

I could see she wasn't going to look at me, but I just waited as she struggled to face what she had to do.

"It was me, at the railway, with Helen," she said quietly. "I didn't want to hurt her, and Monty was only trying to protect me because she was cross with me."

There was no reason for me to say anything.

"It all happened like you said. I took Monty for a walk, out through the gate, and there she was. I couldn't believe it. She was standing right by the track. It was as if she had come to find me. But, of course, she had no idea where I lived. I realise that now.

"Even though it was dark I knew it was her. I knew every line of her face. I had sat and watched her for so long at work, willing her to like me, to want me, but it did no good. So I went up to her and just said her name, and she jumped.

"Where did you come from? she said, and I told her I lived here. And she said: Oh God. Go away. I don't want to see you, and all the time she was raising her voice. Monty didn't like that and he jumped up at her. I suppose I should have had him on his lead. He started barking. Helen fell back and suddenly the train was there and there was nothing I could do. She was on the track, scrambling to get up. The train was braking, but I knew it wasn't going to stop in time."

"It's strange," I said, "that the people in the crossing house didn't report hearing the dog bark."

"Don't you believe me?"

"Yes. I believe you. I suppose the sound of the train was all they heard. Sometimes people only hear what they expect to hear."

"So what happens now?" Gemma's father said.

"What do you think should happen?"

"It wasn't Gemma's fault. You can't blame her for what happened."

"But don't you think it would be fair to Helen's family to tell them what actually happened. It would help them come to terms with losing their daughter."

He was looking at me, desperate to find a way out for his daughter.

"Do we have to tell the police?" he asked.

I replied to Gemma.

"The police already know my suspicions to some extent, but I haven't mentioned you to them by name, because I wasn't completely certain. It's likely they will reopen their enquiries. You could save them a lot of time and effort by coming forward and telling them."

"Will I get into trouble?"

"That's not for me to say. You left the scene of a serious accident, and they might think that you hampered police enquiries by not coming forward or telling your parents what had happened. As a result they weren't able to help the police when they called. Or when I called, for that matter."

"Oh God. What a mess! I've been so stupid."

"What you decide to do is up to you. I can't sit back now and do nothing. Helen's parents have asked me to investigate and I am duty bound to tell them what I know. Even if I didn't choose to go to the police, they might well insist that I tell them. I think it's likely that the police would look more favourably if you go to tell them what happened, rather than leaving them to come looking for you. But I can't speak for them."

"Dad," she pleaded, but I could see from his expression that he could see no way out of what needed to be done.

"Will I lose my job?"

"That's up to Mr Jordan. If you like, I'll go and talk to him."

"That would be very kind of you," her mother said.

"He seems to me to be a reasonable man. He lost a good PA in Helen. He won't want to lose someone else who does her job well."

"Why are you being nice to me?" Gemma asked.

"I'm only doing what I think is right. That's all any of us can do."

Gemma's father reached a decision and stood up without taking his eyes off his daughter.

"Will you come with us to the police?" he asked me.

"Of course, if you want me to," I said.

There was a different desk sergeant, but the procedure was exactly the same as before and we were asked to wait to see the same person I had seen earlier.

"Do you need me in there with them?" I asked him.

"Will they tell me all we need to know?"

"Oh, I think so," I said. "I'll wait here until you've finished, if you like," and I sat back on my chair in the waiting area.

Gemma looked at me before she followed the detective through the door and her father held out his hand, so I stood again and shook it. It was as firm as I would have expected and I got the impression that everything would be all right, at least within the family.

When the detective sergeant returned, a little while later, he told me there was no need for me to stay. They would be in touch again if they needed any clarification, he told me, and he thanked me for what I had done.

Buoyed by his comments, and particularly his thanks, I went home and pondered all that had happened and the changes which had occurred in people's lives as a result.

My thoughts were interrupted by my ringing phone.

"Is that Greg?" It was Sarah from Colbox.

"Yes."

"Mr Jordan thought you would like to know that Gemma didn't come into work this morning. She hasn't called in sick so we don't know what's wrong."

"Ah. Thanks for the call. Would it be possible to speak to Mr Jordan?"

"I'll see. Just a minute."

There was only the briefest of pauses.

248

"Greg." The same brisk, business like voice. I could picture him in his favourite chair behind the desk.

"Frank. Gemma won't be in today. I'm afraid she's at the police station with her father. I just left them there."

"Oh God! Is she in serious trouble?"

"I don't know how serious it will prove to be. That's up to the police. I do know she was there when Helen died, although what happened was not directly her fault."

"So why is she with the police?"

"She's telling them exactly what happened. At least I hope she is. Look, I'm not sure how much I should tell you in detail. It will all come out soon enough, but don't expect to see Gemma today, or perhaps for a few days. No doubt she will be in touch with you in due course."

"Right." He paused. "And thanks, Greg. It seems you were right to be suspicious."

"Listen," I said after a moment's thought, "for what it's worth, I think Gemma's suffered enough for what happened. I've no idea what the police will do, and what you do, if anything, is entirely up to you. But, in a sense, all she did was allow her heart to rule her head. Helen's death was an accident of chance and circumstance. Gemma will have to live with what happened for the rest of her life. And don't forget, Gemma loved her, and that will make dealing with everything even worse for her."

I paused, but I'd said enough.

"Thanks for your help. If you ever need a detective, give me a call."

I couldn't stop myself making such a stupid remark. It hardly sounded professional, I told myself. But I could almost hear the smile in his voice when he replied.

"I will," and the phone went dead.

As my car stopped on Joyce's parents' drive an hour or two later, I sat for a minute looking at the house. Oliver must have bought it to share with his new wife, I thought. She would have been already pregnant with Helen, so this is the only home Helen would have known.

They must have been so full of hope and expectation when they moved in. Pam would be trying to put an unhappy past behind her, and Oliver would be busy with his bank job, buzzing to and from the Far East from time to time. A prosperous, happy family.

Then Joyce arrived to round off the perfect set of two children per couple. Everything must have been rosy and happy for a long time, then it all began to collapse.

Joyce lost her job and her career. Soon afterwards Oliver was made redundant. Then Annie died and the inheritance went to someone unknown. And as if all that wasn't bad enough, Helen was killed in an accident, and I realised now that it was an accident. Nothing was intentional.

Gemma was frustrated and angry, but not murderous. Monty only did what dogs do and protected his mistress. It was hard to blame either of them, yet without the two of them Helen would never had died.

And Doug saw it happen and did nothing. Had he alerted the authorities and told them what he knew and what he saw, the coroner's verdict would have been quite different, the police would have continued their enquiries and Pam and Oliver would not have had to suffer a prolonged period of not knowing.

I considered again the question of Helen falling backwards and how the body was situated when the police arrived. It must have been turned somehow as she fell, I concluded. Surely no police pathologist would consider that someone threw themselves backwards in front of a train.

It was easy to think that for everything that happens, someone is responsible. Some people do good in the world and others do harm. I recalled Oliver's rant about Hitler, and that if there had been no war, none of this would have happened. That would mean no Ilse, no grudge held by Doug, and perhaps a direct inheritance by Helen from Annie. But it would not have changed Gemma. It was her infatuation with Helen which ultimately caused her death, if anything did.

And yet, with no Ilse, Helen would not have been by the railway line to be pushed over by a dog. So, in a sense, Oliver was right. Perhaps it was not possible to apportion blame for all that had happened, not to Gemma, or Monty, or Doug, or anyone else. It was a combination of factors, originating with the war.

Joyce came out of the front door and called something to me. I opened the door to hear.

"I heard you arrive," she repeated. "Are you going to sit there all day?"

I forced a smile. After all that had happened, I didn't feel like smiling very much. But I got out of the car and went into the house which I knew now was going to become part of my future.

"How are you getting on?" Oliver greeted me.

"It's all done. I know what happened."

"Really?" Pam asked from behind him. "Oh dear. Do I want to hear this?"

"I think you might feel better for knowing. Come and sit down."

Those two comforting phrases, come and sit down, and make some tea. How often I had heard them both in the past few days.

We went into the living room and I looked round at the three faces. Pam's still drawn, but expectant. Oliver's tense and rather haggard. And then Joyce's. It shone, and I knew that what I had to say would take the shine away. So I looked at her mother instead when I spoke.

"Helen left work that day, and went to see your solicitor. She took the three photographs she had found, and the solicitor confirmed that they were of Ilse Chambers.

"When Helen got back to the station, she was on her way to the car park when purely by chance; she saw Ilse and recognised her from the pictures. So she followed her home, confronted her with the photographs and Ilse invited her in and told her everything. All about Annie being her mother, who her father was. Everything.

"She left Ilse's house just as Doug, Ilse's brother, arrived on his motorbike, and he watched her walk down the garden, cross the road and go into the lane. He immediately thought the worst and guessed that Ilse had told Helen about her background. So incensed was he that someone should discover Ilse's father was German, that he chased after Helen down the lane. But by then it was dark, and he had to go carefully.

"Up ahead he could see Helen stop by the railway crossing, and then she was joined by someone else. They were only shapes to Doug. It was too dark to see, but it made him stop and watch. He heard voices, then a dog barked, and then he heard the train screeching to a halt. In his panic, he ran back to his motorbike and left.

"Ilse was back in the house by this time, probably in her kitchen at the back of the house where it was warm. She wouldn't have heard a thing."

I paused, but no one spoke.

"The house next to the lane is where Gemma lives. Gemma worked with Helen at Colbox and had become rather infatuated with her."

"You mean?" Oliver began.

"Yes," I said. "Again, by pure chance, Gemma went to take her dog for a walk, through the garden gate and into the lane, and met Helen. She spoke to Helen and there was an exchange of heated words by all accounts. Now Monty, her dog, is big. I mean big." And I opened my arms like a fisherman describing his catch.

"Like all dogs, Monty was very protective of his mistress, and he thought Gemma was in danger. He leapt up at Helen, pushing her back just at the moment the train arrived. Helen lost her footing, perhaps falling over the nearest rail on the track, I don't know, and the train driver had no chance.

"And that's it."

"Poor girl. Oh my poor Helen," cried Pam as she began to sob uncontrollably. Oliver moved across to comfort her. Joyce was just looking at me.

"So we know it all now," she said.

"Yes. All we'll ever know."

There wasn't anything more to say. But there was more to discover, although there was no way of knowing that at the time.

Joyce and I left Pam in Oliver's arms and went out into the hall.

"I'm so proud of you," she said.

"Good. I'm glad. But I couldn't have done it without you and a tremendous amount of luck."

"People make their own luck."

"All right, then. It was all me."

She punched me then, on the arm and I grabbed her and we kissed for a very long time.

I left them soon afterwards to their shared grief. There was one more thing to do, and that was to take Ilse to her mother's bungalow and help her sort through the many artifacts in the trunk. In a sense that was nothing to do with me, but I wanted to help.

Having heard what I planned, Oliver had offered to help, and as the trunk was too heavy for me to lift on my own, I was glad to accept. There was no way Pam could resist the chance to come too, so it was going to be quite a family group.

At least that would be a positive end to one part of the investigation, not that it could in any way diminish the sadness of the family's loss.

Chapter 20

Pam and Oliver arrived bright and early the next day. It looked as if they had enjoyed a good night's sleep and had at least begun the long process of healing and moving on.

They were both wearing jeans and I dared to joke about how similar they looked. Fortunately it was all taken in good part, and Oliver and I began to manhandle the trunk out of the house to the car, while Pam locked up the house for me.

"So where's Joyce this morning?"

"She's at the gym."

"Mmm," I said. "I can see I shall need to get fit to keep up with her."

Pam smiled, and I could see the strain beginning to leave her eyes.

On the way to pick up Ilse the conversation was predictable.

"It will be funny being in the bungalow without Annie," Pam said.

"I hope you get to see a lot more of it when Ilse is living there."

"Yes. I hope so, too."

As we turned into Barn Lane there was a difficult moment when Pam asked, "Is this the way Helen came that night?"

"Come on, darling," Oliver said. "We have to put this all behind us."

"I know. I know. But it's so difficult."

We pulled up outside Ilse's cottage and I went to the door to collect her. It seemed she was getting younger each time

I saw her. She looked smart and colourful in a winter coat and smiled as she opened the door.

"Ready when you are," I said, and she closed the door and followed me along the garden path.

As I held the rear door open for her to join Pam in the back seat, I hoped it would not be too difficult for them to talk together and get to know each other better.

Oliver and I chatted about mundane things in the front, and the journey soon passed.

As I pulled up in front of the bungalow, Ilse repeated what Pam had expressed earlier.

"It's funny coming here on my own. It will seem empty without my mother."

"You'll soon get used to it," Pam encouraged her.

"Come on," Oliver said. "Let's get this trunk unloaded and find out how much work the house needs."

Ilse had been given the house keys by the solicitor, but before she unlocked the door she just stood and looked at it. She turned to us all.

"Oh dear. This is so strange. I can't really believe this is my house."

"It's what your mother wanted you to have," I reminded her. "It's your new home."

"It will take some time to get used to that," she said, and she tried the key in the keyhole almost as if she expected it not to fit. But, of course, it did.

Pam went in after Ilse, and Oliver and I struggled with the trunk behind them, leaving it in the hall for the time being.

The bungalow was just as Annie had left it. The furnishings were a little outdated but looked cosy and comfortable. There were family photographs in every room and considering no one had been in for months, it was not particularly dusty, just a fine coating visible on exposed surfaces. But it was very cold.

Oliver and I went into the kitchen to check the water and electricity systems, and all seemed to be working.

"What kind of central heating is it?" Oliver asked.

"Gas, I think," Ilse said.

We rooted about and found the boiler, relit the pilot light and set the whole thing going.

"It will take a while," I said, "but we should soon have some heat coming through."

Ilse was walking from room to room with Pam. They were talking about wallpaper and curtains, so I left them to it. There was nothing useful I could add to that conversation so I went back to the kitchen to put the kettle on in the hope that there was some tea in the cupboard. There was and, what's more, Oliver went to the car to retrieve a flask of cold milk and I was very impressed with his thoughtfulness and efficiency.

"Tea up," he called and I carried a tray through to the living room. It was still cold in there, but we were all wrapped up, and the tea helped.

The conversation was about practical things. Decorating rooms, tidying the garden, the state of the front gate, which had seen better days.

Ilse was going to have no difficulty getting the work done. She was a rich woman now. She could do what she chose.

"I suggest you leave the house for a day or two to warm up, before you move in," Oliver said. "It will need a lot of airing and there's no point coming here to be uncomfortable."

"You are all being so kind," Ilse looked round at us. "I'm not used to this."

"I hope you can get used to it," I said. "None of us lives very far away. We are going to be almost like neighbours."

Pam began talking to Ilse about the area. What her favourite shops were in Ipswich, how close her parents lived. Ilse began to look quite overwhelmed with all she had to learn and get used to.

"You told me once," I said carefully, "you don't like the countryside very much and that you prefer living in a town. Well, here you are in the perfect place. A town just down the road, with buses to get you there. Lots to do, people to visit. I think you will be very happy here."

"I'm sure you will," Pam added.

"Now," I said, fumbling in my coat pocket, "somewhere in here I have some photographs for you. You can go through the trunk in your own time. All that's in there is yours."

I found the three pictures of Ilse herself and passed them across to her.

"There are also some photographs of the cemetery at Brocton. As soon as I get those back from the Imperial War Museum, I'll let you have them. What's this?"

I'd found the newspaper in which the photographs had been wrapped. It had been in my pocket since then and I began to open it out.

"I love old newspapers," I said. "They always have something interesting in them."

I unfolded the paper, laid it on the floor and began to read the adverts. They always appeal to me. All the products they show trigger immediate memories of things bought or used during my earlier life. Types of chocolate bar no longer available, outdated models of cars, items priced in pounds, shillings and pence, holidays at ridiculously cheap prices, they are all strangely intriguing.

But this newspaper wasn't as old as all that, and it was not until my eyes reached the top of the page that I noticed the date, 11 May 1991. Even then I made no connection to anything particular until I saw the headline.

50th Anniversary of landing at Eaglesham.

"Look at this," I said.

They all craned to read the page. The newspaper was the Renfrew Argus and I read with increasing disbelief.

It was a story virtually unknown to me, but as I read it, I found the final mystery being solved before my eyes.

"Listen," I said. "It says: *Residents of Eaglesham and district were remembering yesterday the strange events which occurred half a century ago.* That would be 1941," I said and I looked at Ilse who was staring at the page.

"*Rudolf Hess, second only to Adolf Hitler in the ruling Nazi party of wartime Germany, landed by parachute in a field on Floors Farm. When questioned by members of the local Home Guard he told them he was on a mission of humanity, and that his Fuhrer did not want to fight Britain. He claimed to be acquainted with the Duke of Hamilton, having met him during the Berlin Olympics, and that he had come to visit him in order to begin negotiations, through the Duke's auspices, with Winston Churchill in order to end the war."*

I looked around at the others and you could have heard a pin drop.

I read on.

"Hess used the name of Alfred Horn at first, but later revealed his true identity. The fact that he was German was always clear as he was wearing the uniform of an officer in the Luftwaffe. His aircraft, a Messerschmitt Me110E, had flown from the airstrip at Haunstetten, close to where it had been constructed in Augsberg. Crash investigators discovered extra fuel tanks fitted in the aircraft, and this confirmed Hess' story that his co-pilot had been due to return directly to Germany. Evidence of severe engine trouble, possibly caused by a collision with a flock of large birds, was also found by investigators."

"I remember reading about Rudolph Hess's flight to Britain," Oliver said.

"Sshh," Pam insisted. "Listen."

I looked from one to the other, smiled and continued.

"Hess is now known to have been a staunch follower of Hitler ever since studying under Karl Haushofer at Munich University. His work in the field of Geopolitics and Haushofer's theory for Germany's future, derived from the earlier concept of lebensraum, had made a major impact on the young Hess, and Haushofer had become a profound influence on his development as a political activist. The arrival of Rudolph Hess has been an event shrouded in mystery and conjecture for many years. Upon receiving the news of the flight, Hitler is reported to have become angry, denying any prior knowledge of the flight and accusing Hess of being mentally unstable."

"My mother said there was a secret mission," Ilse said. "And it said so in her journal."

"There's one last paragraph," I said. "Just listen to this.

"Little was immediately known of Hess' co-pilot, but the description given by Hess fitted that of a man who was run over by a truck in Kilmarnock on the morning of 11 May 1941. His name is now believed to have been Hans Jurgen Schmid, and he is buried at the German Military Cemetery in Brocton, Staffordshire."

Ilse's hands had flown up to her face.

"My father," she said. "That was his name. So that's what it was. He was flying Rudolph Hess."

"Good God," Oliver said. "What a connection."

Pam was looking at Ilse who had tears running down her cheeks.

"Are you all right?" she asked her.

"I think so. It's almost as if my mother left this newspaper for me to find."

"You said it was like a love story," I said. "Her mother was taking him to a station to escape to Ireland," I said to Pam and Oliver. "They'd met before, then he suddenly landed from the sky in her backyard. She must have been so excited to see him. And then she lost him the following day."

"That's awful," Pam said. "How sad. So many sad things have happened to us all."

"But not anymore," I said, having difficulty coping with the emotion around me. "Now we have a happier life to look forward to."

"Thanks to you," Pam said.

"Oh, stop it. I didn't do much. But I'm glad it all worked out."

And that was that. Ilse moved into her new home a couple of days later.

Oliver eventually started a business consultancy and Joyce helped him run things. I started to sort out my outstanding cases and slowly began to think of myself as a detective, on a small scale, of course.

Pam and Ilse became firm friends, if not sisters, and saw each other a great deal.

Oliver had railed against the effects of the war, and I suppose he was right, in a way. Without the war, none of it would have happened. Ilse would never have been conceived and Helen would still be alive. Oliver would probably still have lost his job, but there would hopefully have been Annie's inheritance to help him begin again.

But without what happened, it's likely I would never have told Joyce how I feel about her. So perhaps it's true that everything does happen for a reason.